THE PHILLIP HAZARD NOVELS, NO. 2

THE
BRAVE
CAPTAINS

by

V. A. STUART

MCBOOKS PRESS, INC.
ITHACA, NEW YORK

Published by McBooks Press 2003
Copyright © 1968, 1972 by V.A. Stuart
First published in the United Kingdom by
Robert Hale

Cover: Crimean War, British frigates engaging the Kilburn Forts,
16 October, 1855. Courtesy of Peter Newark's Military Pictures.

Library of Congress Cataloging-in-Publication Data

Stuart, V. A.
  The brave captains / V.A. Stuart.
    p. cm. — (The Phillip Hazard novels ; no. 2)
  ISBN 1-59013-040-5 (alk. paper)
  1. Hazard, Phillip Horatio (Fictitious character)—Fiction. 2. Great
Britain—History, Naval—19th century—Fiction. 3. Balaklava (Ukraine),
Battle of, 1854—Fiction. 4. Crimean War, 1853-1856—Fiction. 5.
British—Ukraine—Fiction. I. Title.
  PR6063.A38B73 2003
  823'.914—dc21

                                        2003005260

Visit the McBooks historical fiction website at www.mcbooks.com.

Printed in the United States of America

9 8 7 6 5 4 3 2

FT
Pbk

AUTHOR'S NOTE

With the exception of the Officers and Seamen of H.M.S. *Trojan,* all the British Naval and Military Officers in this novel really existed and their actions are a matter of historical fact. Their opinions are also, in most cases, widely known and where they have been credited with remarks of conversations— as, for example, with the fictitious characters—which are not actually their own words, care has been taken to make sure that these are, as far as possible, in keeping with their known sentiments.

The remarks criticizing Army organization, attributed to Midshipman St. John Daniels (later V.C.) are based on opinions expressed at that time by a number of Naval Officers and, in particular, by Sir Evelyn Wood, V.C., in his *From Midshipman to Field Marshal,* published in 1906.

The main events described are historically accurate and did actually take place, as described, according to books published, soon after the Crimean War ended, by those who took part in them.

THIS NOVEL IS DEDICATED TO
Commander Charles Gower Robinson, R.N.

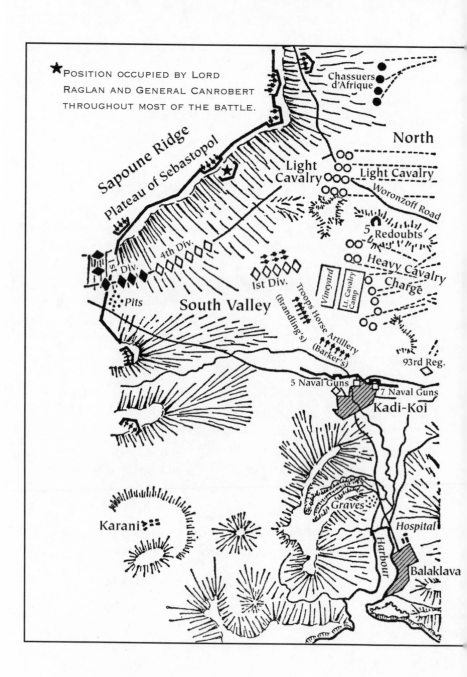

★ POSITION OCCUPIED BY LORD RAGLAN AND GENERAL CANROBERT THROUGHOUT MOST OF THE BATTLE.

Chassuers d'Afrique

North

Sapoune Ridge

Plateau of Sebastopol

Light Cavalry

Light Cavalry

Woronzoff Road

5 Redoubts

Heavy Cavalry Charge

4th Div.

1st Div.

1st Div.

Pits

South Valley

Vineyard

Lt. Cavalry Camp

Troops Horse Artillery (Brandling's)

(Barker's)

93rd Reg.

5 Naval Guns

7 Naval Guns

Kadi-Koi

Graves

Karani

Hospital

Harbour

Balaklava

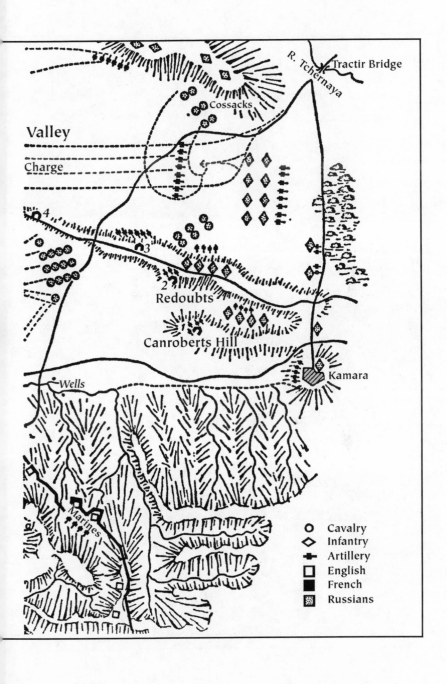

R. Tchernaya

Tractir Bridge

Cossacks

Valley

Charge

4

3

2

Redoubts

Canroberts Hill

Kamara

Wells

Marines

○ Cavalry
◇ Infantry
✚ Artillery
☐ English
■ French
▦ Russians

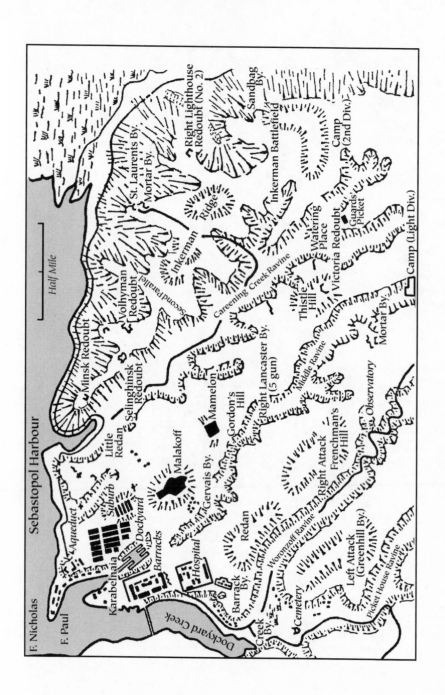

PROLOGUE

1

At 6:30 *a.m.* on October 17, 1854, the siege-guns of the Allied Armies of Britain and France opened fire on the Russian naval base of Sebastopol from their entrenched positions on the Crimean Upland, to the south of the city.

The two armies, with their Turkish allies and supported by their fleets, had landed on the Crimean Peninsula at Kalamita Bay, to the north, on September 14 and, six days later, had defeated the Russians, under Prince Menschikoff, at the Battle of the Alma. Subsequently yielding to the French belief that Sebastopol was impregnable to attack from the north, the invaders had made a flank march inland, landing their siege-trains at Balaclava and Kamiesch. It had taken the better part of three weeks to haul the heavy guns into position on the Upland and to establish the army camps there but, by October 17, all was in readiness for the first full-scale bombardment which, it was hoped, would destroy the enemy's land defenses. Those on the seaward side were to be attacked—as nearly simultaneously as might be possible—by the Allied Fleets.

A well-directed fire was maintained from both works on the Upland for nearly four hours, the Russian garrison replying with spirit, in the awareness that this was a prelude to the long awaited assault on Sebastopol by the two besieging armies which, if it were successful, must lead to the city's capture. At 10 a.m., however, a shell exploded the principal French magazine, causing considerable damage and loss of life and virtually paralyzing the French artillery. After a second explosion not long afterwards, General Canrobert—recently promoted to the French supreme command—sent an aide-de-camp to the British lines to announce that it would be out of the question for his troops to participate in any further action that day. Notwithstanding this news, the British batteries continued to pound away energetically at the Russian defensive works.

At noon the combined Black Sea Fleets, consisting of eleven French, ten British, and two Turkish ships-of-the-line, in addition to frigates and steam gun-vessels, started to maneuver into line to engage the enemy's sea defenses. Sebastopol lay shrouded under a thick pall of smoke from the land bombardment and it was impossible to judge with accuracy what was taking place ashore. No means of communication having been arranged between the naval and military forces, the two Admirals Commanding-in-Chief were unable to obtain information as to the progress of the land-based assault they had been requested to support. In the confident supposition that this must shortly take place—if, indeed, it had not already been launched—both flagships made the signal to their fleets to attack as soon as the line was complete. The maneuver occupied almost an hour, since the battleships under sail had to be towed into station by steamers lashed to their sides, and it was 1:15 p.m. before the first broadside was fired.

In the meantime, despite the fact that the guns of the British Naval Brigade ashore had opened a breach in the Russian perimeter through which an assault might well have been attempted, the British military Commander-in-Chief, Lord Raglan—in the absence of French support—regretfully declined to order it. The regiments under arms detailed to form the first wave of the attack were, accordingly, permitted to stand down but the two fleets advanced valiantly to press home their own attack, unaware that their efforts were now to no purpose. They were met by a withering hail of shell and redhot shot.

As darkness began to fall, the thunderous roar of gunfire from the Upland slackened and then ceased and, it being at last evident that no land-based assault on Sebastopol had been made, the naval signal for recall was hoisted, first by the *Ville de Paris* and then by the *Britannia.* The smoke of battle slowly cleared and, as the attacking ships hauled off, one—H.M.S. *Rodney* of 90 guns and under sail—was seen to have run aground in shoal water in perilous proximity to Fort Constantine. Under a heavy cannonade from the batteries which had her range, she was towed off by two small steamers, *Spiteful* and *Lynx,* each mounting six guns, assisted by the steam-screw frigate *Trojan,* 31, whose commander took his ship close inshore to draw the fort's fire from the stricken *Rodney.*

The French Fleet, under the command of Vice-Admiral Hamelin, set course for Kamiesch Bay to the south, followed by the Turkish flagship *Mahmudieh.* Vice-Admiral James Deans Dundas, Commander-in-Chief of the British Fleet, grimly recognizing that the action had been a failure, ordered his battered ships to return to their own anchorage at the mouth of the Katcha River, to the north of Sebastopol.

The swiftly gathering darkness did not completely hide the melancholy spectacle they presented. Scarcely a ship of the inshore squadron had escaped damage, their Admiral observed despondently, as he studied them through his night-glass. Some had been hulled more than a score of times; *Retribution* had lost her mainmast, *Trojan* her foremast, and *Arethusa* was still fighting a fire on her upper deck. Shrouds and stays hung in tattered shreds from those whose masts had not gone by the board, and blackened, still smouldering decks were littered with a tangle of torn rigging and shattered yards, which their weary crews laboured to salvage or cut away.

For nearly five hours the British fleet had discharged broadside after broadside at the great, stone-built fortress known as Constantine, which guarded the northern approaches to Sebastopol's harbour. They had pitted their wooden ships against casemated batteries protected by immensely thick walls upon which, however rapid and well-aimed their fire, they had been able to make little visible impression. Prevented from storming the harbour by a line of blockships sunk across the entrance, most of the British line-of-battle ships had been out-ranged and out-gunned. Russian batteries, placed behind strongly constructed earthworks on the high cliffs behind the fort and firing bar and chain-shot had, even at extreme range, wrought havoc with their rigging and upper yards.

The seamen had worked their guns heroically, stripped to the waist and half-blinded by smoke, as shells burst on the crowded decks, taking terrible toll of them. But they had carried on in the best traditions of the British Navy, only now to realize that all their heroism had been in vain, their courage and sacrifice wasted by the inaction of the troops on shore. Sebastopol was still securely in the hands of its Russian garrison and, to add to the bitter consciousness of failure, not one of the towering forts at the harbour mouth had been silenced. Save for a few minutes early in the engagement, when a lucky shot from H.M.S. *Agamemnon*, 91, flagship of Rear-Admiral Sir Edmund Lyons, had caused some stored ammunition to blow up, the guns of Fort Constantine had blazed continuous defiance.

Even when, in an endeavour to shorten the range, Admiral Lyons had led the inshore squadron to within a scant six hundred yards of the fort itself, he had been compelled to drop anchor with less than two feet of water under his keel, and this had prevented all except the *Sanspareil*, 70—like *Agamemnon*, a steam-screw ship—from closing him. The other ships of his squadron, although able to bring their starboard broadsides to bear on the fort, had suffered severely from the enfilading fire of the cliff-top batteries ahead and astern of them, to which they had not the elevation to reply. These batteries had thrown hot-shot with devastating effect, setting several ships on fire, among them the *Agamemnon* herself. Her crew had, however, brought the blaze under control and the flagship had held her station, discharging repeated broadsides at her target, at times

almost alone. First *Albion,* 91, then *London,* 90, and then the
50-gun frigate *Arethusa*—all sailing ships and all gallantly commanded—had been forced to break off and permit the steamers
to which they were lashed to tow them out of range.

The Navy had paid a high price for the little—the tragically
little—that the bombardment of Sebastopol's seaward defenses
had achieved, Admiral Dundas thought bitterly. And when, next
day, he waited in the spacious stern-cabin of his 120-gun flagship *Britannia* for reports of damage and lists of killed and
wounded to reach him from individual commanders, he grew
increasingly bitter.

The combined Fleets had suffered 520 casualties in the
abortive action, of which the British Fleet's total was 44 killed
and 266 wounded and, of the latter, the Admiral knew, many
would die from their injuries within the next few days. He felt
understandably resentful as he set about the difficult task of
composing a despatch for the Board of Admiralty later that afternoon, when all the reports had come in. He had advised very
strongly against an attack on Sebastopol from the sea, convinced
that the sinking of the enemy blockships at the entrance to the
harbour must render such an attack ineffective. Lord Raglan
had, however, seen fit to disregard his advice and when, after
lengthy discussion, what had seemed to him a most ill-con-
ceived plan of attack had been agreed upon, the French had
insisted on changing even this . . . and at the eleventh hour,
when his own ships were already clearing for action. He shook
his head in weary frustration.

Their Lordships could scarcely be expected to approve of
the long casualty lists and the damage to so many ships-
of-the-line, he was unhappily aware. A successful bombardment
of the sea forts, culminating in the capture of Sebastopol by the
Allied land forces, might have justified the naval losses . . . but
an unsuccessful engagement, which the Army commanders had
so lamentably failed to turn to advantage, could not possibly
redound to his credit. Conscious that the costly failure was not

his fault, Admiral Dundas knew that, so far as their Lordships
of the Admiralty were concerned, he would be held responsible nonetheless, and he endeavoured to pen his despatch
optimistically, writing it in his own hand, instead of dictating
the carefully phrased sentences to his Secretary.

When it was done, he read it through, frowning. Certain
documentary evidence might with advantage, he decided, be
appended to his report. Copies of letters from Lord Raglan and
of various notes he had sent to and received from Admiral
Hamelin were filed in his Letter Book. In addition there was a
copy of the official communiqué, signed by Lord Raglan
and General Canrobert, in which was set out, in detail, the military plan of action and the request for naval support. These
might possibly absolve him from blame, if not entirely from
responsibility, in their Lordships' eyes. At least they would
serve to demonstrate that he had wanted no part in yesterday's
costly fiasco and that he had agreed to the Generals' demands
because, eventually, he had been left with no alternative. He
could not put into words, could not even hint—in an official
des- patch to the Admiralty—at his dissatisfaction with his
French Allies, whose system of command was such that it left
all major decisions on naval strategy to be made by the military Commander-in-Chief.

Still less, the Admiral reflected regretfully, could he confess
to the growing mistrust he felt for his own second-in-command,
since it was apparently at their Lordships' wish and certainly
with their knowledge that Sir Edmund Lyons occupied the privileged position he did, vis à vis Lord Raglan. Rear-Admiral Lyons,
rather than himself, was regarded as the final authority on naval
matters by Lord Raglan, enjoying his confidence, having his ear,
influencing his decisions.

He blamed the French—and General Canrobert in particular—for yesterday's failure. Although, so far as yesterday was
concerned, Sir Edmund Lyons was, in his opinion, almost as
much to blame as the French were. Had it not been Lyons who

had originally conceived the idea of the ill-starred naval attack on the forts? Had it not been he who, thirsting for action and seeking an opportunity to distinguish himself, had persuaded Lord Raglan of its merits?

The Admiral drew the draft of his despatch towards him and studied it again in frowning concentration, his frown deepening when he re-read the paragraph he had numbered 8. To have linked the name of his second-in-command with that of the Captain of the Fleet, Rear-Admiral Stopford—who, like himself, had watched the action from Brittania's unscathed poop—was perhaps a trifle ungenerous. He had deliberately refrained from singling out for praise the gallantry displayed by Admiral Lyons in bringing his fine steam-screw ship *Agamemnon* so close to the fort but . . . there was a certain justice in the omission.

No one, least of all himself, Admiral Dundas thought wryly, could deny Edmund Lyons's personal courage or his splendid seamanship—although he possessed an exceptionally able Flag-Captain in William Mends. Thanks to their skilful handling of *Agamemnon* in the action, her total casualties had been four men killed, two officers and twenty-four seamen wounded . . . a remarkable achievement, in the circumstances. But no doubt word of this and of Lyons's dashing leadership of his inshore squadron would, in due course, reach the First Lord, Sir James Graham, by other means. Lyons himself regularly exchanged letters with Sir James, and Lord Raglan would probably mention the matter in his despatch to the Duke of Newcastle. There would also be glowing reports in the Press, to the majority of whose "special correspondents" Lyons was already a hero, in the Nelson tradition. He would not be denied the credit he deserved by those to whom courage was the supreme virtue but for himself . . . Admiral Dundas passed an impatient hand through his thinning white hair.

He himself set greater store by forethought and sagacity, in a commander, and by a fitting sense of responsibility. Courage

and dash, of the kind Lyons had exhibited yesterday, were qual-
ities one looked for in junior officers; but when a man accepted
promotion to high rank, he assumed with that rank responsibility for the lives of thousands of other men and the safety of
the ships in which they served. A commander-in-chief was
answerable for defeats, as well as being given credit for victo-
ries, and must, therefore, learn to temper courage with caution.
Nelson—on whom, if rumour were to be believed, Edmund
Lyons had sought to model himself throughout his service
career—had died young.

Nevertheless . . . Admiral Dundas sighed. Lyons would succeed him as Commander-in-Chief of the British Black Sea Fleet
when his own appointment came to an end, in two months'
time, and he found himself wondering, a trifle cynically,
whether this would bring about a change of attitude on the part
of his successor-designate. With the burden of command resting squarely on his shoulders, Lyons might not be quite
so eager as he had been yesterday to send his ships in to shell
Sebastopol's formidable harbour defenses—even at Lord
Raglan's request. He might not be so insistent on defending Balaclava at all costs when the costs would be his own, the lives
sacrificed in its defense his to explain to the Lords Commis-
sioners of the Admiralty, his to remember long after the battles
were over and forgotten.

To give the devil his due, though, Lyons was efficient and
a fine organizer and he had proved repeatedly, since his return
to the Navy after almost twenty years in the diplomatic service,
that he had forgotten none of the seamanlike skills he had
acquired as a frigate captain. He inspired devotion in the officers and men serving under him and he was popular with the
Army, particularly with its senior officers, most of whom—
including Lord Raglan—were only too eager for him to assume
command of the British Black Sea Fleet. Indeed, Admiral Dundas thought, when the time came, even he would not be sorry
to pass on the burden of high office which now rested so heav-

ily upon him, leaving Edmund Lyons, the sailor-diplomat, to make what he could of a difficult and unrewarding task. But . . . he thrust the draft of his dispatch from him, reaching again for his pen. He had not yet done so; he was still Commander-in-Chief of the British Fleet, he reminded himself, decisions as to naval strategy and the employment of the Fleet his to make—his and his alone—until he should haul down his flag.

If *he* decided to abandon Balaclava, neither Lyons nor Lord Raglan could gainsay him. Already the tiny, landlocked harbour was proving totally inadequate for the number of ships and the immense volume of stores, ammunition, and supplies it was required to accommodate. It was difficult of access; everything landed there had to be manhandled up a steep track to the head of a gorge and thence, for a further five or six miles, to the siege-works on the Upland—and it was daily becoming more congested. The choice of Balaclava as the British base had been made by Lord Raglan, on Lyons's advice. Admittedly Lyons had chosen it in the belief that its use as a base would be temporary. He had expected to land the siege-trains and troop reinforcements there and, in the unlikely event that winter quarters might be required for the Army and a secure harbour for the ships of the Fleet he, like many others, had anticipated that Sebastopol would be captured in ample time to afford both.

As indeed, it might have been, the Admiral thought sourly, had the British and French troops launched their expected assault on the place yesterday. Taking a fresh sheet of paper, he wrote Lord Raglan's name at its head.

"*I consider,*" he wrote, his pen moving firmly and decisively over the paper, "*yesterday's action a false one, which I decline to repeat and with which, as a naval officer of fifty years' experience, I am profoundly dissatisfied . . .*" The Admiral paused, to read through what he had written. He had expressed himself without finesse, even harshly, but every word was true and must be said, if he were not to fail in his duty. Sir Edmund Lyons could be requested to deliver the note in person and would, no doubt, exercise his skill as a diplomat in order to make his protest palatable to Lord Raglan and . . . he would defer making any decision concerning Balaclava for the time being. Perhaps the place could be held. He shrugged, added a few meaningless, conventionally polite phrases, and signed his name at the foot of the paper.

This done, he summoned his Secretary. Having given instructions for copies to be made of his despatch and the enclosures and a fair copy of the former to be delivered to him for signature, he asked for a number of other documents to be brought to him, including his Rear-Admiral's report of the bombardment of Sebastopol's sea defenses.

Promotions would have to be recommended, letters written to those Captains whose conduct merited recognition, and the command of several ships settled. *Triton's* commander, Lieutenant Lloyd, had been killed yesterday, *Firebrand's* Captain wounded, and there was the *Trojan* whose Captain, Thomas North, had died of cholera just before the frigate left Balaclava. She had been commanded in the action by her First Lieutenant, Admiral Dundas recalled . . . and very ably commanded. The First Lieutenant's name was Phillip Hazard, he saw, aged 27, with fourteen years at sea, and a son of old Admiral Sir John Hazard, under whom he had served for a short time on the *Cambrian*, longer ago than he cared to remember. There had been a brother—an elder brother, if his memory was not at fault—who had been tried by court martial and dismissed the Service in . . . the date eluded him. But the ship had been the *Comus*, he was certain, and she had run aground at the mouth of the River Plate about ten or twelve years ago.

The Hazards were a fine old naval family but there was the brother and, of course, there were also the extraordinary accusations which the late Captain North had made against his First Lieutenant a few hours before he died. It was possible that he had been delirious—his behavior had been strange, to say the least, and his record as a commander left much to be desired but, in the circumstances, the sooner a new Captain was appointed to the *Trojan* the better, probably.

His Secretary laid the papers he had asked for in front of him and the Admiral thanked and dismissed him. Sir Edmund Lyons's file lay on top of the rest and he read the report it contained again, with even more care than he had given to it initially, noting in particular the glowing tribute his second-in-command had paid to Captain Dacres of the *Sanspareil*.

" *. . . never in the glorious annals of the British Navy . . . was an admiral better supported than I was by the commander of the Sanspareil . . .*" Admiral Dundas frowned. There was praise also for the commanders of several other ships and a lengthy explanation of the circumstances in which the *Rodney* had gone aground, which exonerated her Captain, Charles Graham, of any suggestion of negligence. Admiral Lyons commended the conduct of several junior officers serving in his flagship, and drew attention to that of his Flag Lieutenant, Cowper Phipps Coles who, at the height of the engagement, had volunteered to go in a small boat to *Bellerophon* and *Sanspareil*—which had not seen his signals through the smoke of the guns—to request them to close the *Agamemnon* again.

"A service of great danger," the Rear-Admiral wrote, *"for the water all round the ship appeared a mass of foam from the projectiles which were passing her in all directions. Nevertheless, Lieutenant Coles accomplished his mission and returned in safety. . . ."*

Admiral Dundas' expression relaxed. He had witnessed Lieutenant Coles' act of heroism from *Britannia's* poop, when the smoke had momentarily cleared, and he made a note of the young officer's name. This, at least, was a promotion he could endorse with a clear conscience, together with that of Frederick Maxse—Sir Edmund Lyons's previous Flag Lieutenant—who had distinguished himself when acting as naval aide-de-camp to Lord Raglan, during the flank march to Balaclava. The other recommendations would require more thought. He had himself mentioned Commander Augustus Kynaston of the *Spiteful* in his despatch to the Admiralty, which should suffice to have that officer advanced immediately to post-rank, and there was Mr Codrington Ball, Second Master of the steam-tug *Circassia*, who had undertaken the dangerous and responsible task of piloting the inshore squadron across the shoal to within six hundred yards of Fort Constantine. But Admiral Lyons, he noticed, turning over the pages of his report, had also requested promotion for his senior Lieutenant, William Rolland, and for the commanders of *Lynx* and *Trojan*—Lieutenants Proctor-Luce and Hazard.

Of Lieutenant Phillip Hazard, the Rear-Admiral had written another glowing report, which concluded: *"In view of the exemplary and gallant manner in which, as her First Lieutenant, he commanded the* Trojan, *I should like to recommend that he be confirmed in his command. As, however, this is a post-command and it seems to me probable that your Excellency may have an officer of higher rank in mind as successor to the late Captain North, I would request that Lieutenant Hazard be appointed to the* Agamemnon . . . *until such time as the command of a suitable ship . . . should become vacant. . . ."*

Admiral Dundas picked up his pen once more, his broad, red-complexioned face set in thoughtful lines. He had several officers of higher rank in mind, of course. There were a number of commanders due for advancement, to whom the captaincy of a modern, 31-gun steam-screw frigate would be a fitting reward for good work and devotion to duty. Young Hazard was, as his sponsor had pointed out, too junior to be given the *Trojan*, save in exceptional circumstances. In the last war officials in their early twenties had attained post-rank—including Nelson and Lyons himself—but times had changed and there were now captains, with twice Hazard's service, commanding smaller ships than the *Trojan*.

Besides, the Admiral reminded himself, there had been some ugly rumours concerning the *Trojan* during Captain

North's period of command. Her crew had been said to be disaffected, discipline poor and desertions numerous . . . he frowned, remembering. True, she had made a record passage out from England carrying, as passengers, a member of the Russian Imperial Family and her chaperone—the former a youthful Grand Duchess, who had somehow been overlooked during the course of an educational visit to London—both of whom had been repatriated to Odessa, just before the official declaration of war. It was also true that North had had the reputation of a taut hand but . . . his accusations against Lieutenant Hazard had been specific and damning and he had demanded a court martial under Article Nineteen of the Articles of War. Delirious or not, he had claimed that Hazard had been responsible for the disaffection of his ship's company and had stated, quite positively, that he could prove his charges before a court martial. North was dead now, his proof and his charges dying with him but nevertheless . . . the Admiral's quill spluttered over the paper.

He made a note that Lieutenant Hazard was to be appointed temporarily to the *Agamemnon,* but to serve with the Naval Brigade ashore in his present rank, unless specifically required for staff duties by Rear-Admiral Lyons. Still frowning, he placed a query against the note and laid it aside, whilst applying himself to the difficult task of deciding to which, of at least a dozen equally deserving senior officers, the vacant command of *Trojan* should be given.

He had reached no definite decision when his Secretary returned with a copy of his despatch for signature and the information that Rear-Admiral Lyons's barge had been sighted, putting off from *Agamemnon* for the mile-long pull to *Britannia*'s anchorage.

"The *Banshee* is alongside, sir," the Secretary added. "And mail for Constantinople has been collected from all ships at this anchorage, with the exception of the *Agamemnon,* sir. I understand that they are holding the postbag for Admiral Lyons, sir, who has been ashore at Lord Raglan's headquarters all day."

"Very well." Admiral Dundas appended his signature to the despatch. "You will kindly see that this goes with the *Banshee* to Constantinople. And inform Commander Reynolds that he is to get under way immediately, if you please. The rest of the mail can be consigned to the *Spiteful* tomorrow morning."

His own despatch would thus, he was fully aware, be the first official report of the naval bombardment to reach White-hall . . . but he was conscious of no regrets on this account, as his Secretary took the document and its enclosures from him and went obediently to carry out his instructions.

The *Banshee* was under way before Admiral Lyons's barge had covered more than half the distance which separated the two flagships. Her sturdy paddle-wheels churning the water to foam, the little despatch-steamer was a dark silhouette against the evening sky by the time the barge tied up to *Britannia's* star-board chains. The side party stiffened to attention, as the boatswain's mates raised their calls to their lips, preparatory to piping the Rear-Admiral aboard with due ceremony.

In the stern cabin, sipping a glass of Madeira, the Com-mander-in-Chief awaited his coming with equanimity. He had now made up his mind as to the *Triton's* new commander—a comparatively easy decision, since *Triton* was only a 3-gun paddle-wheel steamer—and he had reduced the list of those he was considering for the command of *Trojan* to four names.

All were equally deserving, so that it might, perhaps, be politic in the circumstances to consult his Rear-Admiral or even to permit him to decide which of the four should be given advancement . . . Admiral Dundas smiled quietly to himself. Loyal as always to his little coterie of one-time *Blonde* or *Mada-gascar* officers, Lyons would almost certainly plump for Charles Crawford who, like Dacres of the *Sanspareil,* had served under his command in the *Blonde* in 1828.

Well, Crawford would not be a bad choice; he was the senior, even if his health was not as robust as it might have been and had put him ashore on half-pay for the last few years, his senior-ity entitled him to a better command than his present one . . . the quill spluttered again, as Captain Charles Crawford's name was underlined. A good man, Charles Crawford, the Admiral reflected—taut enough, yet invariably a well-liked and respected officer. Just the man to put a stop to any disaffection there might still be among *Trojan's* people . . . and it would do no harm to let Lyons imagine that the choice had been his.

Sipping his Madeira, Admiral Dundas wondered what had gone wrong during Captain North's command. Some incident involving the passengers, perhaps? It was a possibility, of course. Women had no place aboard a ship of war; they invari-ably caused trouble, and the presence, on board the *Trojan,* of a Russian Grand Duchess on the eve of the declaration of war might well have caused trouble of the worst kind . . . particu-larly when the *Trojan's* Grand Duchess had, apparently, been young and very beautiful.

Draining his glass, the Admiral wondered, with fleeting curiosity, what had happened to her. Perhaps she had been among the ladies of Sebastopol for whom, it was said, Prince Menschikoff had caused a pavilion to be set up overlooking the Alma, in order that they might witness the victory of his Impe-rial Army over the invaders from England and France. Or on the other hand, she . . . there was a knock on the door of his cabin. He rose heavily to his feet and, forcing a smile, prepared to welcome his second-in-command and successor-designate, Rear-Admiral Sir Edmund Lyons. . . .

2

The heavy coach lurched drunkenly over the rutted, uneven surface of the post-road from Perekop, to Simpheropol, its four sweating, mud-spattered horses urged on by the whips of the postillions crouching low in their saddles. Ahead galloped a dozen cavalrymen in the green uniform of the Chasseurs of Odessa, seeking to clear the way with shouts and curses but having, at times, to use the flat of their sabres in order to force a passage through the packed ranks of plodding foot soldiers, whose weariness made them deaf to commands and curses alike. But they halted thankfully when their own officers waved them to the road verge and stood there, leaning on their muskets, grateful for the unexpected respite which enabled them to draw breath and shift the heavy packs they bore to a more comfortable position.

The coach rumbled past them, showering them with mud and small stones, and those of the waiting infantrymen who troubled to look up saw that its window curtains were drawn, hiding its interior from their gaze. They made no comment, asked no questions, and, even among themselves, indulged in no speculation as to the identity of the passing travellers. The majority of the soldiers were not curious. So far as they were concerned anyone who drove at such speed, with an escort of cavalry riding before and behind, must be a personage of great importance—a General or their Governor and Commander-in-Chief, Baron Osten-Sacken, probably. Someone, at all events, whose presence in Simpheropol was required with much greater urgency than their own. They were simply the rearguard of a force of some thirty thousand men, summoned from Odessa and destined to act as reserves to the army of Prince Menschikoff now based at Bakshi-Serai and gathering, in daily increasing strength, in the Valley of the Tchernaya.

Inside the coach, one of the occupants—a tall, slim young man in the uniform of a Colonel of Chasseurs and wearing the *aiguillette* of an Imperial aide-de-camp—moaned softly as the rear wheels of the vehicle struck some obstacle, almost dislodging him from his seat. His right sleeve was empty, tucked into the front of his frogged green jacket and, unable to save himself with his single arm, he slithered forward, to be brought up with a jolt against the door of the coach, all his weight momentarily on his left leg which—although booted—was heavily bandaged. He contrived to drag himself back into his seat before either of his two companions could offer him assistance, shaking his head firmly to the anxious question in the eyes of the lovely, dark-haired girl who sat beside him.

"I . . . am all right, Sophia. Please do not make a fuss. I . . . it will pass, I promise you."

Her arms about him, endeavouring to give him support, the girl looked down pityingly at his pale, sweat-beaded face and tightly compressed lips. This journey was torment to him, she knew and, turning to the third occupant of the carriage, she addressed him pleadingly. "Cousin Nikita, I beg you . . . tell the coachman he must slow down. I know that you are anxious to reach Bakshi-Serai but Andrei is not fit to be thrown about in this manner. His leg is not yet healed and his arm causes him a great deal of pain still. He—"

"Our hero of the Alma!" The handsome boy she had appealed to spoke derisively. "Of course, we must take the greatest care of him, must we not? But perhaps, my dear Sophia, your husband does not thirst, as I do, for action? It is possible that, having tasted English steel, he is less eager than he would have us believe to wipe out the stain on our country's honour which those thrice-damned English bayonets inflicted upon it."

"He is ill," Sophia defended. She felt her husband's body go limp in her arms and, impeded by the swaying of the coach, managed at last to place him in a position of more comfort with his head pillowed on her lap. "And," she added reproachfully, when her companion made no attempt to help her, "he is in such needless agony that he has fainted. *Why* must we travel at this reckless speed, Nikita? Surely a few hours won't matter to you, will they?"

"But of course they will! Mikail has stolen a march on me . . . he is already there. In action, probably, at the head of his troops, whilst I, his elder brother, am not." With an impatient hand, the boy flicked dust from his impeccably polished Hessian boots. He, too, was in uniform, looking absurdly young for the major-general's insignia and the number of Orders and decorations which adorned his silver-laced blue Hussar jacket. In fact, he was twenty-two . . . "If your husband is unfit to travel, then he is unfit to fight and should have remained at Odessa under his mother's eye."

"You don't know what he has endured," the girl protested. "Have you no pity, Nikita?"

"For Andrei Stepanovitch Narishkin? No, Sophia, I have not. He is an arrogant, strutting *poseur,* brought up by women, his every whim indulged by his adoring mother, who has made a weakling of him. Since his so-called capture of the English frigate *Tiger,* which ran aground under his nose, he has been impossible. I cannot imagine how you are able to endure being married to him."

Sophia Mikailovna Narishkin did not answer her cousin's taunts. They were, she knew in her heart, justified but, even to her cousin Nicolai—whom she had known since childhood—she was not prepared to make any such admission.

"Talking of English frigates," the young Grand Duke went on, his tone deliberately provocative, "there is one in which, I am told, you still take a sentimental and somewhat unpatriotic interest . . . the *Trojan,* yes? Or was it her commander who aroused your—er—your interest during the voyage from England?"

Sophia felt the hot, betraying colour come flooding into her cheeks. "Who," she challenged angrily, "who dared to make any such suggestion?"

Nicolai shrugged. "Servants talk . . . and old Osten-Sacken is an incurable gossip. There was mention of a ring . . . that one, I think,"—he gestured to the fine emerald on her right hand—"was it not? Ah, come now. . . ." When Sophia was silent, "when did we have secrets from each other, little cousin? What was he like, this English sailor of yours? A better man than Andrei, I'll wager!"

Sophia's fingers gently caressed her husband's cheek. Almost against her will, she found herself looking back, remembering the *Trojan* and Phillip Hazard. For a moment it was his face she saw pillowed on her lap, not Andrei's and then, losing interest in his teasing, Nicolai drew back the curtain and pointed.

"We're in Simpheropol at last," he said. As swiftly as it had come to haunt her, Sophia's vision vanished. "Andrei," she whispered softly, "wake up, my dear . . . we have arrived."

CHAPTER ONE

1

The morning of Sunday, October 22, dawned bright and clear with a hint of frost in the air although, as yet, it was by no means cold.

Her Majesty's steam-screw frigate *Trojan*, 31, in company with the rest of the British Black Sea Fleet, lay at anchor off the mouth of the Katcha River, six miles to the north of Sebastopol. As the sun rose, the duty watch—anticipating an early pipe to breakfast—moved about her freshly holystoned upper deck coiling down and stowing hammock.

Vice-Admiral Dundas had assured Their Lordships of the Admiralty that, with the exception of the *Albion* and the *Arethusa*, he hoped to be able to make his squadron serviceable within 24 hours of the attack on Fort Constantine and, in *Trojan's* case, this hope had been fulfilled. Her fore-topmast had been replaced; the tangled network of broken spars and torn rigging, with which she had emerged from the action, had been cut away and replaced, and the gaping holes in hull and upperworks, made by the Russian round shot, plugged and caulked up. The carpenter and his mates had toiled no less energetically than the seamen aloft, their task to rip up and renew splintered or fire-scorched deck planking and to repair what could not be renewed. Only her single, black-painted funnel, which had been riddled by the guns of the Wasp battery, still bore witness to the fury of the engagement in which *Trojan* and her squadron had taken part.

Standing on the quarterdeck, Phillip Horatio Hazard, the frigate's First Lieutenant and acting commander, looked about him with approval. Her newly appointed Captain, he thought, would be able to find little fault with the order *Trojan* was in, when he came to make his inspection later this morning. The entire ship's company had worked with a will, like the good men they were and . . . he bit back an involuntary sigh and, acknowledging the salute of the officer of the watch, who came to meet him, said formally, "Pipe hands to breakfast, if you please, Mr Fox. The ship's company will muster at five bells for Captain's inspection. Captain Crawford will read his commission and then inspect the ship, before conducting Divine Service."

"Aye, aye, sir." Lieutenant Fox nodded to the midshipman of the watch to pass on these instructions, his expression carefully blank and his voice lowered, as he added some routine instructions of his own. Seven bells of the Morning Watch struck; the Boatswain put his silver call to his lips and the pipe, echoed by his mate on the deck below, was obeyed with alacrity by the duty watch, who had all been out of their hammocks since 4 a.m.

As the men gathered in their messes, clustering hungrily about the well-scrubbed deal tables to await the appearance of the cooks, with their mess-kits of steaming cocoa and boiled ship's biscuit, the Boatswain's powerful, full-throated voice could be heard, carrying clearly to the lower deck.

"D'ye hear there, fore and aft? Clean for muster at five bells . . . rig of the day duck frocks and white trousers! Clean shirts and a shave, for Captain's inspection at five bells. . . ."

Phillip Hazard stood by himself on the starboard side of the quarterdeck, a tall and, in that moment, an oddly isolated and even lonely figure as he listened to the shouted orders, his dark brows meeting in a frown. Captain's inspection now meant, of course, Captain Crawford's inspection, not his own, he reflected wryly. In fact, this was probably the last time that he would stand on the weather side of *Trojan's* quarterdeck, clad in the dignified trappings of command, his word law to the three hundred officers and men who made up the frigate's complement of bluejackets, engineers, and marines. In a little under three hours' time, he would cease to enjoy the exclusive right to pace these few yards of narrow deck, which were, by tradition, the commander's prerogative, sacred to him as soon as he made his appearance from below, and to be shared only at his invitation, even by the officer of the watch. All too soon another man would stand here in his place and he himself, stripped of his brief authority, would be merely one of half a dozen watch-keeping lieutenants on board a ship-of-the-line, limited in his responsibilities, anonymous in his lack of importance.

He smothered another sigh and, suddenly aware that the eyes of his own officer of the watch were fixed on him in mute but nonetheless obvious sympathy, felt himself redden.

"Well?" He turned to face the offender. "What is it, Mr Fox?" His tone was discouraging, deliberately so, but Lieutenant Fox appeared to notice nothing amiss.

"Sir?" He came to Phillip's side, giving him the deference due to his temporary rank. "I said nothing, sir."

"No . . . but you were looking uncommonly glum. I wondered why."

Fox hesitated. "It occurred to me that the time had come rather sooner than we had anticipated, that was all," he answered guardedly.

"The time? The time for what, pray?" Phillip's expression did not relax.

"For you to take your leave of us again, Phillip," the younger man told him, abandoning formality, since there was no one else within earshot. "And I was sorry—or glum, if you prefer it. The *Trojan* has been a happy ship under your command . . . a happy and efficient ship, as she was when she was first commissioned. I wish, for all our sakes, that you could have had a little longer."

Phillip's lean, high-boned face hardened in an effort to avoid betraying his feelings. He regarded his senior watch-keeper and closest friend for a moment in frowning silence and then forced a smile. Their friendship had been of long standing, he reminded himself—dating back to their early days in the midshipmen's berth of Captain Keppel's *Maeander* frigate—and he had no secrets from Martin Fox. There was little point in pretending that he wanted to leave *Trojan* or welcomed the circumstances which compelled him to relinquish his temporary command and there was no point whatsoever in clinging to the remnants of a dignity he no longer possessed.

"I wish that too," he said flatly. "I wish with all my heart that I might have had a little while longer. I do not have to tell you with what affection I regard this ship or what it has meant to me to command her. But . . . let's walk, Martin, shall we, until your relief puts in an appearance? Captain Crawford will be taking breakfast with the Commander-in-Chief, he told me, so I do not imagine that he will be here much before five bells. And he doesn't require a boat to be sent for him."

They fell into step together, pacing the starboard side of the quarterdeck with the measured, unhurried tread of men to whom every obstacle and every foot of planking was familiar, both in daylight and in darkness.

"What is he like, Phillip?" Martin Fox asked curiously.

"Captain Crawford, do you mean?"

"Yes. You talked to him yesterday aboard *Britannia*, did you not? What impression did you form of him?"

"An exceptionally favourable one," Phillip answered, without hesitation. "He is not young, in fact he's held post-rank for almost as long as you and I have been at sea. And he has a fine record, of course. He was in Sir Edward Codrington's squadron at Navarino, and served as a midshipman in the *Blonde,* which makes him one of the elite of this squadron. Admittedly, he has been on the half-pay list for several years but that, I understand, was due to ill health . . . Captain Crawford is not a wartime misfit like North. You'll have no occasion to worry on that account,

Martin, I assure you—he's a fine seaman, from all accounts. As to what he's like, as a man . . . well, I spent only a few minutes in conversation with him yesterday. Both Admirals were present, plying him with questions concerning the latest news from home, so he hadn't much time to answer any of mine, but he struck me as a very pleasant individual. In appearance he is small and grey-haired, of rather frail physique, and he speaks very quietly. He seemed considerate and kindly and possessed of a dry sense of humour. I don't think you will find him hard to get along with."

"I trust you are right." Fox's broad shoulders rose in a shrug. The midshipman of the watch approached him diffidently, offering the muster book for his inspection. He excused himself, glanced at it, and nodded in curt dismissal. When he turned to Phillip again, the expression on his good-looking young face was a trifle less glum but he said, with regret, "I shall still be sorry to see you go. And so will this ship's company . . . most damnably sorry, Phillip, believe me."

"It's good of you to say so," Phillip returned, his tone bleak. "I'll be sorry to go but there's no help for it, is there? I had no illusions. I didn't for a moment imagine that I should be left in command of this ship, however much I wanted to be. It was never on the cards, Martin—how could it be, when there are full Commanders and even Post-Captains of twice my age, having to be content with six-gun sloops and out-dated paddle-wheel corvettes? In any event, my dear fellow . . ." He clapped a hand on his companion's shoulder and grinned at him affectionately. "My going will put you one more rung up the ladder and, if anyone has earned his promotion, you have . . . and I mean that, in all sincerity."

"Promotion at your expense?" Martin Fox exclaimed. He flushed indignantly. "That's the last thing I want, the very last! And you know it, don't you?"

"Of course I do. And you, I am sure, know that old proverb about not looking a gift horse in the mouth."

"I have heard it quoted," Fox admitted, still very red of

face. "But all the same, Phillip, Admiral Lyons did promise that you—"

Phillip cut him short. He said, his tone crisp, "The Admiral has done his best for me. Indeed, he's done far more than I had any right to expect, in the circumstances. I have him to thank for my appointment to the *Agamemnon* and—"

"As *third* lieutenant, Phillip! And he had told you, as he told us all, that he intended to recommend you for promotion," Fox put in.

"True," Phillip conceded, his smile widening and his tone now deliberately light. "But it is the Commander-in-Chief who decides whether or not to pass on such recommendations to their Lordships, is it not? I've been given the opportunity to volunteer for service with the Naval Brigade ashore, you know. Replacements are needed and Admiral Dundas himself advised me to take the opportunity. He—"

"Are you trying to tell me that Admiral Dundas has blocked your promotion?" Martin Fox demanded. He halted, staring at Phillip in frank bewilderment. "But why? What reason has he, for heaven's sake?"

Phillip fell silent, his smile fading. He was far from anxious to discuss—even with Martin Fox—what the Commander-in-Chief had said to him the previous evening, when he had been summoned aboard *Britannia* to receive orders to hand over his temporary command to Captain Crawford. The Admiral's words had come as an ugly shock to him, from which he had not yet fully recovered, and Martin Fox—being the loyal friend he was— would insist on coming to his defense should he suspect what had transpired. This, at all costs, must be prevented, Phillip thought wretchedly, since it would inevitably do more harm than good. He shrugged, with simulated indifference, and attempted to evade the question.

"The Admiral has his reasons, Martin, and no useful purpose can be served by going into them now, I promise you."

"But"—Fox was not to be put off—"he told you what his reasons were, I imagine?"

"Yes, he told me. But there's nothing to be done, in the circumstances. Nothing, that is to say, that would not make matters worse for us all . . . you may take my word for that."

"For *us all*, Phillip?" Fox said quickly. "What do you mean? Surely . . ." Comprehension dawned and he swore softly under his breath. "You cannot mean that the North affair is being held against you? If it is, then it's the height of injustice! Oh, I realize that it is considered reprehensible to speak ill of the dead, but where the late Captain North is concerned, my conscience is clear because I can, in truth, say nothing good of him."

"Then say nothing," Phillip besought him.

"Why? Is North to be whitewashed at your expense, without your lifting a finger to defend yourself? In God's name, Phillip, have you forgotten to what a state this ship's company was reduced under his command? Or to what desperate lengths we ourselves were being driven by his tyranny?"

"No." Tight-lipped, Phillip shook his head. "I have not forgotten—nor am I likely to forget. But I should infinitely prefer not to speak of it now, Martin. It is over, it's no longer of any consequence."

"But it *isn't* over!" Fox protested vehemently. "Phillip, we've been friends for a long time, you and I . . . I beg you to tell me what the Admiral said to you, if it concerns North. You can trust to my discretion, you must know that . . . unless, for some reason, I have forfeited your confidence. If I have then, for the sake of our friendship, you owe it to me to say so. At least tell me why."

"Don't be idiotic, my dear Martin . . . of course you haven't forfeited my confidence. Nevertheless I . . ." Phillip hesitated but finally, observing the injured look in Fox's dark eyes, he reluctantly abandoned his attempt at evasion. "Very well, since you wish it, I will tell you what there is to tell—provided I have your word that you will take no action in the matter. No action whatsoever, without consulting me first."

"That's a condition?"

"Yes, it is. I want your promise, Martin."

"Then you have it, naturally. But I—"

"Thank you." Phillip embarked on his explanation, choosing his words with care and hoping that Fox would not press him for too many details. "A few hours before he was stricken down by the cholera, Captain North paid a visit to *Britannia*. He requested an interview with Admiral Dundas, the purpose of which was, I have been given to understand, to accuse me of misconduct and to apply for my trial by court martial. The nature of the charges he made against me was such that, as Commander-in-Chief, Admiral Dundas has deemed it advisable to transfer me to another ship. I accept his decision of course," he added hastily, as Martin Fox endeavoured to interrupt him, "I've no right to question it, Martin. All things considered I have been fortunate . . . Admiral Lyons most generously spoke up for me and, furthermore, expressed his willingness to have me appointed to his own flagship. So you see, it's not a matter concerning which you need lose any sleep. I go to *Agamemnon* very gratefully, even if it has to be without my promotion. Things might have been a great deal worse and I intend, in any case, to volunteer for the Naval Brigade, subject to Admiral Lyons's approval and there I—"

"One moment, Phillip," Fox pleaded. "That isn't the whole story, is it? You are trying to pull the wool over my eyes but please . . . tell me the truth. I must know."

"What else do you want to know?" Phillip asked. "I've told you the essentials." It was almost eight bells, he thought, and Fox's relief would present himself in a few minutes. Although, being Sunday, when it was customary to allow an extra quarter of an hour for breakfast—to enable the men to prepare for inspection—the watch would not change until 8:30, or one bell of the Forenoon Watch. And this, unfortunately, would give his companion ample time in which to ask the questions he had been hoping to avoid . . . he again forced a smile and sought to change the subject but, as before, Martin Fox refused to be put off.

"You mentioned charges, Phillip," he pointed out. "But what possible charges could North have brought against you that he could not have brought against the rest of us? We were all more deeply involved than you were—you had only just rejoined the ship, after serving on the Admiral's staff."

Phillip shrugged. "Very well, if you must know—I was to be charged under Article Nineteen of the Articles of War." His voice was controlled and devoid of feeling. "North informed the Admiral that it was also his intention to bring charges against my brother. He did not specify what these were but he assured Admiral Dundas that evidence to support his charges, against both Graham and myself, would be furnished within a matter of hours. Since, however, he died within a matter of hours, no evidence was forthcoming, so . . ." He spread his hands in a gesture of resignation. "Officially, that is to be the end of the matter. North was ill. The Commander-in-Chief is prepared to accept that he may have been delirious."

"The petition!" Martin Fox exclaimed. "That letter we all signed, Phillip, requesting you to take whatever action was necessary to bring about North's removal from this command—*that* was his evidence, I suppose? He was depending on Smithson and his Marines to obtain possession of it, was he not, while he talked to Admiral Dundas?"

"Yes, I imagine so," Phillip said shortly. His mouth tightened in distaste as he recalled the events which had preceded his late commander's unpleasant and utterly unexpected demise.

Captain North, it was now evident, must have known of the petition to have him removed from command of *Trojan*—known or, at any rate, suspected that his officers were contemplating such a move. He had gone to the *Britannia* in a great hurry, determined that *his* version of the unhappy affair should be the first to reach the ears of the Commander-in-Chief. He had promised to supply proof of the allegations he had made to the Admiral, having left Smithson, the young Lieutenant of Marines, with orders to seize the letter and to place under arrest any officer who attempted to resist him. He had been on his way back to the ship, triumphantly aware that victory was his for the taking, when the cholera had struck him down . . . and he had died, unlamented by a single officer or seaman of *Trojan*'s crew, in the hideous, writhing agony of an acute attack of the disease.

Phillip shivered, as he remembered the scene which, with Surgeon Frazer and his brother Graham, he had been compelled to witness. It was a memory he had tried in vain to erase from his mind ever since, but it was imprinted there still, horrifying in its vivid clarity, to be conjured up at moments when he least wanted to be reminded of it. The tyrant denuded of his power, his final, vindictive triumph snatched from his grasp, had cut a pitiful and undignified figure in his last hours. The sweat broke out on Phillip's brow as he saw again, in memory, that white, twitching face and heard the frightened, sobbing cries, the abject pleas for aid which was no longer of the smallest use to him in his extremity.

No matter how bitterly he had hated Thomas North or how much he had suffered under the sadistic tyranny of his late commander, such an end—however providential it had proved—was not one to wish on a dog, still less on a human being. Yet at the time . . . he stiffened, aware that Martin Fox had asked him a question he had not heard, and thrust the ugly vision from him. Guessing what the question had been and steeling himself to display no sign of emotion, he said with flat lack of emphasis, "Without proof North's charges cannot, of course, be substantiated. And the proof, as you know, has been destroyed, on Admiral Lyons's instructions. He is, apart from ourselves, the only one who saw that petition—therefore, as I told you, Martin, that is the end of the matter. No official action is to be taken against either Graham or myself."

"Apart from your removal from this ship," Martin Fox reminded him indignantly. "And the Commander-in-Chief's refusal to recommend your promotion. Graham, no doubt, will remain rated an A.B.—or is he also to be transferred to an other ship?"

"No, he is to stay—subject to Captain Crawford's approval—as acting Second Master."

"Then you will be the only one to suffer, that's what it amounts to, Phillip. You, who are the least culpable of any! In justice to yourself, you cannot leave matters as they stand or expect us to. Surely you know that we, that all of us—"

"There's nothing to be done, Martin," Phillip interrupted, an edge to his voice. "As Admiral Dundas was at pains to make clear to me, officially I am being given the benefit of the doubt. But allegations of misconduct *were* made against me by my late commander and these have not been disproved. Nor can they be, unless I am brought to trial and there's no question of that. My accuser is dead and there were no witnesses to his interview with the Commander-in-Chief. I grant you, it's something of a vicious circle but you'll only make matters worse if you attempt to intervene on my behalf." He sighed in frustration, losing a little of the rigid control he had imposed on himself. "Don't you see, Martin, the fear that you would want to intervene was what made me reluctant to confide in you? And, I confess, why I had to extract a promise from you that you would do nothing without first consulting me—a promise to which I intend to hold you! Now, let's talk of something else, shall we? Something calculated to leave a pleasanter taste in the mouth than this has done."

"But for heaven's sake . . ." Martin Fox began, very white of face. Eight bells struck and, with commendable punctuality, Lieutenant Cochrane, who was his relief, mounted the after-companion way, saluted the quarterdeck, and stood waiting for a pause in the conversation, his smile innocently cheerful as he glanced from one to the other of his two seniors. Despite the fact that he was a conscientious and efficient officer, Anthony Cochrane had been one of the late Captain North's most frequent victims, Phillip recalled, and he had narrowly escaped a court martial for alleged insubordination, as the result of an attempt to save the men of his division from their commander's wrath. He acknowledged the red-headed young watchkeeper's salute but Fox, seemingly unaware of his presence, went on talking.

"This is monstrous, Phillip!" he said explosively. "If you are guilty of misconduct, then we all are . . . if, that's to say, the action to which North had driven us constitutes misconduct. Consider the fact, I beg you. We had agreed to draw up a petition, signed by every officer aboard this ship—with the exception of Smithson, who was only on temporary duty—and addressed to the Commander-in-Chief, to request the removal from command of a sadistic madman, who was quite unfitted to hold *any* command! Our request was justified, God knows. The letter was simply a means of putting our agreement in writing, so as to enable you, as First Lieutenant, to draw up the petition and present it to the Admiral, with our statements to back it up. Does that make it a breach of Article Nineteen or the petition itself an act of mutiny?"

"Both could have been so construed by a naval court martial," Phillip returned. "Ask Mr Burnaby, he's an expert on naval law. Besides, we're at war, don't forget and—"

"Is that supposed to be justice?" Martin Fox challenged, with bitterness. "When there's not an officer or seaman in the entire ship's company who would not have been willing to testify, on oath, to the truth of every word contained in those statements? For that matter, there isn't one who would not go to the Admiral now, if North's allegations against you require to be disproved. Believe me"—he halted, his eyes pleading as they met Phillip's—"they all think the world of you. They know what you did, what you were prepared to do . . . Laidlow, Cochrane, Surgeon Frazer, even old Burnaby, and, it goes without saying, myself. Any or all of us would gladly bear you out, Phillip—so why will you not permit us to do so?"

"Because, my dear fellow," Phillip told him, losing patience at last, "we should all be ruined if you did. And I most certainly should, I assure you. Study Article Nineteen, notably the references to 'mutinous assembly' if you've any doubt as to the inferences which could—and would—be drawn from them by a court martial board, however just and unbiased." He controlled himself and gestured to the patiently waiting Cochrane who, already attired in frock coat and cocked hat, served as a mute reminder that time was passing and he and Martin Fox had yet to change into full dress to receive their new commander. "Mr Cochrane is here to relieve you of the deck. I am sure, when you have broken your fast, that you'll feel more optimistic regarding this situation—as, indeed, I do myself, now I've had time to think about it."

"Do you truly, Phillip?"

"I do. So . . . let us drop the subject, shall we, and breakfast together? All things considered, my dear Martin, we have had a narrow and extremely lucky escape from disaster and we can, at least, start anew with a clean slate, can we not?"

"I suppose we can," Martin Fox admitted, but without conviction. "Nevertheless it's a gross injustice and you—with less reason to reproach yourself than any of us—are the loser. *That* sticks in my throat, Phillip."

"Forget it," Phillip advised. "Thanks to Admiral Lyons, I'm losing much less than I might have done and I've every reason to be grateful to him . . . every reason in the world. He is giving me the opportunity to vindicate myself and I ask no more than that." He laid a hand briefly on Fox's shoulder and added, with an abrupt change of tone, "Have the watch called, if you please. And leave instructions with Mr Cochrane to keep a sharp look out for Captain Crawford's gig. I wish to be called as soon as it is sighted."

"Aye, aye, sir," Martin Fox acknowledged automatically. He passed on the order and, as the pipe sounded and the duty watch came scrambling up on deck in response to the call, he prepared to hand over to his relief.

Phillip crossed to the starboard rail to wait for him, listening without impatience to the thud of bare feet on the deck planking and the familiar shouted orders. A midshipman's high-pitched, boyish voice called out names from the muster book, reeling one off after the other with scarcely a pause, and the men answered gruffly, smart in their clean white frocks, their faces freshly shaven, ready for inspection. On board other ships at the Fleet anchorage, similar scenes were taking place and, from where he stood, Phillip could glimpse the fine steam-screw two-decker *Agamemnon*—soon to be his destination—lying at anchor a quarter of a mile to the east and closer inshore than the rest of the line-of-battle ships. He expelled his breath in a longdrawn sigh, conscious once again of regret. It was going to be a wrench leaving this ship, he knew . . . an appalling wrench.

He had put *Trojan* in commission, standing for the first time on her quarterdeck when she had been lying in dry dock at Devonport, with her masts out . . . a lifeless and unlovely hulk, to whose taffrail he had secured a small staff with a narrow pennant flying from it, as a symbol of her future in the Queen's service.

Her future? He repeated his sigh, remembering the dreams he had had, the hopes, and the pride he had felt that day. *Trojan* had been the first ship for whose fitting-out and manning he had been solely responsible, since Thomas North had not been appointed to command her until, under his supervision, she had been put into full seagoing trim and her crew entered.

During the weeks of dockyard preparation, when she had been masted, rigged, stored, provisioned, and armed, this ship had occupied a special place in his heart. As indeed, Phillip thought sadly, she always would. He had seen her lofty masts and yards swayed into place from the dockyard sheers, had seen her rigging set up, dead-eyes and ratlines squared, the worn copper on her bottom stripped off and replaced by newly rolled sheets, and her over-hauled engines tested and tuned. Under his critical eye, painters had applied the finishing touches to the black and white checker of her gundeck, with its hinged portlids—their number increased by two on each side, to allow for the extra armament she was to carry—and to deck fittings, upperworks, and funnel. He had inspected her two suits of sails and seen one bent to the yards, the other—completely fitted, ready for use—stowed in the sailroom.

Trojan had been his ship then, his ship and his responsibility. As he had watched her grow into a thing of grace and beauty, he had come to love her with the single-minded devotion and the passionate, heartfelt pride that only a seaman can feel for his ship. Even the ill-fated advent of Captain North had not changed his feelings for the ship herself or for the officers and men who made up her crew. If anything, Phillip realized now, it had enhanced them, involving him more deeply in *Trojan*'s destiny and causing him to assume a greater measure of personal responsibility for her people.

As First Lieutenant he had endeavoured to stand between the ship's company and their new Captain's ruthless attempts to enforce a system of discipline which daily became more harsh and unreasonable. He had, as a result, borne the brunt of North's outbursts of savage rage, his frequent accusations of disloyalty . . . Phillip's hands gripped the rail, tightening convulsively as he looked back, remembering.

Thomas North had been the *Trojan*'s evil genius as well as his own and he found himself wondering whether, as Martin Fox had suggested a short while before, their late commander had, in fact, been a madman. Certainly no sane and responsible captain could have behaved as North had behaved to those unfortunate enough to have had to serve under him, regardless alike of the consequences and of the hatred he had invited. No normal man, with an ounce of human feeling in him, could have gone on day after day, driving other men to the limit of their endurance, without justification or excuse and completely without pity. Yet the late Captain North—if the rumours which persisted concerning his previous command, the brig *Guillemot*, were true—had done so twice in his lifetime. . . .

Phillip relaxed his grip on the rail in front of him. The nightmare was over, he reminded himself. North was dead and the rest must be forgotten and it was best that it should be forgotten. *Trojan* was to have a new commander; Martin Fox was, most deservedly, to become her First Lieutenant. He himself, although the dead hand of Thomas North had reached out to touch him with brief malice, had nothing on his conscience to trouble him, nothing he need seriously regret. The morale, discipline, and efficiency of the ship's company had been fully restored. *Trojan* had gone into action against the stone forts of Sebastopol under his command and had acquitted herself well. She had earned Admiral Lyons's commendation and the cheers of other ships in the fleet when, with *Spitfire* and *Lynx,* she had emerged from the smoke of the Russian guns, escorting the stricken *Rodney* out of their range.

Therefore if he were honest, Phillip reflected, he could not—except for purely sentimental reasons—regret his forthcoming transfer to *Agamemnon.* In the circumstances, as he had told Martin Fox, he could consider himself extremely fortunate to have been given an opportunity to serve aboard the flagship or, as one of her officers, to join the Naval Brigade ashore. His appointment, the Commander-in-Chief had told him, had been made at Admiral Lyons's behest and this, in itself, was an indication of the Rear-Admiral's continued confidence in him. It also meant that he was being granted a second chance to secure his promotion, for which he had every reason to be grateful . . . and, indeed, more than grateful.

Like all who had ever served under his command, he had the highest admiration and respect for Rear-Admiral Sir Edmund Lyons, as well as a warm personal regard which had grown up over the years. He had been a very junior midshipman when he had first made Sir Edmund's acquaintance and, with his shipmates, had sampled the generous Lyons's hospitality at the British Embassy in Athens. . . . Phillip smiled reminiscently. It had been there that he had met the other members of the family, including Jack—the younger of the Admiral's two sons and also in the Navy—with whom, despite Jack's eight years' seniority, he had formed a close and lasting friendship.

Jack—Captain Edmund Mowbray Lyons—was now in command of H.M.S. *Miranda* and on his way to join his father's flag in the Black Sea. *Miranda*, a steam sloop of fourteen guns, had been the first British naval vessel to enter the Baltic and, under Jack Lyons's able command, had subsequently greatly distinguished herself in operations in the White Sea. In company with the *Eurydice*, 26 and the *Brisk*, 16, she had maintained a successful blockade of Russia's Arctic shipping for nearly four months—no mean achievement on the part of three small steamers, virtually alone in enemy waters. Phillip's smile widened. It would be good to see Jack again and . . . "If you're ready, sir—" Martin Fox was at his elbow.

He roused himself. "Yes, indeed, Martin—I'm decidedly peckish, I don't know about you. But we shall have to bestir ourselves or Captain Crawford will be alongside before we're properly attired to receive him. Lead on."

"After you, sir," Fox answered. He stood aside to permit Phillip to precede him, offering him the last courtesy he would enjoy as *Trojan*'s commander.

2

They breakfasted together in the gunroom and, as if by common consent, their conversation was of the ship and of the war and they avoided all personal topics. There were other officers seated at the long table—Lieutenant Laidlaw, Surgeon Fraser, Paymaster Oliphant, Sutherland, the young Mate who was acting gunnery officer, and the white-haired Master, Mr Burnaby. All were oddly subdued, wearing long faces, their reluctance to see him go greater than he had expected, Phillip recognized, but tempered with an embarrassment, when it came to expressing their feelings, which he sympathized with and shared. He choked down his food and said his farewells as briefly as he could, anxious to spare them, as well as himself, the added embarrassment of prolonged good-byes and too many meaningless expressions of goodwill.

His hand aching with the warmth of their handshakes, he made his escape at last and hurried to the Captain's cabin to change into full dress uniform. His steward had already packed for him and hastened to complete the task by adding his pilot jacket and cap to the valise as he took them off. When all his gear had been removed, the cabin took on a curiously empty and characterless air, as if waiting for the new occupant to enter and imprint his personality upon it. Phillip looked about him, as he picked up his cocked hat, and bit back a sigh, seeing North, as he had so often seen him in this cabin, hearing his voice raised, as always, in reproof or resentful anger. But North had gone, as he was going, he reminded himself, and *Trojan's* destiny in the Queen's service would be in another's hands, whilst he . . . there was a knock on the cabin door and, on receiving permission to do so, the Marine sentry on duty outside thrust it open. Phillip recognized his brother's tall, slightly stooping figure in the dimly lit alleyway and called out to him to come in.

Graham Hazard did so, bare-headed and standing to attention, his seaman's straw hat tucked correctly beneath his arm, until the sentry withdrew, closing the door of the cabin behind him. Then he relaxed and turned to Phillip, a smile lighting his gaunt face.

"Have you ten minutes to spare, Phillip? If you haven't, say so and I'll go."

"Of course I have," Phillip assured him. "Sit down, won't you . . . and here, let me offer you a cigar."

"Thanks." Graham accepted the cigar and, when it was lit, puffed at it appreciatively. He was the elder by only seven years but he looked forty, rather than thirty-four, his thinning fair hair already touched with grey at the temples. Of course, since a naval court martial had put an end to his promising career, his life had been hard, and the past eight months—spent on the lower deck, as a seaman under Thomas North's command—had aged him almost beyond recognition, Phillip thought, conscious of an overwhelming pity.

In their boyhood days Graham had been a hero to him, already at sea as a midshipman, when he himself had still been at school. Now, anxiously studying his face, Phillip wondered whether his brother still resented those lost, bitter years, cut off from family and friends and disowned by their proud old father or whether, at last, he was becoming reconciled to the blows an unkind fate had dealt him.

As one of the survivors of the steam frigate *Tiger*, after she had run aground off Odessa, he had been a Russian prisoner of war and had only recently been released, under an exchange agreement made with the Governor of Odessa, Baron Osten-Sacken. The Russians had treated all the *Tiger* survivors well and ironically, for Graham, his captivity had probably been—so far as personal comfort went—a considerable improvement on the conditions under which he had now to exist. Yet he had returned, rejecting the Russian offer of a commission, to the British fleet where—despite a commendation for gallantry from *Tiger*'s First Lieutenant—his chances of regaining officer status were, to say the least of it, remote. And Captain North, had he lived long enough, would have rewarded his act of patriotic altruism with a second court martial . . . Phillip's mouth hardened.

Graham said, meeting his gaze, "I trust you weren't thinking of leaving the ship without permitting me to wish you Godspeed, were you, Phillip?"

Phillip shook his head. "No," he answered, not entirely truthfully, since he was aware that his brother's questions—if he were given an opportunity to ask them—would be no less difficult to evade than Martin Fox's had been a short while before. "I was not . . . but my orders to join the *Agamemnon* came a trifle sooner than I had anticipated. And with Captain Crawford due to read his commission aboard this ship at five bells, I haven't had very much time for leave taking, as I am sure you will appreciate."

Graham's brows rose in a surprised curve. "You were expecting an appointment to the *Agamemnon,* then?"

"Let us say I was hoping for it," Phillip qualified.

"That's odd!"

"Why should it be odd?"

"Lower deck rumour, which is seldom wrong," Graham returned, "has it that you are about to join the Naval Brigade on shore. In fact, my dear Phillip, so strong is that particular rumour—and so great your popularity with the men—that at least half the Starboard Watch, led by Able-Seaman Joseph O'Leary, are determined that they will volunteer in a body to serve with you. O'Leary has already been to his Divisional Officer about it and he intends to make his request to the new Captain tomorrow morning."

"It won't be granted, Graham."

"Why not? O'Leary's the best gunlayer we have."

"The steam squadron has to be maintained at full strength," Phillip explained. "No seaman volunteers, apart from those already in the batteries, are to be accepted from any of the steamers, least of all from the frigates. Replacements for men killed or wounded ashore are to be found by the sailing ships—that is a Fleet Order."

"I see." Graham sighed. "Well, the news will break poor O'Leary's fighting Irish heart, but I fancy it won't lessen his determination to follow you ashore. Aside from his devotion to you, Phillip, he's convinced that the Naval Brigade and the Marines will see more action than the Fleet is likely to now. He could well be right. I pray, for all our sakes, that he *is* right, if it means an end to this infamous delay and an attack on Sebastopol, with all the resources at our command!"

His brother had spoken with such feeling that Phillip stared at him in frank bewilderment. "*Infamous* delay?" he questioned.

"What do you intend to imply by that remark? Presumably you have some good reason for making it?"

"Yes, indeed I have," Graham asserted gravely. "Phillip, unless an assault is made very soon we shall be here for the winter. Or else compelled to evacuate the Crimea, with the loss of all that has been so hardly won. Either would be a disaster, you know. The Crimean winter is quite appalling in its severity, according to the Russians and, for troops under canvas, it would be unendurable. . . ." He enlarged on this and then asked, frowning, "What had gone wrong, do you know, Phillip? *Why* has there been no assault? In Odessa they were expecting Sebastopol to fall for weeks and, even in St Petersburg, the outcome was regarded as inevitable. After his defeat at the Alma, Prince Menschikoff withdrew all his troops from the town, considering it to be indefensible. The Allies could have walked in virtually unopposed, once they had crossed the Balbec. The Russians expected them to do so."

"That can't possibly be true!" Phillip protested, doubting the evidence of his own ears.

"It is, I give you my word . . . and you can believe me or not, as you choose."

"I believe you. But I don't understand, Graham. What do you mean by virtually unopposed?"

"Well . . ." Graham shrugged. "These are the facts, as I know them. Once the army had withdrawn, there were only a handful of seamen left to defend the town . . . less than eight thousand men drawn from Admiral Korniloff's fleet, with three or four thousand soldiers and a few hundred militiamen. Sebastopol's sea defenses are formidable, as we now know to our cost, but the forts on the landward side had long been neglected and allowed to fall into disrepair. They could have been stormed, with small loss, a week after the battle of the Alma . . . even two weeks, perhaps. The only guns which could have put up an effective resistance on the landward side were those of the ships in harbour."

"I find that hard to believe," Phillip demurred.

"Nevertheless it is true," his brother asserted. "It was said that Admiral Korniloff—who, by all accounts, is a brave man—wanted to put to sea with his ships and fight it out with our fleet. But Menschikoff, as supreme commander, over-ruled him . . . he, apparently, ordered the seven line-of-battle-ships to be scuttled and sunk across the harbour mouth, so as to close it to us. He intended it as a temporary measure, to delay the entry of our fleet. Menschikoff had abandoned Sebastopol, Phillip. He was expecting the navy to defend the town only for long enough to enable him to withdraw his main body of troops to Bakshi-Serai, from whence he could receive supplies and reinforcements, and preserve his lines of communication with Russia . . . aiming eventually at a counter-attack. Once he had gained his objective and had covered the post-road to Simpheropol, the garrison of Sebastopol—such as it was—would have served its purpose. They say he's a shrewd old man and a ruthless tactician. As far as he was concerned, Korniloff could either have surrendered or endeavoured to make a run for it, after blowing up the naval arsenal and docks and scuttling the rest of his ships. So you see. . . ." Graham smiled, his smile lacking any vestige of amusement. "The Allied armies *could* have walked into Sebastopol a month ago. Surely the Generals cannot have been so ill-informed as not to be aware of the situation? Lord Raglan must have known that Menschikoff's army had withdrawn . . . didn't he have a brush with the rearguard?"

"I don't imagine that any of the Generals could have known how small a garrison had been left to defend the place," Phillip told him wryly. "I am, of course, not *au fait* with such matters but I did hear that Lord Raglan and most of his Divisional Commanders were only too eager to press on when they reached the Balbec. In fact, there's a story currently going the rounds that Sir George Cathcart volunteered to carry the town with his Fourth Division alone, supported by our steam squadron under Admiral Lyons. But the French wouldn't have it."

"In heaven's name why not?" Graham exclaimed.

"Well, Marshal St Arnaud was dying and General Canrobert had just succeeded to the French supreme command. It was he, apparently, who insisted that the assault must be made from the south and who, I was told, refused to agree to any assault at all, until the siege-guns had been landed to support his infantry. I believe that both Sir George Brown and Sir John Burgoyne shared his opinion and advised Lord Raglan accordingly." Phillip's tone was bleak and he added, remembering Admiral Lyons's bitter disappointment when the Generals' final decision had been made known to him. "None of us liked it, Graham, least of all our Admiral. But Lord Raglan had no choice . . . and he could not attack without the French. In any case, an attack from the north side of the town would have meant ferrying our troops across the harbour. With the blockships sunk across the roadstead, the navy could have given them no assistance and that octagonal fort—which we call the Star Fort—mounting about fifty heavy guns, lay directly in the French line of march. So perhaps their caution was justified."

"Perhaps," Graham conceded, doubtfully. "But having made the flank march and reached the south side of the town, they could still have walked in. *Why* did they not?"

"Because it took three weeks to land the siege-guns and haul them into position for the bombardment," Phillip said.

"To bombard a town that was ready to surrender?" Graham spread his hands in a gesture of despair. "What madness! The delay and the Allies' inaction puzzled everyone in Odessa— there seemed no reason for it. Well, the Russians have made good use of their unexpected respite—Sebastopol is, alas, no easy nut to crack now! Even Baron Osten-Sacken, who prophesied its fall almost daily, has since inclined to the belief that if the place can be held for a few more weeks, then the Crimean winter will do the rest."

"Do you agree with him? Do you think Sebastopol will hold?"

Graham sighed. "Yes, if we delay our assault much longer. Menschikoff has been pouring in reinforcements since early in

October, Phillip. His troops use the post-road from Simpheropol, through Bakshi-Serai, and enter from the north, which—although they are supposedly besieging the town—the Allies have conveniently left open for them! General Luders, with sixteen thousand men, joined the garrison on the fourth of October and, according to the talk I heard in Odessa, the total strength of Sebastopol's defenders must now be doubled. Menschikoff is prudently holding his main body outside the town and adding to its numbers as each day passes. One of the best of the Russian generals, Liprandi, who distinguished himself in the Danube campaign, is said to be in the Tchernaya valley with a considerable force, including cavalry and field guns. And I can tell you for certain that over thirty thousand reserve troops left Odessa three weeks ago for Perekop . . . because I saw them leave."

Unable any longer to doubt the accuracy of his brother's information, Phillip said, "But we have a squadron blockading Odessa, under the command of Captain Goldsmith. He has the *Sidon* and the *Inflexible,* and two French steam frigates, and is patrolling the coast between Cape Tarkan and the mouth of the Dnieper and he—"

"Oh, yes, Goldsmith's squadron was in action against the rearguard," Graham interrupted. "They were being ferried across from Kinburn to Ochakov but all that happened was that the boats went into shoal water, where his frigates could not get within range of them, and the fort at Nicholaief eventually drove him off. It was a gallant effort but our naval blockade is powerless to stop a large body of troops marching overland—they cross the isthmus to Perekop where Baron Osten-Sacken has, no doubt, joined them by this time. He told me he intended to . . . and the Prince Narishkin with him, with his regiment of Chasseurs of Odessa."

"Prince Narishkin?" Phillip said, an edge to his voice. He had not thought of Mademoiselle Sophie or her husband for a long time, had steeled himself not to, but he thought of them now and his hands clenched involuntarily at his sides.

Graham affected not to notice anything amiss. He went on, as if there had been no interruption. "Menschikoff was beaten at the Alma, Phillip, but he outnumbers us now or he soon will. When that happens, he will launch a counter-attack . . . probably on Eupatoria, with his Cossack cavalry, and almost certainly from the valley of the Tchernaya, in an attempt to turn our right flank and drive us out of Balaclava. Both possibilities were being talked about quite freely in Odessa. Russian communications are notoriously slow but a courier from Menschikoff reached Osten-Sacken just before I joined the *Fury*, and there was great jubilation at the news he brought, concerning our failure to take Sebastopol. No one could understand it."

Which, Phillip thought grimly, was hardly surprising. "Have you spoken of this to anyone else?" he asked. "Anyone in authority, I mean? Because it may be of vital importance."

"No one in authority appears to be even remotely interested in the observations of a mere A.B., Phllip," Graham returned, his tone faintly derisive. "Indeed I was regarded with grave suspicion when I said I had been well treated by the Russians! Oh, I tried . . . I tried very hard all the time I was aboard the *Fury*. I made a full report to Commander Chambers, who promised to pass it on—perhaps he did but I've heard no more. I took it that most of what I had found out would already be known to the Allied High Command, so I did not press the point. By the time I rejoined this ship I had rather given up hope of finding anybody who would listen to me."

"You said nothing to me," Phillip reproached him. "I would have listened to you, you must know that."

"We have both of us been occupied with other matters," Graham pointed out. "First with the late unlamented Captain North and then with our naval bombardment and its consequences. Until this moment, I've had no chance to talk to you. But you'll be joining *Agamemnon* very soon, Phillip . . . if you can gain the ear of Admiral Lyons he, at least, might listen. It may be stale news but will you tell him?"

"At the first opportunity," Phillip promised. "But now . . ."

He flashed his brother an apologetic glance and took his watch from his pocket. "I'm afraid that I must go, I—"

"I know." Graham rose, crushing out his cigar. "You have to hand over your command. I'm sorry about that, Phillip. You commanded *Trojan* well. The whole ship's company will regret your going."

"Thank you."

"Don't thank me for giving you your due." Graham held out his hand. "I wish you well in your new appointment."

Phillip took the extended hand and wrung it. "*Au revoir,* Graham. You are to stay, you know, as Second Master, subject to Captain Crawford's approval."

"So I've been given to understand by Mr Burnaby. I trust that Captain Crawford *will* approve . . . if he does not, you may yet find both O'Leary and myself manning a gun in the Seaman's Battery. Captain Crawford may be thankful to be rid of us, whatever Fleet Orders ordain . . . we're both Queen's hard bargains, are we not?" Graham grinned wryly and, tucking his hat under his arm again, moved to the cabin door. "Good luck, Phillip my dear lad . . . may God be with you."

"And with you," Phillip responded, meaning it with all his heart. He donned his cocked hat and went on deck.

Punctually at five bells, Captain Crawford's gig came alongside. He was received with the ceremony to which his rank entitled him and, having read his commission to the assembled ship's company, became officially Captain of *Trojan.*

At the conclusion of Divine Service, Phillip stepped into the boat which was to take him to *Agamemnon.* As the midshipman in charge called out the order to give way, he looked back, once. After that, he kept his gaze fixed resolutely on the flagship, drawing rapidly nearer, as the boat's crew bent with a will to their oars. . . .

CHAPTER TWO

1

Sir Edmund Lyons was ashore at Lord Raglan's headquarters when Phillip reported aboard the *Agamemnon*.

"He is likely to remain there until well into the afternoon," his friend Tom Johnson, the flagship's senior watchkeeper, told him. "After that, I understand, he will go straight to Kadi-Koi for a conference with Sir Colin Campbell. Tell me . . . is your business with him urgent, Phillip?"

"In my view it is," Phillip answered. "The Admiral may be aware of something I have learnt recently but, if he is not, then I think he would wish to be made aware of it."

"In that case, I'd have a word with his Secretary, Frederick Cleeve," Lieutenant Johnson advised. "You know him, of course. Well, ask him to arrange for you to report to the Admiral first thing tomorrow morning . . . and I mean first thing. His barge is called away as soon as he has broken his fast which, when he is going ashore, is seldom later than five bells of the Morning Watch."

"Does he go ashore daily?" Phillip asked.

"Almost daily. Once of the small steamers conveys him to Balaclava and then he rides to Lord Raglan's headquarters which, as you know, is nearly seven miles." Tom Johnson sighed. "It's taking it out of him, and he's beginning to feel the strain, for he doesn't spare himself. But we have to remain here, in order to conserve our fuel, if you please! There's talk that we are to be permitted to shift from this anchorage to Kherson, which would be a blessing from our Admiral's point of view. It would greatly shorten the fatiguing journey for him and would also lessen the risk he's compelled to take. Imagine it, Phillip . . . this morning the *Beagle* took him to Balaclava, yesterday it was the *Arrow,* and both ships landed their Lancasters to help with the siege!"

"You mean they're unarmed?" Phillip asked, shocked.

Tom Johnson nodded, tight-lipped. "I do. And the Russians, as you'll have observed, have several steamers anchored just inside the boom, ready to sally forth on the chance of picking up a prize. The *Vladimir* is especially active in this respect. Her gunnery is excellent and she's well and boldly commanded— our troops on shore had to erect a battery for the express purpose of returning her fire. And I imagine you heard of the occasion ten days ago, when she would have taken an Austrian bark—on passage from Eupatoria to Balaclava, with hay for our commissariat—but for a very smart piece of work on the part of *Beagle* and *Firebrand?*"

"No, I hadn't heard. What happened?"

Lieutenant Johnson smiled. "Oh, it was a splendid thing! The bark ran herself aground on the shoal off Fort Constantine, with all the guns the fort could bring to bear blazing away at her, and the *Vladimir* and another Russian running at full speed out of harbour to take her in tow and bring her into Sebastopol. But in went Boxer, the Second Master, who was in command, with the unarmed *Beagle,* to slip a tow-rope to her and, as he got her away, *Firebrand* stood by to cover him. Captain William Houston Stewart, in *Firebrand,* got the worst of it . . . she was hulled four times. But neither *Beagle* nor the bark received a hit. The Russian gunners have improved since then, alas! You took a pounding from Fort Constantine in last Tuesday's action, did you not?"

"We did," Phillip agreed. They exchanged news and then, Tom Johnson being due on watch, Phillip went, as he had sug-gested, in search of Frederick Cleeve. The Secretary promised to put forward his request and the following morning, at five bells, he was summoned to join the Admiral at breakfast in his quarters. He went with alacrity.

"Well, Phillip my dear boy, it's good to have you aboard again . . ." As always, Admiral Lyons's greeting was warm and friendly but he looked tired, Phillip observed. His thin, pale face—which, in his youth, had borne so strikingly a resemblance to that of the great Admiral Nelson—was unusually lined and haggard and there were dark shadows beneath his eyes, as if he were sorely in need of sleep. As Tom Johnson said, he never spared himself and he was now in his middle sixties, a man of frail physique but—like Nelson—of indomitable courage. Phillip returned his greeting respectfully and the Admiral waved him to a seat.

"Sit down, my dear boy, and help yourself. You are fortunate . . . I have a rare treat to offer you this morning. Grilled kidneys, no less, and obtained, I am given to understand"—he smiled engagingly—"from an animal that strayed inadvertently into the bivouac of the 93rd Highlanders at Kadi-Koi."

A rare treat indeed, Phillip thought, as he helped himself from a silver entrée dish offered by the Admiral's steward—and a welcome change from his accustomed breakfast of stewed salt pork and ship's biscuit. The steward poured his coffee and then the Admiral dismissed him.

"I believe that you wish to see me on a confidential matter, Phillip? Well, I have half an hour to spare, as it happens so . . ." Sir Edmund refilled his own coffee cup and regarded him expectantly. "Say what you want to. If it concerns your lack of promotion—a promotion which, in my opinion, you have fully merited—then I can only tell you that I did my best to get you your step, but I failed."

Phillip reddened. "It doesn't sir. I—"

"Does it not? Good . . . but since we're on the subject, I should like to give you my assurance that you will get your promotion—and a command of your own—when I am Commander-in-Chief of this fleet. In the meantime"—the Admiral's small, slim hand rested lightly on his guest's shoulder—"you are appointed to this ship as third lieutenant, since there was no other vacancy available. But with the experience you have had as a staff officer and the ability you have shown, I can find employment for you on my staff."

"Thank you very much indeed, sir," Phillip acknowledged with sincere gratitude. "There is no service I would rather perform and I will do all in my power to be worthy of your confidence. You have already done much more for me than I deserve, sir."

"Nonsense, boy! More kidneys?" The dish was pushed invitingly across the table. "Finish them up, Phillip. I've had all I want . . . my appetite is poor these days and it would be a pity to waste such excellent fare."

"Indeed it would, sir . . . thank you." Phillip needed no second bidding and, as he obediently emptied the dish, Sir Edmund eyed him thoughtfully.

"You know, I imagine, the reason why the Commander-in-Chief was unwilling to promote you?"

"Yes, sir, I do. In the circumstances—"

"Quite . . . there was nothing else he could do, in these particular circumstances."

Phillip stopped eating, feeling suddenly nauseated.

"I understand that, sir, perfectly."

"Good." The Admiral's smile was both warm and approving. "It takes courage to accept injustice but you'll get your chance again, Phillip, don't worry. Admiral Dundas expressed the wish that you should serve for a time ashore with the Naval Brigade, unless I needed you for staff duties. Well, I do need you but I can find very useful employment for you ashore. Officially you will be under the orders of Captain Lushington and quartered with the Naval Brigade, as from today. But your responsibility will be to me and your duties those of a liaison officer, wherever I may find it expedient to send you . . . is that clear?"

The feeling of nausea slowly passed. "Aye, aye, sir," Phillip acknowledged. Lower deck rumour, as Graham had claimed, wasn't wrong after all, he reflected. Officially, at any rate, he was to join the Naval Brigade and, if O'Leary's supposition should also prove to be correct, he would see more action ashore than afloat . . . a prospect he could not but welcome in his present situation. He finished his kidneys with relish.

"Then that is settled," the Admiral said. "I trust as much to your satisfaction as to mine. And now . . . what is this confidential matter of which you wish to speak to me? What—or whom—does it concern?"

Phillip looked up to meet his gaze. "It concerns my brother, sir. You may recall that he is serving with the fleet as an able-seaman, acting as Second Master . . ." He hesitated but Sir Edmund nodded to him to continue. "He was with the *Tiger*, sir, and he rejoined *Trojan* recently, having been a prisoner of war in Odessa since May. The information he gave me may already be known to you, sir, and to Lord Raglan, but I thought it might be of some importance. May I be permitted to tell you what he told me?"

"When did you receive this information from your brother?"

"Yesterday, sir. But he made a full report to the Captain of *Fury* immediately after leaving Odessa and it's possible—"

"That the report was passed on to me?" Admiral Lyons put in. "It was not. Carry on, Phillip, I should be interested to hear what your brother learnt in Odessa."

"Aye, aye, sir . . ." Phillip repeated, as concisely as he could, everything that Graham had told him. The Admiral listened, for the most part, in silence, occasionally interposing a question when some detail was not quite clear to him, his brow deeply furrowed as the recital continued.

When it was over, he said quietly, "Thank you, Phillip—I am glad that you, at any rate, wasted no time in bringing me this information. Had it reached us earlier, it might have been of inestimable value . . . although I doubt whether even this would have influenced the decision, made by the French

General Staff, to delay the assault on Sebastopol until the siege guns were in position. I doubt it very much—and Lord Raglan mistrusts any intelligence of the enemy's strength or movements received at second-hand. But I wish that *I* had known how few men stood between us and final victory on the twenty-fourth of September!" He smothered a sigh. "However, your brother did not rejoin the fleet until a week or so ago, did he? By then, of course, it was too late."

"Yes, sir," Phillip confirmed, hiding his disappointment at the Admiral's reaction to his report. What he had said was true, admittedly. By the time that Graham had returned from Odessa, the garrison of Sebastopol had been substantially reinforced; and the landward defenses—which Sir George Cathcart had once contemptuously described as "being in the nature of a low park wall"—were now almost as formidable as those guarding the approaches to the harbour.

In three short weeks, while the British and French had labouriously set up their siege-batteries on the Upland and hacked out their parallels in the rocky ground, the Russians had not been idle. Working night and day like so many busy, purposeful ants, soldiers, sailors, and civilians had constructed a defensive system four miles in extent—earthworks, interspersed with strong redoubts and bastions—between the original stone-built forts. As Graham had remarked, Sebastopol was now no easy nut to crack and, if Prince Menschikoff launched a counter-attack on Balaclava, then the tables might well be turned and the besiegers become the besieged. . . .

As if he had read Phillip's thoughts, the Admiral went on, still in the same quiet voice, "Your brother's information confirms what Sir Colin Campbell and I have feared for some time . . . that the Russians intend to drive us from Balaclava if they can. Sir Colin, as you may be aware, has been placed in command of the Balaclava defenses, but these have been hastily prepared and he is by no means satisfied that they are adequate. I saw him yesterday, on my way to confer with Lord

Raglan, and he told me that a Turkish spy had reported that a Russian attack was imminent . . . and coming, as your brother suggests it will, from the valley of the Tchernaya. That is on our right flank, which Sir Colin considers to be dangerously undermanned. And, if a general of the caliber of Liprandi has been sent here, I do not for a moment imagine that he will fail to exploit the weakness on our right, once he becomes aware of it . . . as he undoubtedly will. Rustem Pasha's spy reported that he has at least thirty squadrons of cavalry under his command."

"Cossacks, sir?" Phillip suggested.

The Admiral shook his head. "Not merely Cossacks, Phillip . . . crack regiments of Hussars and Lancers, it seems, if the Turk is to be believed. His report worried Sir Colin and, in response to his request for aid, Lord Raglan ordered Sir George Cathcart's Fourth Division down from the Upland plateau, and Lord Lucan had the Cavalry Division standing-to all night. But no attack materialized so . . ." He shrugged. "The Fourth Division returned to their position, too exhausted to undertake their normal duty in the trenches it would seem, according to their commander, who was far from pleased when the alarm proved to be a false one."

"And our right flank, sir?" Phillip inquired diffidently.

"Is still dangerously undermanned and vulnerable," Admiral Lyons returned, his mouth compressed. "The Russians have reconnoitered the position several times during the past week, with both cavalry and infantry, but Lord Raglan says he has no troops to spare to reinforce it. He has requested that we land more Marines from the fleet. I shall make his wishes known to Admiral Dundas this morning, before I go ashore, and I hope he'll comply with them. The *Algiers* is due to reach this anchorage some time today—she is from England and has a full complement of Marines. With these and, if the Commander-in-Chief agrees, a further two hundred from the *Sanspareil*, our contribution to the defense of Balaclava can be brought up to over fourteen hundred men. But Sir Colin Campbell has few enough under his command, God knows! He has the 93rd, from his own Highland Brigade—his other two regiments are with the First Division—and about a hundred invalids and convalescents, newly returned from hospital in Scutari. In addition he has Captain Barker's troop of Horse Artillery and about fourteen hundred Turco-Tunisian irregulars."

"Turks, sir?" Phillip exclaimed. "To defend Balaclava?"

The Admiral inclined his head gravely. "Yes. And they are ill-equipped and badly disciplined, from all accounts, and Sir Colin says he places little reliance on them. But nevertheless, for want of better troops, he has been compelled to post them on the Causeway Heights, in the redoubts constructed by Major Nasmyth. There are six of these but only four have, as yet, received the guns with which they are to be armed . . . naval twelve-pounders, placed so as to command the Woronzoff Road. They constitute our first line of defense, in conjunction with Canrobert's Hill, on which Sir Colin has placed a Turkish battalion with three of the twelve-pounder guns. Cowper Coles made a sketch map of the position for me this morning. I'll show it to you."

Phillip waited in silence, as the Admiral rose to look for the sketch map. The force at Sir Colin Campbell's disposal sounded wholly inadequate, he thought grimly, yet it was expected to defend the harbour on which the very existence of the British infantry divisions on the Upland depended.

The Marines from the fleet, manning the parapet on the eastern heights above the harbour, would form its last line of defense but they were thinly spread along a wide perimeter and possessed no guns heavier than 32-pounders . . . and few enough of these. Even if reinforced from *Algiers* and *Sanspareil* they, too, must eventually be driven back once their supply of ammunition was exhausted and then . . .

The Admiral returned to the table, his Flag Lieutenant's

sketch in his hand. "Here is the map, Phillip. It will give you an idea of the position."

"Thank you, sir." Phillip took the proffered map and subjected it to a careful scrutiny. Having been in charge of the shore party from *Trojan,* which had assisted in the task of hauling the heavy naval guns from Balaclava Harbour to the Upland, he was familiar with the terrain in general. In particular, every twist and turn of the rutted, three-mile-long track which led through the gorge to Kadi-Koi, and thence to the Woronzoff Road, was etched indelibly in his memory. Climbing steeply from the valley of the Tchernaya—or Black—River, this road crossed the Plain of Balaclava and, following a ridge of high ground known as the Causeway Heights, passed through the camps of the British infantry divisions on the Upland and eventually entered the town of Sebastopol.

The whole area of the Balaclava Plain was about three miles long and two wide, divided into two by the ridge and forming a valley on each side of it, which Cowper Coles had marked on his sketch map as North and South.

In the South Valley, at the head of the gorge and a mile above the harbour, was the village of Kadi-Koi. Here the 93rd Highlanders were positioned, their encampment to the rear of the village, two strong gun emplacements to their left and the Marines on the Balaclava Heights, in an extended semicircle, to their right rear. With the limited means at his disposal, Sir Colin Campbell, Phillip saw from the plan, while concentrating on covering the entrance to the gorge, had also done his best to defend the Causeway Heights and the road it carried, which was of immense strategic importance as the British army's main line of communication with the harbour and ships. To lose the Causeway would be to lose the only good road to the camps of the infantry divisions and the siege-batteries overlooking Sebastopol, which must be kept supplied with shot and shell . . . whatever else they went without.

But Phillip frowned, as he studied Cowper Coles' neatly labelled sketch map.

There was, he reminded himself, Lord Lucan's Cavalry Division, consisting of the Light Brigade under Lord Cardigan, and the Heavy Brigade under Brigadier-General Scarlett, encamped in the South Valley but, strictly speaking, this was a separate command. As a Lieutenant-General Lord Lucan was not under Sir Colin Campbell's orders—despite his 44 years of distinguished military service, Sir Colin ranked only as a brigade commander in the British Army—and in any case, if faced with a heavy concentration of fire from the field guns which accompanied every Russian infantry attack, what could fifteen hundred lightly armed horsemen do? Lucan was known to be difficult and obsessed with trivialities, on bad terms with his brother-in-law and immediate subordinate, Major-General Lord Cardigan, and the cavalry had by no means distinguished themselves so far in the campaign.

As if guessing his thoughts, Admiral Lyons said, "Lord Lucan and Sir Colin Campbell are cooperating most admirably with each other. Undoubtedly, if an attack is made on Balaclava, Lucan will do all in his power to help in its defense. And *I* have promised him a navel battery, with guns from *Niger* and *Vesuvius,* to support the 93rd. The guns are already on their way up and a strong redoubt has been prepared to receive them . . . they'll be in position by this evening."

"Here, sir?" Phillip pointed to the map.

"Yes, at Kadi-Koi," the Admiral confirmed. "Which is where I am going to send you, Phillip . . . to act as naval liaison officer to Sir Colin Campbell. Report to him at Kadi-Koi today." Phillip made to rise but he was waved back to his seat. "Not yet, boy. The Commander-in-Chief won't be ready to receive me until eight bells. He never is, no matter what the urgency but . . ." the Admiral broke off, smiling wryly. "I've some paperwork to attend to, before I go to the *Britannia,* which will give us time to get your brother here. He's acting as Second Master of the *Trojan,* I think you said. Good, then we'll send for him. I'd like to hear what he has to say myself and, in all probability, I shall take him with me to make his report to Admiral Dundas in person. The Admiral will not like denuding the *Sanspareil* or the *Algiers* of their Marines, but your brother's intelligence may help to convince him that such a course is necessary and urgent, if we're to hold Balaclava . . . and hold it we must."

"Do you wish me to have my brother sent for, sir?" Phillip offered.

"You can pass the word for the Flag Lieutenant to report to me—he can attend to it. I haven't quite done with you, Phillip. And you'll need an orderly . . . if you'd prefer one of your own men from the *Trojan,* now's your opportunity."

"Thank you, sir." Phillip thought of O'Leary, as he carried out his instructions, and smiled to himself. When Lieutenant Coles had gone, Frederick Cleeve brought some papers for the Admiral's attention and signature. These dealt with, Admiral Lyons turned to him again.

"According to a Polish deserter from Sebastopol, Phillip, Admiral Korniloff was mortally wounded during our bombardment . . ." To Phillip's surprise, there was a note of sadness in the Admiral's voice, as if he mourned the departed enemy and he added, in explanation, "Korniloff was a very courageous officer, from what I have heard of him and, if your brother's information on this point is accurate, it must have broken his heart when he was ordered to sink his ships, instead of leading them out to do battle with ours. He was killed as a result of his own reckless heroism, the Pole said . . . to encourage the defenders, he rode from one strong-point to another, exposing himself to our fire. He was on the ramparts of the Malakoff Tower when a round shot shattered his thigh."

The Admiral paused, his gaze fixed on some object above Phillip's head and it was a moment or two before he resumed, in his normal quiet, controlled voice. "But now our immediate concern is Balaclava—the place *must* be held, no matter what the cost. When I recommended it to Lord Raglan as our base, I did not anticipate our having to use it as such for more than a week or so, at the outside. I believed that a few days would suffice for the Allied armies to gain possession of Sebastopol . . . and, had it not been for General Canrobert's excessive caution, a few days *would* have sufficed. But . . . the Allied High Command estimated that an assault on the town from the Balbec might result in five hundred casualties, and that was considered too high a price to pay for a successful end to our campaign." He spread his hands, the gesture one of mingled resignation and despair. "Now, if we are not to lose all hope of taking Sebastopol, we cannot afford to abandon Balaclava, Phillip. And, I daresay, we shall deem ourselves fortunate if we lose only twice the number of men, in its defense, that the Generals feared to risk a month ago, when the prize was of infinitely greater value."

Phillip still remained respectfully silent. It was evident that the Admiral was speaking as much to himself as to his newly appointed liaison officer and would welcome no comment. He looked weary and downcast as he bent over the table on which Cowper Coles' sketch map of the Balaclava defenses was spread, studying it despondently, as if in search of inspiration which he did not expect to find. But Sir Edmund Lyons, Phillip knew from past experience, was not a man to lose heart easily. Nor, indeed, was it in his nature to admit defeat if an answer could be found to a complex problem, and now his fine white brows met in a frown of deep concentration as he stared at the map in front of him.

"In this situation, our fleet is of even less use than Korniloff's," Phillip heard him murmur bitterly, beneath his breath. "Save for its guns, and we can land no more of those. But . . ." His mood changed with startling suddenness. "By gad, boy, I have it! Of course . . . why did I not think of it before?" His voice was clipped and decisive, full of confidence. "We can hold Balaclava, if need be, with a ship-of-the-line!"

"With a ship-of-the-line, sir?" Phillip echoed incredulously, unable to restrain himself any longer. True, he reminded himself, Captain Mends had taken the *Agamemnon* into Balaclava Harbour to meet Lord Raglan and his staff, at the conclusion of the army's flank march to the south of Sebastopol . . . but then it had been virtually empty, apart from *Niger* and *Highflyer* and the two small steam-sloops which had preceded her, sounding as they went. He had a swift mental vision of the harbour as it had been when he last saw it, choked with shipping, the wharves overloaded with supplies of every kind, and the temporary Captain of the Port—the *Simoom*'s able commander, Captain Tatham—working far into the night in a vain attempt to bring order to the chaos about him. . . .

"Yes, a ship-of-the-line, Phillip," the Admiral declared. He sprang to his feet, galvanized into action as if impelled by some inner reserve of energy that his frail body looked unlikely to possess, yet seemed always able to summon up when it was needed. In an instant, his depression vanished and he was once again the bold resourceful leader so beloved of the officers and seamen he commanded. Quick thinking and determined, every detail of the plan of action he had conceived was, Phillip realized, already taking shape in his mind.

"A steamer, moored bow and stern across the upper end of the harbour, to sweep the approaches to it with an over-whelming battery of fire from her broadside! It's the only solution. Even should the enemy carry the position of the 93rd at the head of the gorge we could drive them back . . . we could prevent the harbour falling into their hands. A channel will have to be cleared to permit her to enter, of course, but with the assistance of two or three steam frigates, the tugs can see to that, and the depth of water is more than adequate, as we know. With the Marines on the Heights above her, one ship will suffice, well commanded . . . although I think the *Diamond*'s remaining guns might also be manned. *Niger* and *Vesuvius* are in the harbour . . . they can find the guns' crews and if the rest of their seamen join Sir Colin and the 93rd at Kadi-Koi, then I fancy . . ." He broke off, to ring the bell at side. His Secretary answered it and was told to request the immediate presence of the Flag Captain, William Mends.

"Come back, Frederick," Admiral Lyons bade him. "I shall need you and Cowper Coles before I call on the Commander-in-Chief. And tell my steward to clear this table, if you please." He consulted his pocket watch, stifling an impatient sigh. "We haven't very long." Phillip again attempting to efface himself was, for the second time, waved back to his seat.

"I am going to anticipate the Commander-in-Chief's orders, Phillip," the Admiral told him. "You will go at once to the *Sanspareil*. Here . . ." As his steward hastily cleared the table of its breakfast debris, he reached for pen and paper and started rapidly to write. "Take this as your authority. Request Captain Dacres to get steam up and prepare to take his ship to Balaclava, as soon as he receives a signal to proceed from the flagship. You can explain matters to him in detail. He's to anchor outside the harbour to land his Marines but be prepared to enter and defend it, with every gun he can bring to bear, should the Russians attack and, by some ill chance, carry the position of the 93rd at Kadi-Koi. I shall be outside, with this ship, to support him. If he is short of shot or experienced guns' crews, I'll see that he is given whatever he needs . . . tell him that, will you?"

"Aye, aye, sir." Phillip placed the note in his breast pocket.

"The harbour must be cleared of all empty transports and storeships . . . and that infernal yacht of Lord Cardigan's—the *Dryad.*—if she's in the way. The depot and hospital ships cannot be moved, of course but . . ." The Admiral sighed. "Precise instructions will be sent, Captain Mends will work out what is likely to be required whilst I'm with the Commander-in-Chief. In the meantime, it may avoid unnecessary delay if you call on Captain Tatham, Phillip, to warn him of what is in the wind. When you've seen him, call on Commander Heath and give him the same warning . . . say that he will probably be required to take command of a party of seamen from his own ship and *Vesuvius,* to reinforce the 93rd, but he's to await confirmation."

"Aye, aye, sir." Phillip was on his feet.

The Admiral smiled at him. "After which, my boy," he said, "report to Sir Colin Campbell at Kadi-Koi. Inform him fully of what I intend to suggest to the Commander-in-Chief and tell him that I shall call on him myself at the earliest possible opportunity. But if Sir Colin has any immediate communication to make, concerning this or any other proposal, then bring it back to me, because I may not manage to get ashore today. You had better take one of my horses and . . ." Again he consulted his watch, as a knock on the door of the cabin heralded the arrival of his Flag Lieutenant, which was followed a moment or so later, by that of Captain Mends and the Secretary.

"Gentlemen, we have work to do," the Admiral announced, when he had greeted *Agamemnon's* commander and, with his usual courtesy, invited him to be seated at the table. "Carry on, Phillip . . . you know what you have to do. The *Beagle* can convey you to Balaclava—she's standing by to perform this service for me, but I doubt if I shall require her until this afternoon, if at all." His hand rested briefly on Phillip's shoulder. "Godspeed to you, my boy. I shall see you, no doubt, at Kadi-Koi."

"Aye, aye, sir," Phillip acknowledged, drawing himself to attention. He bowed his farewells to the other occupants of the Admiral's cabin, whose brows had risen almost in unison at the mention of Kadi-Koi, and, having hastily packed his immediate requirements into a valise, made his way to the quarterdeck. The duty boat, with Graham and O'Leary on board, came alongside as he made his orders known to the officer of the watch and he had barely had time to exchange a dozen words with his brother before the senior midshipman of the watch came to inform him that his valise had been stowed, and the boat was now ready to take him to the *Sanspareil.*

The huge, red-headed O'Leary beamed his gratification in a gap-toothed smile when Phillip told him why he had been sent for and followed him into the boat with alacrity, lest some unexpected change of plan should rob him of the opportunity he wanted so badly.

2

The call on Captain Dacres did not take long. Like all the officers in his squadron now holding post-rank, Sidney Colpoys Dacres had been privileged, over twenty years before, to serve as a junior officer under Sir Edmund Lyons's command in the *Blonde* and *Madagascar* frigates, and no order the Rear-Admiral might choose to give him was ever questioned. He looked tired and ill and confessed that he was feeling a trifle off-color but his eyes lit up as Phillip, in accordance with his instructions, outlined the proposal that the *Sanspareil* should undertake the defense of Balaclava Harbour. The only criticism he expressed was the fear that clearing the upper anchorage might take longer than anticipated, thus delaying his ship's entry.

"The Russians won't wait for us, Mr Hazard," he said dryly. "But, so long as they postpone their attack until my ship is at her station, then the Admiral need have no cause for anxiety. It is a brilliantly conceived plan of defense. We'll hold Balaclava. They could send an army against us, but the gorge is too narrow to permit more than a hundred or so to attack at one time . . . and with the Marines' 32-pounder howitzers to enfilade them from the Heights, I don't fancy many will get through. Should there be a chance of it, I'll position a couple of extra batteries there myself." He smiled, clearly pleased with the role assigned to him. "Well, I shall get steam up at once, as the Admiral desires but . . . I am to await a signal from the flag before proceeding, you say?"

"Those were the Rear-Admiral's instructions, sir."

"I see." Captain Dacres' smile faded momentarily. "Does that

mean that our Admiral is in any doubt as to whether the Commander-in-Chief will approve his plan for the defense of the
harbour?"

"I don't know, sir. Admiral Lyons will be on his way to *Britannia* by this time to confer with the Commander-in-Chief, sir,
but . . ." Phillip hesitated. It was common knowledge throughout the Fleet that Admiral Dundas had not approved of the
choice of Balaclava as the British base, which had been made
by Lord Raglan on the advice of Sir Edmund Lyons, and he wondered suddenly whether the Commander-in-Chief would agree
to risking a line-of-battle ship in its defense. "My instructions,"
he ended, choosing his words carefully, "were simply to request
you to prepare to take the *Sanspareil* to Balaclava on receiving
a signal from the flagship, sir."

"Ah! And whom else have you been instructed to—er—to
warn of this matter, Mr Hazard?"

"Captain Tatham at Balaclava, sir, in case it should be necessary to clear the harbour at short notice. I understand that
Lord Raglan himself has requested a reinforcement of the
Marines, sir, and that Admiral Lyons intends to suggest that
your ship and the *Algiers* should find the reinforcements."

"Good . . . then the Admiral means business," Captain
Dacres decided. He looked relieved. "Give Captain Tatham
plenty of warning, Mr Hazard, because it will take time to get
that shipping cleared and . . . he's another one who doesn't like
Balaclava. One can scarcely blame him, in the circumstances
but, whatever its disadvantages, now we're there, we're committed to hold the place. Tell me—how are you to get to
Balaclava? With us?"

Phillip shook his head. "No, sir, aboard the *Beagle.*"

"The *Beagle,* eh? Excellent! Then carry on, my young friend,
I won't detain you." The captain was smiling again, enthusiastic as a schoolboy. "I'll send you across to the *Beagle* . . ." He
gave the necessary order to the officer of the watch and turned
to Phillip again. "*Au revoir,* Mr Hazard. I trust that we may meet

again very soon . . . in Balaclava. And perhaps you will be so good as to convey my compliments to Sir Colin Campbell and tell him that, should his duties permit, I shall be happy if he will dine with me aboard this ship, when she takes up her station in the harbour. As his naval aide-de-camp, no doubt he will wish you to accompany him."

Thanking him, Phillip found himself echoing that infectiously boyish smile as he took his leave. The *Beagle* conveyed him at top speed and somewhat uncomfortably to Balaclava. She was a flat-bottomed, steam-screw gunboat, useful because of her light draft but inclined to roll unpleasantly in any kind of sea, and Phillip did not envy her Master, Mr Boxer, his temporary command. She was short of both officers and seamen; her Captain, Lieutenant Hore, and his second-in-command, a young mate, William Hewett, were both ashore with the two 68-pounder Lancaster guns with which the *Beagle* was normally armed, together with the guns' crews and two midshipmen. With his ship in constant demand as a despatch vessel, Mr Boxer and the rest of his crew got little rest; but they were keen and smart and having, by this time, become accustomed to the *Beagle*'s eccentricities and immune to her rolling, were united in their esteem for their ungainly craft and proud of her record.

Learning something of his passenger's mission, the Master glumly expressed the opinion that Balaclava was "hardly worth fighting for," but he blamed the army commissariat and the lack of land transport for the state of disorganized congestion which now existed there.

"You'll see a change, Mr Hazard," he added, still glum. "And not, I fear, one for the better."

Phillip decided to reserve judgement but certainly the harbour, when they reached it, presented an even more alarming picture of over-crowding than he recalled from his last sight of the place. It was, in fact, an inlet from the sea rather than a harbour, lacking roads and hemmed in by massive, almost perpendicular cliffs of dark red sandstone, whose summit was marked by the ruins of an ancient Genoese fort built, many years before, to command the entrance. This was narrow and difficult of access, so that ships under sail had usually to be towed into and out of harbour by a steamer . . . and there were few available for the task.

In consequence or because there was no room for them inside, a great many transport vessels were at anchor beneath the towering cliffs, their crews idling on deck. Others beat back and forth, presumably awaiting permission to enter or the arrival of a steam tug and, in the meantime—like those at anchor—they lacked shelter and protection from the prevailing northerly wind. Within the harbour itself, the five hundred-foot-high cliffs afforded ample protection from wind and weather but the anchorage was barely half a mile long, with a maximum width of three hundred feet and, although its depth of seven fathoms permitted the entry of large vessels, the northern end, Phillip knew, was blocked by shoal water a few feet deep. In order to reach her station, the *Sanspareil* would require skilful pilotage and adequate room in which to maneuver, or she would run the risk of tailing on to the shoal but . . . he drew in his breath sharply. There *was* no room; ships were moored everywhere and he counted over a score tied up, head to stern, in two tiers, along the eastern shore alone. Most of these, Mr Boxer told him, were provision ships waiting to discharge cargoes, for which—owing to the length of time required to clear the wharves of cargoes previously unloaded—no space could yet be found.

The wharves themselves were makeshift platforms, fashioned from planks, and only one had sheers, erected originally by Captain Lushington of the *Albion* to enable his Naval Brigade guns to be landed. Balaclava was, of course, little more than a fishing village with a Greek population, whose sympathies in the present conflict were, Phillip was aware, open to doubt. A cluster of picturesque white houses and green-tiled roofs, it possessed few facilities for serving the needs of an invading army . . . least of all an army which, as Mr Boxer had reminded him, was deficient in land transport. The British Army had been compelled to leave most of its pack-animals, as well as its ambulance wagons, behind in Varna. Some of these had since been shipped to the Crimea, but not nearly enough, and a disastrously high proportion of cavalry horses and pack mules had died during the voyage across the Black Sea in bad weather. As a result, supplies were taken to the infantry camps in Maltese carts or Turkish *arabas* drawn by bullocks; even camels had been pressed into service as pack-carriers and the rest dragged or borne on the backs of weary soldiers, sent down to Balaclava after a night on picket or in the trenches. The sick and wounded came down, agonizingly, in the same way. . . .

The French at Kamiesch were better provided for in this respect, Mr Boxer observed, as the *Beagle* slowly nosed her way through the narrow channel at half-speed. "I was there a few days ago, with the Admiral, and *their* transport system leaves nothing to be desired. They have a fine wharf built by their engineers, and every convenience is provided for the prompt landing and disposal of stores. One of their naval officers told me that, at Kamiesch, there's a place for everything and everything in its place . . . and he was making no idle boast, Mr Hazard, I assure you. They've even set up a small town of tents, with each street named and numbered and, believe it or not, two Parisian restaurants have recently been opened there, under canvas. Whereas here . . ." he grunted in exasperation. "It's a shambles, is it not?"

Phillip was forced to agree that he was right. "It's beginning to smell like that, I grant you, Mr Boxer."

"And do you know why?" the *Beagle*'s Master asked. "Because half the bullocks we brought back from Yalta died before they could be disembarked and there being nowhere to house the miserable creatures which did get ashore, they had to be slaughtered too. Not that our men fare much better. Over there"—he pointed with an indignant forefinger—"is the so-called hospital wharf, Mr Hazard. The sick and wounded soldiers from the trenches lie there for hours, without food or shelter, until an empty transport is found in which to take them to Scutari. There's talk of rigging an awning for them but I've seen no sign of one yet although, on Captain Tatham's orders, the *Simoom's* sailmaker had the canvas ready a week ago. Still, given time, I suppose . . ." he spoke with weary cynicism, "some army quartermaster will take the responsibility of signing the necessary requisition for it and it will go up. Our Jacks are better off than the soldiers—they've at least got the *Diamond* in use as a hospital ship. They're fed and their wounds are dressed and they don't have to wait in the open. But . . . well, you can see why I say that Balaclava isn't worth fighting for, can you not, Mr Hazard?"

Again Phillip could only incline his head in shocked acquiescence. Yet, he thought, Balaclava *had* to be fought for, it had to be fought for and held, if the British Army were to remain in the Crimea as an effective fighting force. The alternative—unless Sebastopol could be taken within the next few weeks—was, as Graham had reminded him, evacuation . . . with the loss of everything that had been so dearly won. Remembering the ghastly scenes of carnage he had witnessed after the Battle of the Alma, he shuddered. So many gallant men had sacrificed their lives in order to gain this tiny, crowded harbour which was now the army's lifeline, that it could'nt be abandoned . . . however inadequate for the purpose it had proved.

To lose Balaclava would be to lose the war, or so it seemed to him, standing on the *Beagle's* narrow quarterdeck as she drew slowly closer to the wharf. Captain Tatham could scarcely be expected to welcome the warning he brought, since it must inevitably add to the congestion and chaos if a Russian attack materialized and the *Sanspareil* had to take up her station in the harbour as a matter of urgency. Nonetheless, the warning must be delivered. . . .

Phillip thanked Mr Boxer and, experiencing some trepidation at the thought of the interview before him, he stepped ashore from the tender, O'Leary behind him with his valise.

"I may be here for some time, O'Leary," he told his new orderly. "So perhaps you had best make your way up to Kadi-Koi. Make what arrangements you can there for our accommodation. There's a naval party already there, I believe—the guns' crews from *Niger* and *Vesuvius*—so presumably there will be tents."

"Leave it to me, sorr," O'Leary answered, with the confidence of a seasoned campaigner and, content to do so, Phillip went in search of Captain Tatham, finding him in his cabin aboard the *Simoom*. He explained his mission and, contrary to his somewhat pessimistic expectations, the Captain received his news with evident relief.

"The *Sanspareil* cannot come too soon, so far as I am concerned, Mr Hazard. Oh, admittedly clearing the harbour for her will present its problems and cannot possibly be done without help from the steam squadron . . . but you say the Admiral has promised us this?"

"Yes, sir, he has. But the sanction and approval of the Commander-in-Chief have yet to be confirmed, for which purpose Admiral Lyons has now gone aboard *Britannia*. My instructions are to request you to make such preparations as you may deem advisable for the reception of the *Sanspareil*—possibly at short notice, sir—but to take no action, pending further orders from the Admiral . . ." Phillip supplied what details he could.

"Very well." Captain Tatham shrugged resignedly. "I'm very grateful to the Admiral for giving me prior notice of his intentions, but I trust confirmation will not be too long delayed . . . because everything points to an attack on Balaclava being imminent. One is constantly hearing reports of our army patrols and pickets being driven in, and of large bodies of Russian troops gathering in the Tchernaya Valley. They can be there for no other purpose and must know, by this time, I imagine, how thinly our line is held."

"That is the Admiral's view, sir," Phillip confirmed. "And also, I believe, that of Sir Colin Campbell."

"But they don't propose to evacuate Balaclava?"

"No, sir. To the best of my knowledge, no such proposal has been put forward. Very much the reverse in fact."

"H'm." Captain Tatham pursed his lips. He seemed about to offer some criticism, but, after a moment's consideration, evidently thought better of it. "Frankly, Mr Hazard," he confessed, "I should welcome the presence of the *Sanspareil* in this port, if for no other reason than because the command would then devolve on Captain Dacres, who is considerably my senior. Don't look so shocked"—as Phillip's brows rose in an astonished curve—"I'm not shirking my responsibilities, I assure you. Given the requisite authority, I should fulfil them to the best of my ability . . . but I have *not* been given that authority. Since the steam squadron was withdrawn, as Senior Naval Officer I have been designated commander of the port. But any orders I issue in this capacity are liable to be countermanded by the Principal Agent for Transports, who out-ranks me, or by General Airey, on Lord Raglan's behalf. No doubt you have observed the haphazard berthing arrangements I've been compelled to make, and the laden ships outside harbour won't have escaped your notice either, I feel sure." He sighed, not waiting for Phillip's answer. "I'm responsible for ships entering and leaving Balaclava Harbour, Mr Hazard, but not—unhappily—for the disposal of their cargoes."

Feeling that some remark was now expected of him, Phillip managed a non-committal, "Yes, I see, sir."

"I doubt if you do," the port commander retorted bitterly. "But to give you one example . . . before the Alma, the Guards Division entrusted their knapsacks to the Navy's care, to enable them to go into action unencumbered. The vessel into whose hold the knapsacks were consigned has twice entered this port and, on both occasions, the Guards sent fatigue parties down to take delivery of them . . . but, having no written authority, the officer in charge was sent back to camp empty handed. The ship in question—still with the knapsacks occupying valuable space in her hold—has been ordered first to Varna and subsequently to Constantinople, where she now is and *I* am blamed for it! I have even received a note on the subject from His Royal Highness the Duke of Cambridge, reproaching me for the fact that his guardsmen lack such essential items of personal equipment as razors and combs. I could go on, Mr Hazard, but I will spare you, since I am sure you have other commissions to perform on the Admiral's behalf."

Phillip rose. He felt intensely sorry for the unfortunate Captain Tatham, whom he knew as an efficient and thoroughly reliable officer, but there was no consolation he could offer beyond the assurance that, if he could, Admiral Lyons intended to come in person to Balaclava.

"Even if he is unable to do so, sir, detailed instructions are to be sent to you which will give you full authority to have the harbour cleared, should this be necessary."

"Heaven be praised!" the Captain said, with feeling. He looked more cheerful, however and, when Phillip left him, he was already making plans to evacuate as many of the sick and wounded from the hospital wharf as time and the Principal Agents for Transports would permit.

CHAPTER THREE

1

Phillip's *final call* before leaving Balaclava was on Commander Leopold Heath of H.M.S. *Niger* with whom, in response to his hospitable invitation, he dined. *Niger,* having landed guns for No. 4 Battery at Kadi-Koi, was at anchor within sight of the harbour entrance, preparing to return to the Fleet anchorage off the Katcha and Phillip, to his annoyance, experienced some delay in obtaining a boat to take him across to her. The warmth of the welcome he received, however, soon restored his good humour.

Commander Heath was a stocky, blunt-featured man with dark hair and whiskers, whose lovely wife had been with him at Therapia when the *Trojan* had first arrived in Turkey, but had now gone to Malta to await the birth of their first child. Phillip enquired for her and his host replied, with a beaming smile, that he was expecting news at any time. They had worked together during the disembarkation at Kalamita Bay and, in spite of the difference in their ranks—Heath was the Fleet's senior Commander of Sloops—were on terms of friendship, born of mutual respect and liking.

"Well, Hazard, what brings you to this benighted place?" the Commander asked curiously, when they were seated at his dining table. "I thought you were commanding the *Trojan?*"

Phillip shook his head. "I handed over my command to Captain Crawford yesterday, sir, on appointment to the *Agamemnon.*"

"Crawford, eh? Charles Crawford . . . wasn't he one of Sir

Edmund's young gentlemen in the midshipmen's berth of the *Blonde?*"

"He was Acting-Mate, he told me, sir, promoted after Navarino, when he served with the Admiral's brother in the *Rose.*"

Leopold Heath nodded wisely. "Then his appointment is no surprise, is it? But what of your own . . . you're on the Admiral's personal staff again, I've no doubt?"

"Temporarily, sir, yes . . ." Phillip explained his mission as they ate and saw his host's dark eyes light up in eager anticipation, as for the same reason, Captain Dacres' had done.

"Capital, my dear Hazard! You could have brought me no more pleasing news since, I must confess, I find harbour duty—in this harbour—somewhat frustrating. Poor Tatham does his best—indeed, he is doing all a man can do in this situation, but his is an impossible task and my heart bleeds for him. You have seen and talked to him, I imagine?"

"I've just come from the *Simoom,* sir."

"Then you'll have heard of the difficulties which beset him. I fancy, between ourselves, Hazard"—the Commander's expression was admirably controlled but the corners of his mouth twitched—"that the unfortunate affair of the Guard's knapsacks upsets him most of all, although it is certainly not *his* fault that they've gone astray. My problems are negligible by comparison but you've saved me from serving on a wearisome court of inquiry, for which I am grateful. Furthermore I've always cherished a secret yearning to play the soldier."

"Have you, sir?" Phillip, too, was careful to conceal any hint of amusement but, abandoning pretense, Leopold Heath permitted himself a full-throated laugh. "Yes, by gad, I have! And it went decidedly against the grain to send my guns and their crews, under the command of my First Lieutenant, to Sir Colin Campbell's support at Kadi-Koi, while forced to remain here myself. I wonder . . ." He broke off, eyeing Phillip speculatively. "When do you leave for Kadi-Koi, Hazard?"

"My orders are to report to Sir Colin after informing you and Captain Tatham of the Admiral's plans for the defence of Balaclava Harbour, sir. But . . ." Phillip hesitated. Time was passing but, so far as he knew, there had been as yet no confirmation of Admiral Lyons'ss tentative orders, and he had been due to meet Admiral Dundas aboard his flagship at 8:00 a.m. . . . he frowned. *Niger*'s officer of the watch would have informed his commander, had the *Sanspareil* been sighted off the harbour entrance and the appearance of four hundred Marines in Balaclava—by whatever ship had conveyed them thither—would certainly also have been reported.

Sensing his anxiety, Commander Heath rose. "Let us try to ascertain what, if anything, is happening, shall we? I imagine that Sir Colin will prefer confirmation concerning his reinforcements to vague promises of future help. If you delay long enough to bring this to him, it will be all to the good."

They went on deck but neither the officer of the watch nor the midshipman he sent scurrying to the masthead were able to make out any signs of unusual activity, save for the fact that a small steam transport had tied up alongside the hospital wharf and was starting to load sick and wounded. Captain Tatham, true to his promise, had taken the first step towards clearing the harbour . . . but surely, Phillip thought, fighting against a strong feeling of dismay, surely the Commander-in-Chief could not have rejected the proposals of his second-in-command out of hand? Lord Raglan had made a personal request for the Marines' position on the Balaclava Heights to be reinforced—a request which, in normal circumstances, could hardly be refused. To risk a ship-of-the-line was, admittedly, a more serious matter over which any naval Commander-in-Chief might hesitate, yet . . . he glanced uneasily at Commander Heath.

"I ought to leave, I think, sir," he began. "But—"

"I'll get word to you, Hazard," the Commander offered. "As soon as there's anything definite to report. You'll be staying at Kadi-Koi, I suppose?"

"Yes, sir. That is unless Sir Colin Campbell wishes to communicate urgently with the Admiral, in which case I am to return with his despatch."

"Then you may rely on me. To tell you the truth, I'm tempted to ride up with you myself, however . . ." Heath sighed, "perhaps I had better not, in the circumstances. But inform my First Lieutenant—and Commander Powell of *Vesuvius* if you come across him—that I hope to be joining them under canvas very soon, all being well."

"Certainly, sir." Phillip thanked him for his hospitality and the Commander smiled.

"You've relieved the tedium of a harbour watch and given me at least some hope of action. And I could do with it, just now . . . waiting for news of one's first-born, at this distance, one tends to brood, you know, and to worry. My Mary is very precious to me . . . you've met her, so you'll understand why. By the bye"—his eyes searched Phillip's face curiously—"what happened to that extraordinarily beautiful young lady of mystery you brought out from England in the *Trojan,* and then transferred with such unseemly haste and secrecy to the *Furious* in Constantinople?"

"Mademoiselle Sophie, sir?" Taken by surprise at the question, Phillip reddened.

"Yes, I believe that was what she called herself . . . but it wasn't her real name, was it?"

"No, sir. She was travelling incognito and—"

"Did you ever learn who she was, Hazard? My officers were all vastly intrigued by the mystery."

"She was a Russian Grand Duchess, a niece of the Tsar, and *Furious* took her to Odessa just before official news of the declaration of war reached us." His emotions under control now, Phillip was able to supply this information quite matter-of-factly, his voice without a tremor. "In Odessa she married Prince Andrei Stepanovitch Narishkin, to whom she had been betrothed since childhood. Prince Narishkin is a Colonel in the

Russian cavalry and was wounded at the Alma, later sent back to Odessa in an exchange of wounded prisoners of war. I heard a rumour that he may be joining Prince Menschikoff here quite soon, sir, oddly enough."

"That is indeed odd," Commander Heath agreed. "In fact the whole story is odd, is it not? But you seem to be remarkably well informed . . . how did you come to hear the rumour, Hazard? Don't tell me"—the question was asked in a bantering tone—"don't tell me the lady still communicates with you?"

Phillip smiled faintly. "No, sir, she does not. I heard the rumour from my brother, who was taken prisoner when the *Tiger* ran aground off Odessa and subsequently . . ." He was interrupted by a shrill hail from the masthead.

"Deck there! The *Sanspareil* is off the port, sir, in company with two steam sloops. *Wasp*, sir, and . . . *Lynx*, I believe, with Marines aboard."

Phillip's spirits rose. So Admiral Lyons had, after all, obtained the Commander-in-Chief's approval, he thought with elation, and Sir Colin Campbell was to receive his Marine reinforcements. The *Wasp* was, he knew, a steam-screw corvette of fourteen guns, commanded by Lord John Hay and, when another shrill hail from the masthead announced that she was signalling for permission to enter harbour to land troops, his spirits rose still higher. Beside him, Commander Heath exclaimed with satisfaction, "Good! Now, perhaps, we may see some positive action . . . and not before time." He had his glass to his eye. "The signal station is making acknowledgement."

"I think, sir," Phillip said, "that I had better take this news to Kadi-Koi without delaying any longer. But I should be very greatly obliged if you could send word should the *Sanspareil* make any signal concerning her intentions. If—"

"I'll do better than that, my dear fellow," Commander Heath put in. "I'll bring you word in person, God willing." He clapped a hand on Phillip's shoulder in smiling farewell and then, shaking his head to some question his officer of the watch asked him, swung himself with the swift ease of long practice, into the mainmast shrouds. He had reached the crosstrees and had his glass to his eye once more before his guest had left the quarterdeck.

Niger's duty boat took Phillip across the harbour to the wharf at which he had landed earlier from the *Beagle.* Fifteen minutes later, mounted on one of Admiral Lyons's horses and accompanied by a midshipman on a white pony, who had mail for the Naval Brigade, he set off at a brisk canter along the narrow, rutted track which led through the Balaclava gorge to Kadi-Koi. Before he had gone very far, however, he slackened speed on the midshipman's advice, for the track rapidly became as congested as the harbour he had left.

A steady stream of wagons, loaded with provisions and drawn by bullocks, creaked up the steep ascent at snail's pace, meeting mule carts or an occasional camel train proceeding in the opposite direction. Artillery wagons bearing shot and shell and others laden with fascines and gabions lurched over the churned-up, uneven surface, making little better progress than the bullock carts, despite the fact that they were horse-drawn. Here and there, having to draw rein to let them pass, they encountered an infantry fatigue party, the men in faded scarlet coats and a variety of headgear, plodding wearily along like so many sleepwalkers, ration sacks instead of muskets slung over their shoulders. One melancholy little party they met consisted of sick and wounded, on their way to Balaclava for evacuation. A dozen or so stumbled painfully down the track supported by their comrades or hobbling with the aid of roughly fashioned crutches. The rest, too ill to walk, lay huddled in a springless Turkish *araba,* inert and barely conscious, a few bundles of filthy straw all that was provided to ease the appalling discomfort of their jolting, carelessly driven conveyance.

The suffering they endured must, Phillip thought pityingly, have been indescribable, especially for those sent down from the field hospitals with shattered or freshly amputated limbs.

The manner in which the wounded had been brought down from the Alma had been bad enough, in all conscience, but this—when a distance of almost seven miles had to be covered— seemed to him infinitely worse. Casualties in the batteries and field trenches were high, the midshipman told him, mostly from grape and cannister, and fire from the Russian men-of-war anchored in Sebastopol Harbour, which was usually very accurate.

"The *Vladmir* and another steamer caused us a lot of trouble early on, sir. Both ships took a leaf from our book at Odessa, steaming in a circle and firing their broadsides in turn, as they came on target. I was in the One-Gun Battery at the time and it took us all day before we disabled one of them and drove the other off . . ." He described the action, with evident relish but added regretfully, "Our Lancaster guns are not proving as satisfactory as had been hoped, sir, to tell you the truth. We take the greatest care in laying and in putting in the exact charge and length of fuse but at maximum range—which is supposed to be three thousand six hundred yards—only about one shot in thirty is effective. Even at half this range, we don't seem to do much better and when you think, sir, that each shell is made by hand and costs about twenty pounds, it's expensive work, isn't it, sir?"

Phillip listened with interest, encouraging the intelligent youngster to talk of his experience with the Naval Brigade and of conditions ashore of which, for a fifteen-year-old, he seemed to have a remarkable grasp. He was, he said, aide-de-camp to the second-in-command of the Naval Brigade, Captain William Peel of the *Diamond*—the frigate that, stripped of her guns, was now in use as a hospital ship in the harbour at Balaclava. It was evident, as the boy talked on, that he had the greatest admiration for Peel who, according to his enthusiastic account, had already proved at least half a dozen times that he was of the stuff of which heroes were made.

"The other day—the day after the Fleet bombarded the

Sebastopol Forts, it was, sir—a Russian 42-pounder shell fell right in the middle of one of our guns' crews in the Koh-i-nor Battery, just as some cases of powder were being passed into the magazine. The men threw themselves flat on the ground but Captain Peel, cool as you please, stooped down and picked up the shell. Holding it against his chest, he carried it back to the parapet, stepped up onto the *banquette,* sir, and rolled it over . . . whereupon it burst! Our men all think the world of him, of course, and so do I. I feel it's a great honor to serve as his aide, although it . . . well, it takes a bit of living up to, as you can imagine, sir."

"Indeed I can, Mr Daniel," Phillip assured him. He knew the gallant Captain Peel well by repute and had met him during the arduous days when the siege-guns were being dragged from Balaclava to the Upland. A son of Sir Robert Peel, he had gained early but well merited promotion and, at thirty, was the youngest officer in the Black Sea Fleet to hold post-rank.

"I spoke to him about it once, sir," Midshipman Daniel went on, reddening a little. "And asked his advice . . . about being afraid, I mean. He told me that everyone was afraid at times, including himself, and the thing was never to show it. He advised me to walk with my head up and my shoulders well back when under fire, and not to do anything with undue haste . . . he said that was what he did himself, sir, because as officers it was up to us to set the men an example. Well, I took his advice and it was wonderful how much better it made me feel. I don't like being under fire—the shells aren't too bad because, when you've had a little practice, you can judge pretty well where they're going to burst. Especially at night, when you can see the glow of the fuses. But when it comes to round shot and cannister . . ." He looked up to meet Phillip's gaze, his thin, boyish face suddenly adult in its bitter disillusionment. "I hate to see men killed and wounded, sir . . . still, in spite of seeing so many, and I fear I always shall hate it, sir."

"That's nothing to be ashamed of, youngster."

"No, sir. I suppose not. But . . ." The boy hung his head. "Our bluejackets take so little care of themselves, it worries me. They lark about and they can't resist jumping on to the parapet, trying to make out whether we've scored a hit, sir. When we do, they cheer their heads off and most of the time it's all you can do to make them take cover. That's why our casualties in the Naval Brigade are higher, in proportion to numbers, than the Army's. But we lose fewer men from cholera than the soldiers do. Our men are fitter and, although they draw the same rations when they're ashore as the Army, they're better fed. I also believe they're better officered, sir."

"Oh? What makes you think that, Mr Daniel?" Phillip prompted.

"Well, sir . . ." The midshipman hesitated. "Perhaps this may sound an odd thing to say but I think our officers look after their men better than the Army officers do. Most of *them* don't seem to trouble when they're not actually on duty. They go to their tents, and the men are left to their own devices, with only the non-commissioned officers to supervise them—but our bluejackets always have at least one officer to supervise everything they do. Usually three or four, even if they *are* only mids, sir . . . they know their duty."

"Go on, Mr Daniel, I should like to hear more." Phillip was impressed and the boy, sensing this, lost all vestige of shyness.

"Our men parade before going down to the battery, sir, and each man has to drink his cocoa or coffee and take his issue of quinine and lime juice in the presence of an officer. When they return to camp, the cooks—who aren't sent to the batteries, sir— have hot soup ready for them and an officer on duty to make sure that it *is* hot and that the men drink it before they're dismissed. But the soldiers don't have company cooks, I've noticed, sir. Each man is given his ration of meat and expected to cook it for himself and often he's too tired or there isn't enough firewood for him to cook it properly. Our camp regulations are much stricter than the Army's, too, sir, and again it's the officers who make sure they're obeyed, on Captain Lushington's orders. I realize these are only small things, but I believe they *matter,* sir."

"I'm quite certain they do," Phillip agreed. And, indeed, he reflected, such things mattered a great deal where morale was concerned, as well as bodily fitness and resistance to disease. He had heard that Captain Lushington was having wells dug, so that his seamen might have access to pure, uncontaminated drinking water, and that he insisted that every man should have three hours' sleep and a supply of dry clothing, before being sent down to Balaclava for rations or to bring up ammunition.

"Another thing I've noticed, sir," Midshipman Daniel told him, "is that very few of the Army officers know their men by name, as we do . . . although in the Scottish regiments they do, I think. I'm not saying they are bad officers, sir, or that this is their fault, but their training is different from ours, I suppose. Perhaps it has something to do with being at sea for a four-year commission . . . going foreign, sir, when we're all members of the same ship's company. We train *with* our men, as cadets and mids—we work together all the time, so that we get to know our men as individuals and think of them as . . . as fellow human beings. Ours is a different relationship, sir, if you see what I mean. In the Army, the officers—some of them, any-way—seem to . . . well, to . . ." He broke off, searching for words and eyeing Phillip anxiously, as if fearing that he might already have said too much. "To hold themselves aloof, as it were, and care only for their own comfort, as if—" Again he broke off uncertainly.

"To hold themselves aloof and take their privileged status for granted?" Phillip finished for him, smiling. "As if they were a different breed from their men and entitled, on this account, to their respect . . . whether or not they merit respect on the grounds of professional competence. Is that what you mean, Mr Daniel?"

"Then you've observed it too, sir?" The boy looked relieved.

"Yes, that's exactly what I was trying to say. Oh, they aren't all like that, of course. The artillery and engineer officers are professionally competent and so are those in the infantry regiments who have seen service in India. But some of the others . . ." Again he was at a loss for words. "I don't know how to put this, sir, quite . . . but they're amateurs, playing at war, taking command without knowing how and without . . . well, without regarding command as we're taught to regard it, as responsibility for men who . . . who *trust* us, sir."

Out of the mouths of babes and sucklings, Phillip thought wryly. But the boy was right; he had put his finger on the essential difference between the naval and military attitude towards the men they led. A naval officer shared the hardships and dangers of each voyage with his men and their relationship was based on mutual dependence—on the men's loyalty and trust and on the officer's ability to command these. Joining the Service at an early age, he very soon learned that the privileged status of an officer was not granted to him, as to his military counterpart, by right of purchase of a Queen's commission. As a mere boy, when others of his age were still at school, he was given responsibility for the safety, the well-being, and often the lives of adult seamen and he learned by hard and bitter experience what this responsibility meant. He was put in command of a boat, a gun's crew, a shore party and, at sea, he went aloft in all weathers with the men of his division, constantly on his mettle and always aware that his command was nominal until, by his men's measure of his competence, this became actual. And he could not buy promotion, he . . .

"Look, sir, who's coming!" Midshipman Daniel pointed along the track to where a small mounted party was approaching the head of the gorge from the direction of the Cavalry Camp in the South Valley. The riders came at a fast canter, raising a cloud of dust in their wake and a plodding file of infantrymen, laden with sacks of provisions and dragging a handcart, hastily scattered to avoid being ridden down.

The leader of the cavalcade was a tall officer in the magnificent blue and cherry-red uniform of the 11th Hussars, astride a blood chestnut draped with a crested shabraque. Riding beside him was a curiously incongruous figure in a black civilian frock coat and flat-brimmed "bell topper," while two aides-de-camp and four troopers, all wearing the uniform of the 11th, clattered at his heels to complete the party.

"Major-General Lord Cardigan, sir," Midshipman Daniel explained unnecessarily, for Phillip had already recognized the commander of the Light Cavalry Brigade. Indeed, he thought, there was no mistaking that eye-catching figure in the resplendent uniform for any other as, with typical arrogance and without acknowledgement, the Earl swept past the weary foot soldiers. The sunlight struck bright reflections from the thick rows of gold lace frogging which adorned his brief, perfectly fitting jacket and from the richly braided, fur-trimmed pelisse slung by its cords from one shoulder. He sat his big thoroughbred with the easy grace of an accomplished horseman, long legs encased in cherry-red overalls, a handsome man, his erect and well-proportioned body belying his 57 years. So, too, did the flowing, carefully trimmed moustache and the luxuriant ginger whiskers, neither of which appeared—at first glance—to be touched with grey.

Having regard for the speed of their approach and not wishing to suffer the fate of the infantry fatigue party, who were now brushing dust from their faces, Phillip kneed his horse to the side of the track so as to permit the Earl his escort free passage and young Daniel, after a momentary hesitation, followed his example. Both saluted and Lord Cardigan, recognizing their naval uniforms, raised a hand in casual response and then, as if struck by a sudden thought, reined in beside them.

"Who are you?" he asked, his tone peremptory, addressing Phillip. His civilian companion, taken by surprise at his unexpected change of direction, brought his sweating horse, with difficulty, to a standstill some yards away.

Phillip introduced himself. At the mention of his ship, his questioner grunted with evident satisfaction.

"*Agamemnon,* eh? Good . . . I thought I recognized that bay you're riding. One of your Admiral's is it not?"

"Yes, sir. I'm appointed temporarily to the Rear-Admiral's staff. If there's any way in which I can serve your lordship, I—"

Lord Cardigan did not let him finish. "You can tell me if the Admiral is coming ashore today."

Phillip started to explain that this was uncertain but, as before, he was interrupted. "Never mind, the matter is of no great consequence . . . it can wait until tomorrow. Capital fellow, your Admiral—but like all you sailors, he's no judge of horseflesh. Tell him from me to get rid of that spavined brute you're on. It will give him nothing but trouble." Lord Cardigan nodded, in curt but not unfriendly dismissal and, turning to the black-garbed gentleman who accompanied him, said with a complete change of tone, "All right, Squire—we'll go on, shall we? Sorry to have delayed you . . . it was just an idea I had."

The cavalcade reformed and continued on its way.

"Meaning no disrespect, sir," Midshipman Daniels remarked, when they were safely out of earshot, "But that's an example of what I was trying to say concerning the difference between the Army officers and our own."

"You're referring to his lordship, I imagine?" Phillip returned, aware that he ought not to encourage the youngster to criticize his superiors, yet tempted to do so, since his own feelings were similar.

Daniel nodded, "Yes, sir. Captain Lushington, with my Chief and Captain Moorsom, command the Naval Brigade and, although the *Diamond* is in harbour and they could . . . well, be quite justified in living aboard her, sir, they don't. They're under canvas with the rest of us. But his lordship is commanding the Light Cavalry Brigade from the harbour sir, isn't he? And not even from a naval ship—from his own private yacht, the *Dryad* which, they say, his friend, Mr Hubert de Burgh, brought out here to accommodate him. I don't know if this is true, sir, but I've heard he has a French chef aboard. We . . ." He grinned mischievously, "we've nicknamed him 'The Featherbed Soldier,' sir, and the Army call him 'The Noble Yachtsman,' I believe." He added, quite seriously, "How can you command a Brigade of Cavalry from a yacht, sir?"

Phillip wisely refrained from comment. But, once again, he thought, this boy was right—he had cited the supreme example of the assumption of privileged status. James Thomas Brudenell, Earl of Cardigan, was wealthy and influential; he had an extremely bad reputation as an army officer and had been removed from command of the 15th Hussars some twenty years previously . . . yet this had not prevented his military advancement. Less than two years after a court martial had censured him severely, he had been permitted to purchase—for a price rumoured to be in the region of forty thousand pounds—command of the 11th, then a light dragoon regiment, serving in India. And now he was a Major-General, commanding the Light Cavalry Brigade and, if the gossip of the camps were to be believed, constantly at logger-heads with his immediate superior, the Earl of Lucan, who was in overall command of the Cavalry Division and his brother-in-law.

Not that Lord Lucan had much to recommend him . . . again if gossip were true. He, too, had purchased his promotion and there had been frequent criticism of the manner in which he had commanded the British cavalry Division which, to say the least of it, had done very little up till now to distinguish itself. Lucan had earned himself the derisive nickname of "Lord Look-on," bestowed upon him, it was said, by Captain Edward Nolan of the 15th Hussars, A.D.C. to General Airey and an expert on cavalry tactics, who was his fiercest and most outspoken critic. Phillip suppressed a sigh and, beside him, Midshipman Daniel said, with youthful scorn, "One cannot imagine 'The Noble Yachtsman' risking *his* life for his men, as Captain

Peel did in the battery the other day, can one, sir?"

One could not, Phillip was compelled to concede, but he did not say so. Instead, his conscience pricking him, he suggested to his young companion that, the way now being clear, they might quicken their pace. Daniel obediently kicked his pony into a canter and, when they came in sight of the tents of the 93rd, he prepared to take his leave, thanking Phillip politely for being allowed to accompany him. He said, on parting, "You want to keep your eyes peeled for Russian spies, sir."

"Spies, Mr Daniel?" Phillip echoed, his tone faintly repressive. "What in the world are you talking about?"

"Oh, I mean it, sir, I assure you. One of the *Queen*'s mids—Wood, who's a messmate of mine in the Naval Brigade—spotted a mysterious fellow in the uniform of the French Chasseurs d'Afrique, who seemed to be taking a great deal of interest in Gordon's Battery a day or so ago. Wood pointed him out to my Chief, Captain Peel, sir, and he sent him to invite the French officer to dine with us. But as soon as Wood approached him, the supposed Frenchman took to his heels and couldn't be seen for dust!"

"That's scarcely a valid reason for believing him to be a spy, Mr Daniel."

"Well, I don't know, sir." The boy's voice was grave. "Young Wood is convinced of it—and he could be right, sir. I've heard that there have been some supposed British officers seen prowling about the French positions, who didn't stay to be questioned either. Anyway, I thought I should warn you because . . . well, because Kadi-Koi would be a likely place for a spy to visit just now, if the Russians *are* planning to attack Balaclava, would it not, sir?" He smiled, touched his cap smartly, and made off before Phillip could think of a suitable rejoinder.

Daniel was a bright, intelligent youngster, he thought indulgently, his only fault, perhaps, the fact that he had too vivid an imagination, but his entertaining conversation had been the means of enlivening an otherwise long and wearisome ride. Phillip found himself echoing young Daniel's smile, as he turned his horse's head in the direction of Kadi-Koi. . . .

2

The Highlanders' tents, pitched some distance behind the village, proved to be deserted when Phillip reached them, save for a few women gathered in a small chattering group about their wash-tubs, sleeves rolled up and aprons of coarse sacking girded about their waists. They eyed him incuriously as he approached but broke off their conversation to give him the time of day in response to his greeting. Like most of the womenfolk who had followed their men to war, they were—collectively, at any rate— unprepossessing and notable rather for the toughness of their physique than for their looks, but Phillip found an unexpected pleasure in the soft, lilting sound of their voices.

It was a long time, he reflected, with a twinge of sadness, a very long time since he had last listened to a woman's voice, speaking his name. And then it had been the voice of Mademoiselle Sophie heard, it had seemed to him, in a dream, when she had bidden him farewell in Odessa, on the eve of her wedding . . . he reined his horse in, leaning back in the saddle, as the animal picked its way slowly between the tent-ropes. What had Mademoiselle Sophie said to him as he lay in that room in the Governor's residence, more dead than alive, seeing her face indistinctly through pain-dimmed eyes, as if it were the face of a ghost?

"We shall not meet again, Phillip—we cannot meet again, I . . . I know my duty." He felt his whole body tense, as memory stirred and the words came back to him. "You will live, for my sake, Phillip . . . you must live. To know that you are living somewhere in the world will comfort me. I shall think of you and pray

for you . . . for you and your valiant Trojan." Her voice was quite
clear now, sounding above the faint murmur of the other
women's voices, as if she were close beside him. *"The heart does
not forget,"* she had whispered. *"However sad it is . . . may God
be with you now and always, my dear English sailor . . ."*

Momentarily, as the unmanly tears pricked at them, Phillip
closed his eyes. It was foolish to think of her now, he told himself, ashamed of his weakness. She was no longer Mademoiselle
Sophie but the Princess Narishkin, wife of a Russian officer—
an enemy officer against whom, if destiny so willed it, he might
have to go into battle. Hadn't Graham told him that Andrei
Narishkin had left Odessa for Perekop at the beginning of
October, with the Governor, Baron Osten-Sacken, and thirty
thousand troops? He was one of Prince Menschikoff's aides-de-
camp and Colonel of a regiment of Chasseurs—a regiment
which might, even now, be with those gathering in the Tchernaya Valley—and, although he had been so severely wounded
at the Alma, Narishkin might . . . the bay horse, allowed to wan-
der at will among the tent-ropes, suddenly stumbled.

Phillip was flung forward and as the bay, receiving no assistance from its rider, came down heavily, he found himself
precipitated over the animal's head. Horse and rider rolled over
together and, as ill luck would have it, Phillip's right foot caught
in the stirrup-iron and, as the horse rolled over on top of him,
his injured leg was trapped. The horse was up a moment after-
ward but the damage was done. White with pain, Phillip lay
where he had fallen, clutching at his leg and unable to stifle
the agonized cry that was wrung from him.

The Highland women, observing his mishap, abandoned
their wash-tubs and clothes-lines and crowded about him, talking in their lilting Gaelic but hesitating, apparently, to touch
him. Then a girl emerged from a near-by tent and came to kneel
beside him, her fingers, deft and skilled, gently probing.

"I do not think your leg is broken," she said in English, her
voice as lilting as the others but her accent unmistakably

educated. "We will carry you into my tent, where I will tend it for you and you may rest for a while."

Phillip looked up at her, trying vainly to focus his gaze on her face but seeing it as a white blur, whose only distinguishing feature was a pair of smoke-blue eyes, alight with pity and concern as they met his own.

"The . . . horse?" he managed to ask, from between clenched teeth.

"The horse is all right," the soft voice assured him. "You are the only one who has been hurt."

"But it . . . it's my Admiral's horse and I . . . that is—"

"Do not concern yourself about the animal. We shall take care of it. Now if you'll lean on me . . ." The girl's voice seemed to be coming from a long way away and her face, when Phillip searched for it, receded and was lost to his sight in a swirling mist of pain as two of the women lifted him. He tried to tell them that he had an urgent message for Sir Colin Campbell and, on this account, must continue on his way but seemingly they did not hear or, at all events, did not understand him, since no one responded to his plea. He must have fainted then, he decided, for he had no recollection of being carried into the tent in which—evidently some time later—he found himself. Someone had ripped open his trouser leg and, glancing down, he saw that the cloth was deeply stained with blood.

"This is an old wound," a strange voice said, still sounding distant. "The fall has opened it, I am fearing. A bad wound it was, by the looks of it, poor young man. But it is clean. Maybe if we . . ." The voice lapsed into Gaelic, in reply to a question someone else had asked.

"I will attend to it . . ." Phillip recognized the girl's voice, a note of authority in it, as if its owner were one who was accustomed to being obeyed. "The surgeons all have their hands full and I am quite capable of doing what is necessary."

"Not you, Mistress Catriona . . . you are not accustomed to such sights and there is bleeding. Leave him to me."

"Is it not time that I became accustomed to the sight of blood, Morag? Fetch me water and clean cloths, if you please. And there are unguents in my small valise . . ." Grumbling to herself, the other and—judging by the sound of her voice—older woman departed on this errand and Phillip was again aware of the gentle, probing fingers touching his leg with infinite care. "Lie still please," the girl bade him. "Your leg isn't broken, only badly bruised. I shall try not to hurt you but I must stop the bleeding . . ." There was a pause, pressure was applied and Phillip's teeth closed over his lower lip in an effort not to cry out, as a fresh wave of pain swept over him. "There . . . that is all. I am sorry if I hurt you. How did you receive this wound?"

"From a . . . from a shell-burst."

Water was brought, his leg cleansed and firmly bandaged, and the pain began gradually to lessen. Phillip was able to sit up, the girl supporting him, and to take a few sips from the cup she held to his lips, which contained some bitter tasting liquid he could not identify. He tried to turn his head away, nauseated, but she was persistent. "Drink it all, if you can," she pleaded. "It will do you good and help the pain. I am sorry . . . it isn't very pleasant, is it? Morag MacCorkill brews it from herbs and it is all we have. But we have found that it is effective."

Controlling his aversion from the evil-tasting concoction, Phillip managed to finish the draught and murmur his thanks.

"Well done . . ." His self-appointed nurse set the cup down and he was able to see her then, quite clearly, for the first time. He stared at her in unconcealed astonishment for, despite the fact that she wore the same makeshift sacking apron as the other women, she did not resemble them, any more than her voice or her accent sounded like theirs. She was slender and young—about nineteen or twenty, as nearly as he could judge— and, beneath the apron, the dress she wore was of a good quality woollen material, well, if not fashionably cut. But it was her face which held Phillip's bewildered gaze . . . small and lovely, it was so obviously the face of a lady of breeding that there could be no question as to who or what she was and, had there been any doubt, her hands would have dispelled it. They, too, were small and the skin smooth and white—far too smooth and too white to be the hands of a soldier's woman, roughened and calloused by hard work. Her hair was raven-black, in striking contrast to the blue eyes . . . Celtic colouring, Phillip reminded himself, and as rare, in its true form, as it was beautiful.

"Who . . . who *are* you?" he asked, his bewilderment in his voice. Hearing it and guessing its cause, his rescuer reached for a shawl and hastily draped it about her slim shoulders, concealing her hands and the top of her dress beneath its folds.

"I am . . . Catriona Lamont," she answered, after a barely perceptible hesitation, and then, her cheeks flushed, she added, "You will be feeling a mite better now, sir, I don't doubt?" The "sir" and the clumsy attempt to coarsen her accent did not deceive him but, realizing that he had startled her by his sudden interest, Phillip affected to notice nothing and replied gratefully that he did.

Catriona Lamont rose. "That's fine"—again the clumsy, unconvincing attempt to disguise her accent—"then I'll away and leave Mistress MacCorkill to care for you. Her husband, Sergeant MacCorkill, has been sent for and will be here soon. But you'll rest here for an hour or so, maybe, and when you're able, the Sergeant will escort you to the naval camp."

"No . . . no, I cannot stay here." Belatedly recalling his mission, Phillip shook his head. "It is kind of you but I must go on. I have my orders, I . . ." He struggled into a sitting position, moving his leg experimentally, and the tent whirled about him.

"Wait!" In an instant, the girl was on her knees beside him, her hands on his shoulders, once more easing him back on to the rough pallet bed. "You cannot go on as you are. Please, you must rest that leg for a little while longer or it may start to bleed again. Mr . . . that is, Lieutenant . . . I don't know your name, but your orders cannot be so important that you would risk re-opening and perhaps infecting that old wound of yours by being too precipitate in trying to carry them out. You—"

"My name is Hazard, Mistress Lamont," Phillip put in. "Lieutenant Phillip Hazard of Her Majesty's ship *Agamemnon*, serving at present on Admiral Lyons's staff. I was on my way to Sir Colin Campbell when my horse put me down. I have a message for him from the Admiral which may be of considerable importance and which it is my duty to deliver to him without delay. Thanks to my own stupidity, I have already delayed far too long, so if you would be so kind as to help me . . ." He made another effort to sit up. "I shall be all right once I am on my feet."

"Will you, Mr Hazard?" Catriona Lamont gave him the help he had asked for and then sat back on her heels, regarding him anxiously.

"Sergeant MacCorkill would, I am quite certain, gladly deliver your message to Sir Colin if it is urgent. As I told you, he will be here soon—Morag has gone to fetch him. He is in the 93rd and a most reliable man . . . you can trust him, I assure you."

"Mine is not a written message," Phillip explained. "So that I cannot entrust it to anyone else. And it is also possible . . ." The tent roof steadied and he cautiously got to his feet, this time unaided. "It is also possible that Sir Colin may wish to send me back to the Admiral with his reply, so you see, Miss—that is, Mistress Lamont—I must go myself."

"I think you are unwise," the girl told him, with disconcerting frankness. "And I am Miss Lamont, Mr Hazard. I am unmarried." Apart from this statement, she offered no further information concerning herself but she had now abandoned her attempts to feign an uneducated accent, Phillip noticed, as if sensing that, on this score at least, she had failed to deceive him. Wisely, he refrained from both comment or question and instead repeated his thanks, which she accepted with a shy, charming smile.

"I am only too pleased that I was able to be of assistance to you, Mr Hazard. But, if what I have done is not entirely to be wasted, may I beg that you permit Sergeant MacCorkill to escort you to Sir Colin? And, if a reply *has* to be sent to your Admiral tonight, let somebody else deliver it . . . because you are really not fit to ride back to Balaclava again, least of all in darkness."

"In darkness?" Phillip echoed, in some dismay. "You mean that it is dark already? How long have I been here, then?" He moved unsteadily towards the tent flap and Catriona Lamont, guessing his intention, came quickly to his side.

"Lean on me, until you get your balance," she invited. "You must have been here for nearly an hour, I should think . . . you were unconscious for half an hour, anyway. And, as you can see" —she opened the tent flap and pointed, with a small hand— "the sun is setting. It will certainly be dark by the time Sir Colin has prepared an answer for you to take back to your Admiral, Mr Hazard."

Indeed it would, Phillip thought, his conscience troubled as, with a hand on the girl's shoulder, he hobbled to the opened tent flap and looked out. Several of the Highlanders' women-folk were moving about outside the tent and they raised a good natured murmur of pleasure at the sight of him and one—noticing his ripped trouser leg—fetched a needle and thread and, ignoring his embarrassed protests, swiftly stitched it up for him, kneeling at his feet in order to do so. He thanked her, putting out his hand to assist her to rise, but she flashed him an amused smile and scrambled up without taking his proffered hand. Another went to fetch his horse and Phillip hobbled to meet her when Catriona Lamont drew his attention to a red-coated figure approaching them.

"Here is Sergeant MacCorkill at last," she announced with relief. "Wait, if you please, Mr Hazard . . . I will tell him what he is to do."

The Sergeant, a big, broad-shouldered man, drew himself up as the girl went to him, and stood bareheaded, listening respectfully to what she had to say. Then he took the horse's rein from the woman who was holding it and led the animal over to where Phillip was waiting, saluting him smartly.

"You are wishing to go to Sir Colin, sir?"

"Yes, Sergeant, I am . . . and as quickly as possible, if you don't mind. I've wasted rather a lot of time already."

"So they are telling me, sir." The Sergeant permitted himself a ghost of a smile. "Will I be giving you a leg up, sir?"

"I'll manage, thank you, Sergeant." To prove his point, Phillip clambered back into the saddle a trifle awkwardly but unaided. Once there, he looked round for Catriona Lamont, intending to take his leave and to ask if he might call next day to offer his formal thanks, but to his sirprise, she was no longer anywhere to be seen and, when he asked for her, the women shook their heads, eyeing him blankly, as if they did not understand to whom he was referring.

"We should be going, sir," the Sergeant prompted, "if you are wanting to speak with Sir Colin." He laid a big hand on the bay's bridle, his manner still respectful but a mute warning in his eyes which—although mystified and more than a little put out—Phillip decided to heed. He ventured a question, as his guide led him towards the village of Kadi-Koi, but as the women had, Sergeant MacCorkill affected not to understand him and, still puzzled, he did not pursue the enquiry. For reasons of their own, obviously, Catriona Lamont's presence in the Highlanders' camp was not a subject to be discussed with a stranger but, Phillip reflected, there would probably be an opportunity during the next few days for him to call on her. And he would take it, if he could. . . .

The Sergeant, despite his unwillingness to speak of Miss Lamont, was communicative enough where other topics were concerned. The 93rd, he said, had not seen the inside of their tents for the past two nights . . . whatever Sir George Cathcart might think, Sir Colin Campbell was, it seemed, expecting and prepared for a Russian attack.

"We sleep in our lines, sir," Sergeant MacCorkill explained, "on the bare ground, with no bivouac fires permitted, and each man with his rifle at his side. Yonder, sir . . ." He gestured ahead of them, to a fold in the rising ground. "And Sir Colin with us, for he is never asking his men to put up with hardships that he himself does not share. The naval gun battery is away over there, to our left, sir . . . with your Jacks still working like beavers on their parallels. Fine lads they are indeed, sir, and we are proud to have them with us. But the Turks . . ." He shrugged, evidently as mistrustful of the Turco-Tunisian auxiliaries as Admiral Lyons had told him Sir Colin Campbell was, Phillip thought. "'Tis a pity that we are having to leave *them* to hold the redoubts on the Causeway. Now if we'd the rest of our Brigade—the 42nd, and the 79th, sir—there would be no fear of the Russians over-running us, for there's not a man in the whole of the Highland Brigade who wouldn't follow Sir Colin to hell and gone, sir, if he bade them. He's a bonnie fighter and the best commander in the British Army, you may take my word for that, sir . . . the best, aye, and the bravest, too!"

"I believe you, Sergeant," Phillip assured him, with sincerity, reminded of his conversation with young Midshipman Daniels on the subject of army officers. It seemed a grave reflection on the British Army's system of promotion that a man like Sir Colin Campbell, with over forty years of active and very distinguished service behind him, should merit only the command of a brigade. True, he had been given a brevet promotion to Major-General quite recently but so also had Lord Cardigan and others of the same caliber. Officers who had seen no fighting since Waterloo out-ranked him and even those few who had lacked his experience. Indeed, with the sole exception of Sir George de Lacy Evans, who was 67, none of the present Divisional Generals could come anywhere near to equalling his record. Sir Colin Campbell had fought under Moore and Wellington; there was scarcely a battle in the whole Peninsular War in which he had not taken part and, in India, at Chilianwala and

Gujerat, he had commanded a division under Lord Gough, and later under Sir Charles Napier, whose glowing tributes to his courageous leadership and outstanding ability had won him a K.C.B. in 1849. At the Alma, he had led his Brigade magnificently, his three fine regiments putting some twelve Russian battalions to flight in a display of disciplined valour that . . .

"I am thinking, sir," Sergeant MacCorkill said, breaking into his thoughts, "that there is one of your naval young gentlemen who is wanting to speak with you. Over younder, sir . . ." Phillip turned and a perspiring boy, with the white patches of a midshipman on the collar of his uniform jacket, came panting up to him.

"Lieutenant Hazard, sir?" the boy asked, when he could get his breath.

"Yes, that's right, youngster. And you?"

"From the *Niger*, sir." The midshipman touched his cap. "Captain Heath sent me to tell you that four hundred Marines from the *Algiers* and the *Sanspareil* have been landed at Balaclava, sir. The *Wasp* has been placed under the orders of Captain Lushington and she is finding reinforcement for the Naval Brigade. Captain Heath is to command a force of two hundred officers and seamen, sir, to reinforce the position here, and I am to tell you, sir, that the Captain expects to report to Sir Colin Campbell at Kadi-Koi first thing tomorrow morning. An advance party of volunteers from *Niger* and *Vesuvius* are on their way up now, sir, with ammunition."

"Thank you," Phillip acknowledged. He waited but when the midshipman said no more, asked frowning, "That's all?"

"Yes, sir, I think so. Except that I am to inform Lieutenant Dunn—our First Lieutenant, sir—who is in Number Four Battery before Kadi-Koi. He—"

"Your Captain did not mention the *Sanspareil*? Apart, that is to say, from the Marines she landed?"

The youngster shook his head, clearly puzzled. "No, sir, he didn't. But she was lying off the port during my watch and she was still there when I left *Niger*, sir. The Marines were landed by *Wasp* and *Lynx* and one of the small tenders, together with some 32-pounder howitzers and shot and shell, sir, for the Marine Artillery positions on the Heights."

Phillip asked one or two more questions and then thanked and dismissed the lad. The *Sanspareil*, it was evident from his replies—although she was anchored outside Balaclava—had not as yet signalled for permission to enter the harbour which meant, he supposed, that Admiral Lyons had failed to persuade the Commander-in-Chief of the need to risk a line-of-battle ship in its defense. According to *Niger*'s midshipman, the Admiral himself had not come ashore and no orders from him had been received in Balaclava, so that . . . he sighed and motioned Sergeant MacCorkill to continue their interrupted journey.

Sir Colin Campbell, with members of his staff and Colonel Ainslie of the 93rd, was eating a frugal meal in a ramshackle farmhouse adjoining No. 4 Battery when Phillip reported to him. The meal was cold but—having been compelled to forbid his men to light bivouac fires, lest these betray their position to the enemy—he could not, Sir Colin explained, permit his staff to do so either.

"But you are welcome to share our repast, such as it is, Mr Hazard," he invited cordially, in the strong Scottish accent he had never lost. "Sit you down and tell us what news you have brought us from the Admiral. I trust that it is good news?"

"I hope you may consider it good, sir, in the circumstances . . ." Phillip made his report, ending with an apology for the mishap which had delayed his arrival, and saw his hosts exchange wry glances as they listened.

The Brigade Major, Anthony Sterling, asked him a number of pertinent questions, but Sir Colin himself was silent, thoughtfully tugging at his moustache and at the small tuft of greying dark hair which adorned his chin. In appearance the redoubtable commander of the Highland Brigade was a spare, slightly built man who, at first sight, looked far from robust but, from previous experience of him, Phillip knew that—like Admiral Lyons—he was possessed of reserves of energy and a wiry strength that many a man half his age might have envied. Like the Admiral, too, he drove himself hard and, although something of a martinet, his men loved him . . . he was "a bonnie fighter," as Sergeant MacCorkill had said, and his Highlanders took a fierce pride in the stern discipline he imposed on them.

His years of service in the health-sapping climates of China and India had, however, taken their toll of him. Sir Colin looked much older than his 61 years and his deeply lined, sallow-complexioned face was a legacy of those years of almost ceaseless campaigning, as also was the ague, to which, when it attacked him, he was wont to refer as "this cursed old enemy of mine." He was evidently suffering from this now, Phillip noticed but, in spite of it, he firmly shook his head to the mess servant's offer of whisky when, his unappetizing meal finished, he pushed his plate away. His senior aide-de-camp, Lawrence Shadwell, eyed him anxiously but, when his own turn came he, too, shook his head to the whisky, and most of the others followed his example.

"Your Admiral and his Commander-in-Chief have done a great deal for us, Mr Hazard," Sir Colin said. "And we are grateful . . . particularly for your Marines, who are as fine a body of men as I have ever seen. Would there were more of them! It is a pity that Lord Raglan cannot spare me the rest of my Brigade but . . ." He shrugged philosophically. "We have done the best we can with the men and materials we've been given. You may tell your Admiral, when you see him, that he need not concern himself unduly about the need for a line-of-battle ship in the harbour. It will not be needed, save as a last resort, and I do not believe it will come to that. The Russians will not carry our position here whilst we are alive." The statement was made quietly, a statement of fact, not a boast. "Our only real cause for anxiety are the Causeway redoubts."

"You do not think the Turks will hold them, sir?" Phillip asked, recalling what Admiral Lyons had told him.

"If they were adequately armed and supported, Mr Hazard, the Turks—who, in point of fact, are Arab irregulars—would probably fight as well as any of us," Sir Colin returned, a trifle tartly. "But they are most inadequately armed, their gun emplacements have been hurriedly constructed and offer them little protection . . . and I have neither the men nor the means to give them support. The most I have been able to do is to place a non-commissioned officer of the Royal Artillery in each redoubt, to steady them and to assist them in working their guns. Frankly, I should have preferred to post them as an advance screen, without guns, and let them fall back to our lines if an attack should materialize. They are trained as skirmishers, it is the type of fighting they understand and for which they are best suited." He sighed. "The Russians, when they do attack—and there is every sign that this is their intention—will attack in overwhelming numbers. I do not think that even a division of well trained and disciplined British troops could hold the Causeway with only nine 12-pounder guns, positioned in four widely separated redoubts . . . the two westernmost are unarmed, since there has been no time to place guns in them. Rustem Pasha, the Turkish commander, is a good soldier, trained in Austria, who knows his business—and he shares this view. As, indeed, do most of my officers, do you not, gentlemen?"

There was a murmur of assent from those seated about the table. Phillip said nothing and Sir Colin went on, speaking calmly and dispassionately, "Our task is to prevent the Russians dispossessing us of Balaclava Harbour, Mr Hazard, which—God willing—I am confident we can do. But I have told Lord Raglan that, unless he can spare us at least a division, I cannot guarantee to hold the Causeway. His lordship has replied that he cannot spare us even a battalion from the siege unless we are attacked by overwhelming numbers, when he will send what help he can. So we can only pray that Rustem Pasha's Arabs *will* hold until support reaches them from the plateau."

"I see, sir." Phillip hesitated. "Do you wish me to take any message back to Admiral Lyons, sir?"

"Tonight? No, Mr Hazard, there is no need. In any event, you should rest that leg of yours, should you not, whilst you have the chance?" Sir Colin gave him one of his rare smiles. "Find yourself a place to sleep and report to me tomorrow morning. I shall be making the rounds with Lord Lucan at daybreak and you may accompany us, if you wish, and having visited our posts, you will be in a position to inform Admiral Lyons of what is going on." He rose, reaching for the Highland bonnet which, adorned with the hackles of the three regiments of his brigade, had been presented to him after the Alma and which, with Lord Raglan's permission, he now wore in place of his general's plumed hat. He donned it, bade Phillip a pleasant good night, and went out, with Colonel Ainslie and his staff, to pay a final visit to the 93rd's lines.

Phillip himself went in search of O'Leary and found him, eventually, in the darkness, working to unload ammunition with *Niger*'s guns' crews. The big Irishman was doing the work of two men and keeping his comrades in fits of laughter with his droll Irish stories, so—having learnt that his gear had been stowed in a tent he was to share with two of *Niger*'s officers—Phillip told him to carry on. The tent was close by and he found it without difficulty. Wrapped in a blanket, he lay down on the bare ground and fell asleep almost instantly.

CHAPTER FOUR

The next day, Tuesday, October 24, was a day of feverish activity and also of considerable anxiety for the defenders of Balaclava.

Time, they were all aware, was running out and they were racing against it, spurred on by reports from patrols and outlying pickets which, throughout the day, were constantly coming in to tell of large concentrations of Russian troops in Tchergoun area of the Tchernaya Valley. Some estimated the number at between fifteen and twenty thousand; others put this higher, but all were agreed that the Russians had several thousand cavalry, consisting of Hussars and Lancers, as well as Cossacks, and that the number of field guns was much greater than earlier reports had suggested. From the Heights above Balaclava, Colonel Thomas Hurdle, in command of the Royal Marines, sent word to say that Cossack *vedettes* had crossed the river in order to probe and reconnoiter the British right flank. When fired on, they simply retreated out of range and continued to keep his gun positions under close observation.

On the Marine Heights and before Kadi-Koi, men sweated and strained to haul the last guns into position, to bring up and store reserves of ammunition and to do what they could to strengthen the emplacements. Engineer officers talked of constructing *abatis* and *trous de loups* in front of No. 4 Battery, with its seven naval guns but there were no men to spare for the work involved, so that finally all they could do was to hack a few more shallow trenches in the rock-hard ground.

Only the 93rd scorned to dig trenches. The Highlanders were unaccustomed to the use of spade and mattock and strangers to the shelter-trench exercise and they displayed an obstinate unwillingness to fight behind cover. Ordered to deepen the ditch to their front, they made deliberately slow progress with their task, on the grounds that, if it were made too deep, they would be unable to get out of it to attack the Russians. Knowing the quality of his splendid regiment, Sir Colin Campbell wisely allowed the order to be ignored.

Phillip spent the whole day in the saddle, snatching a few moments' rest when and where he could. Roused before dawn by O'Leary, he shared the pannikin of rum and lime juice his orderly brought him with the two other occupants of his tent and had nothing else to eat or drink until evening. His injured leg had swollen and stiffened during the night, so that he could scarcely walk, but he managed to limp over to retrieve the Admiral's bay from Sir Colin Campbell's groom, who had volunteered to care for the animal overnight and, once mounted, he was able to carry out his duties as naval liaison officer with reasonable efficiency, if with some discomfort.

At first light, he accompanied Sir Colin Campbell and his staff from the 93rd's position to the Cavalry Division's camp, situated about a mile away in the South Valley, at the foot of the Sapouné Ridge of the Upland plateau, on which the infantry divisions were encamped. The cavalry were already standing to their horses and Lord Lucan arrived, with a large staff, to carry out his usual early morning inspection of both brigades. The Heavy Brigade paraded first, under the command of Brigadier-General the Honourable James Scarlett, a pleasant, red-faced man who, Phillip noticed, had two officers in Indian Army uniforms riding with him as aides. The elder of the two appeared to be about fifty and, of truly magnificent physique, he made a striking figure in the green and gold laced *alkalak* of an Indian irregular cavalry regiment. His insignia proclaimed him a full colonel but, although General Scarlett frequently turned to him to address some remark, Lord Lucan somewhat pointedly ignored his presence. His companion, a captain in the French grey and silver of the East India Company's regular native cavalry, was a good deal younger and, with Scarlett's other aide-de-camp, Lieutenant Elliott—whom Phillip had met —kept himself very much in the background.

"That," Captain Shadwell said, pointing to the big man in colonel's uniform, "is the famous Colonel William Beatson, one of the greatest experts on cavalry tactics living today. He commanded the Bashi-Bazouk cavalry at Silistria but . . ." He lowered his voice, "his services having been successively refused by Lord Raglan, Lord Lucan, and Lord Cardigan, he remains officially in the Turkish service—in which he ranks as a general—and acts *unofficially* as General Scarlett's military adviser."

"And the other?" Phillip asked.

Shadwell smiled wryly. "The other is Alex Sheridan, one of the heroes of Silistria, my friend . . . but he, too, is unofficially attached to Scarlett's staff. Indian Army officers are out of favour with our High Command . . . even Elliott, though he now holds a Queen's commission, is regarded with some suspicion because most of his service was with the Company's Army in India where, I may say, he greatly distinguished himself and commanded Lord Gough's bodyguard. Needless to tell you, Sir Colin does not share the general prejudice against the Company's officers. He thinks very highly of all three and especially of Alex Sheridan, who served temporarily on his staff at the Alma. I will introduce you, if the opportunity should arise . . . you will like Alex, I am sure. I have worked with him and I know his worth."

"Thank you. I should like to meet him."

"Then it shall be arranged," Captain Shadwell promised. "A word of warning, however, Mr Hazard . . . Sheridan was once in the 11th Hussars and Cardigan drove him to sell his commission. I believe, as an impetuous youth, he challenged the noble earl to a duel so, as you may imagine, the subject of his lordship is . . . well, let us say, one to avoid. But he is the best of fellows. He married a sister of Phillip Dunloy, of the 11th, a most charming girl who is now, I believe, in Constantinople."

Phillip repeated his thanks, studying the younger of the Heavy Brigade commander's unofficial aides with interest, and liking what he saw in the handsome, slightly austere face.

The inspection over, Lord Lucan prepared to ride on to the Light Brigade camp but Sir Colin, deciding to visit the Turkish redoubts on the Causeway, took his leave and, as the larger party which accompanied Lucan detached itself, he trotted over to General Scarlett with a request that he might borrow one of his aides.

"I am going to do what I can to put heart into our Turkish allies in the Causeway redoubts," Phillip heard him say. "And for that purpose, I should, I am sure, be the better for the services of one who knows them and speaks their language. Could you spare us Captain Sheridan for an hour or so, do you think?"

The genial Scarlett beamed his assent. "Of course, Sir Colin . . . Alex Sheridan will, I know, enjoy a few hours with his old Chief and there's nothing for us to do now until we go on patrol, save water our horses. Thanks to Lord Lucan's passion for this dawn inspection, we usually have time in hand." He raised a hand in salute, his smile widening. "No doubt, sir, we shall have the pleasure of your company at inspection tomorrow morning?"

"It seems highly probable, General Scarlett," Sir Colin agreed dryly. "Unless we are attacked in the meanwhile, that is to say. In which case, I may be otherwise engaged." But he echoed the Heavy Brigade commander's smile and took cordial leave of him, before leading his small party off. Alex Sheridan rode at his side for a time, replying to Sir Colin's questions and then, when the A.D.C. finally dropped back, Lawrence Shadwell introduced him to Phillip.

"A sailor on horseback is becoming quite a common sight

these days, Mr Hazard," the Indian cavalryman observed. "And, from all accounts, your bluejackets fight as well on land as they do at sea. I have the most stirring recollections of a party from the *Britannia,* under the command of Lieutenant Glyn and the young Prince Leningen, who made a very opportune appearance in two small gunboats on the Danube, just at the moment when were endeavouring to persuade a Turkish force to cross over from Rustchuk and drive the Russians from Guirgevo. Had it not been for their arrival, complete with sappers and bridge-building equipment, our attack would have failed. As it was . . ." He smiled reminiscently, "the Turks won a resounding victory and I have entertained the greatest respect and admiration for the Royal Navy ever since. This was enhanced by what I witnessed of the Fleet's valiant engagement with the sea forts a week ago. Tell me, Mr Hazard, were you by any chance in that engagement or have you been ashore with the Naval Brigade all the time?"

Phillip shook his head. "No . . . I was in the attack on the forts, Captain Sheridan." In response to the other's urging, he described it briefly, "Now I am getting my first taste of soldiering and so far"—the confession was rueful—"I haven't acquitted myself very well, I fear. My horse and I parted company yesterday and, as a result I am lame . . . though he, thank heaven, since he is the property of my Admiral and only on loan to me, does not appear to have suffered any ill effects." He glanced admiringly at his companion's superb grey Arab. "That is a very fine animal of yours, if I may say so."

"Shahraz comes from Omar Pasha's own stable," his owner said, leaning forward in his saddle to caress the grey's proudly arched neck. "He has carried me nobly since I landed in Bulgaria over five months ago. Quite a number of officers in my old regiment have tried to purchase him from me but now I would not part with him for a king's ransom, for I feel about him as I imagine you sailors feel about your ships. Shahraz represents one of the perquisites—I might almost say one of the few compensations—for being in the Turkish service, Mr Hazard."

"Does that require compensation, then?" Phillip asked curiously and was puzzled by the look of pain he glimpsed in Alex Sheridan's eyes. But it swiftly vanished and the A.D.C. answered quietly, "Yes, it does, I'm afraid, when one's own countrymen are engaged in a war. There is a . . . barrier, I suppose you might call it although, in fairness, the barrier, is caused rather by the fact that I hold a commission in the East India Company's Army than because I happen temporarily to be serving with the Turks. We are all made very much aware of its existence, from General Cannon downwards. But—again in fairness, Mr Hazard—it stems only from a certain section of the British Army. There is no barrier where officers of the caliber of Sir Colin Campbell are concerned, of course . . . and I have not noticed anything of the kind where the Navy are concerned."

"I'm glad of that, Captain Sheridan," Phillip said, with sincerity, once more reminded of his conversation the previous afternoon with Midshipman Daniels and their meeting with Lord Cardigan. But he did not pursue the subject and Alex Sheridan seemed only too glad to drop it. As they trotted towards the Causeway, he talked of the Turkish troops in general and of those to whom defense of the redoubts had been entrusted in particular.

"Ably led, the Turk is as fine a soldier as any in the world," Sheridan asserted. "In the Danube campaign he proved himself, time and again, a match for the Russians. The trouble is that, all too often, he is *not* well led . . ." He cited examples, to which Phillip listened with interest and ended, with a taut little smile, "Do not judge the Turkish army by these men here, Mr Hazard. They are, I fear, an undisciplined rabble, untrained by our standards and badly officered, with the notable exception of Rustem Pasha . . . and, as possibly you've been told, they are Arab irregulars, not Turks. Given time, we might have been able to make something of them but . . ." He shrugged. "You'll see what I mean in a few minutes. It is doubtful whether they will have noticed our approach, for one thing and—"

"But surely they will have posted sentries?" Phillip put in, shocked.

"Oh, yes," Alex Sheridan returned. "But they will be watching for the appearance of Russians, not a British general. Apart from the sentries, the rest will be sleeping or smoking their hookahs, including the officers, and they will not welcome us at so early an hour, believe me."

His forecast proved to be quite accurate. The first two redoubts, which had no guns, were occupied by riflemen, and all—with the exception of the sentries—were asleep. In No. 4, which overlooked the Woronzoff Road, there were two naval twelve-pounders and an alert British Artillery sergeant, who had somehow contrived to make all his men stand to their guns— although the officers continued to sleep. At No. 3, the Turks were also on the *qui vivre,* their British N.C.O. drilling them at their guns but at No. 2 the Artillery sergeant had been driven to despair by the Turkish officers' indolent refusal to co-operate and by his failure to make himself understood by his charges.

Sir Colin Campbell's unexpected arrival and the terse exchange between Alex Sheridan and the Turkish officers wrought a salutary change in their attitude, however, and by the time his small party started for Canrobert's Hill, all the Turco-Tunisian auxiliaries were standing to their guns, looking considerably chastened. The redoubts, Phillip saw, were—as Sir Colin had said—hastily constructed and afforded scant protection to the gun's crews. Major Nasmyth had started them, Alex Sheridan explained, but had been invalided to Scutari before the works were completed and since then, due to the failure of the Turkish officers to instil any sense of urgency into their men, little more had been done.

"Shadwell and I talked our heads off," he added ruefully, "but the results are, as you have seen, hardly to be termed successful. We urged them to dig communication trenches between their positions and to construct earthen defenses, in the Russian pattern, loop-holed for riflemen. They duly made a beginning, but little progress, I'm afraid. No. 1 battery, on Canrobert's Hill, is the only one which is strongly fortified. It has three guns and is garrisoned by a full Arab battalion, all picked men, under an able and conscientious commander, whose guns were sited by Captain Pipon of the Royal Artillery. It is, however"—he shrugged—"the most vulnerable to attack, if the Russians cross the Tchernaya by the Tractir Bridge and then advance on Kamara which, as you will observe, stands on high ground to the right rear of Canrobert's Hill." He indicated the village of Kamara and forestalled Phillip's question with a regretful, "Yes, I know . . . we should have guns there. But alas, Mr Hazard, we have no guns, nor have we sufficient troops to man them."

The garrison of No. 1 Redoubt, in encouraging contrast to the rest, was very much on the alert. Sir Colin was received by the commander with every appearance of pleasure and invited to make an inspection of troops and guns, which he did, afterwards congratulating officers and men on their vigilance and smartness, his words translated by Alex Sheridan into Turkish. A flag pole to the rear of the redoubt flew the Turkish crescent and star and it was arranged that in the event of a Russian attack, two flags should be hoisted, as a warning signal. Escorted courteously to his horse, Sir Colin took his leave, the expression on his lined face a trifle less anxious than it had been, Phillip noticed.

On returning to Kadi-Koi, the sight of Commander Heath and his seamen, who had brought up shot, shell, powder, and tents with them, served still further to lessen Sir Colin's depression. Heath said that Admiral Lyons was expected to come ashore within the next hour and Phillip was despatched to meet him, bearing a written report of the situation from Balaclava's commander. He rode back to Balaclava Harbour, to learn that the Admiral had landed from *Beagle* half an hour before and had gone to the Marine Heights, to confer with Colonel Hurdle. The *Sanspareil* was, it seemed, still lying at anchor off the harbour entrance and, within the harbour itself, *Wasp* and *Vesuvius* had joined *Simoom* and skeleton crews were exercising their guns.

Regretfully refusing several hospitable invitations to dine on board, Phillip set off once more in search of Admiral Lyons and eventually delivered Sir Colin's letter to him an hour later. Sir Edmund read the report with furrowed brows and then looked up to meet Phillip's anxious gaze.

"This needs no answer," he said, his frown relaxing. "Save my felicitations, which you will be good enough to convey to Sir Colin, Phillip. He is confident that he can hold any Russian attack, unless it is made in overwhelming numbers, in which case—typically, I think—he tells me that he will delay an advance on Balaclava until reinforcements can be brought down from the plateau. Colonel Hurdle is equally confident that his Marines can hold their positions on the Heights and the *Sanspareil*—although Admiral Dundas is reluctant to order her into the harbour unless it is necessary—is to remain outside, prepared to enter should the situation warrant it. I am on my way to see Lord Raglan now . . ." He hesitated, glancing down at Sir Colin Campbell's letter again. "He is a remarkable man, Sir Colin, is he not?"

"Indeed he is, sir," Phillip agreed warmly.

The Admiral folded the note and placed it in his breast pocket. He asked a few crisp questions concerning the general defensive position at Kadi-Koi and the Turkish redoubts on the Causeway, on learning that Phillip had visited them and then, consulting his pocket watch, prepared to continue on his way.

"Tell Sir Colin that I will endeavour to call on him later this evening, after my conference with Lord Raglan, Phillip."

"Aye, aye, sir. Is there anything else I can do, sir?"

The Admiral hesitated, exchanging glances with Captain Mends, who was with him. Finally, as if reaching a decision concerning which, until then, he had been uncertain, he

inclined his head. "Yes, there is. It places a grave responsibility
on you, but I fancy you are capable of bearing it. Phillip, you
will be with Sir Colin and the 93rd if—or perhaps I should say
when—the Russians launch their attack."

"Yes, sir," Phillip confirmed and waited, wondering what
was in the Admiral's mind.

"Should it appear to you that the 93rd's position is likely to
be carried," Admiral Lyons went on, his tone grave, "you are to
ride down to the harbour with all possible speed and inform
Captain Tatham that he is to signal the *Sanspareil* to enter . . ."
He added precise and detailed instructions. "Is it quite clear to
you? You understand what I want you to do?"

"Yes, sir, I understand."

"Good. Then return to your post, Phillip . . . and God go
with you."

The small naval party, on their somewhat ill-matched
horses, cantered off and were soon lost to Phillip's sight in the
dust cloud raised by their passing. His own horse was showing
signs of weariness and, since the Admiral's message for Sir Colin
was not a matter of urgency, he let the tired animal choose its
own pace. Passing the Highlanders' encampment, he was careful to give the tent-ropes a wide berth but, observing a crowd
of women gathered, as they had been the previous afternoon,
about their wash-tubs, he rode over to them, intending to offer
his thanks for their timely help following his fall.

They greeted him with smiles and the woman who had
repaired his trouser leg for him came over to inspect her handiwork, beaming up at him when she saw that her stitches were
holding.

"These could be doing with a wash, sir," she remarked. "We
are a trifle hard put to it to get enough water at times for our
laundering but, if you have a second pair to change into and
you would leave these with me, I would gladly attend to them
for you."

"You are very kind. But . . ." Phillip indicated his bandaged and swollen leg. "I have had to continue to wear them, since no others would go on over this. I was wondering . . ." He broke off, looking about him, hoping to see the girl who had dressed his leg the day before. "Is Miss Lamont here? Could she, perhaps, spare me a few minutes? I should like to express my gratitude to her and . . . " There was a sudden silence and the faces about him lost their smiles as if, for some reason, he had offered them a deliberate affront. "I mean Miss Catriona Lamont," he explained carefully. "The . . . the young lady who came so opportunely to my rescue yesterday afternoon when my horse threw me."

The women looked at each other but remained silent. At last, after a whispered conference in Gaelic among themselves, a tall, gaunt, middle-aged woman detached herself from the rest and came to Phillip's side. "I am the wife of Sergeant MacCorkill of the 93rd, who escorted you to Sir Colin Campbell's headquarters, Lieutenant," she stated. "'Twas to my tent you were brought after your fall and 'twas I who dressed your leg . . . do you not remember?"

"I remember only a dark-haired young lady, Mistress Mac-Corkill. A dark haired young lady with blue eyes," Phillip asserted. "She told me that her name was Catriona Lamont and she—" he was interrupted by a chorus of derisive laughter and Sergeant MacCorkill's wife said, with brusque finality, "You must have been confused, sir, or else you dreamed that you saw her. There is no Mistress Lamont here. But *I* have blue eyes!"

The laughter was redoubled. "You were falling on your head, sir," the woman who had stitched up his rent trouser leg pointed out. "When that is happening, strange notions come sometimes into the mind. Maybe there is some young lady of whom you dream or you have a wife, perhaps?" She spoke gently, not deriding him and, as if her tone were a rebuke, the laughter of the other women ceased abruptly. "A man is lonely out here in this alien land and such dreams are coming unbidden from his heart because . . . why, because the heart does not forget, you see."

The heart does not forget, Phillip thought, and felt as if a knife had been twisted in his own. Mademoiselle Sophie had whispered these same words to him a long time ago, when she had bidden him farewell and he had heard them as in a dream, so . . . perhaps the woman was right. Perhaps Catriona Lamont was a vision conjured up by his imagination, a strange, pale ghost of Mademoiselle Sophie—now the Princess Narishkin, who had married a Russian officer to whom, since childhood, she had been betrothed. For him, neither Sophie nor Catriona had any real, tangible existence, he told himself sternly and, in any event, he had no business to linger here. He thanked both the woman who had spoken to him kindly and Sergeant Mac-Corkill's wife and, as he turned towards Kadi-Koi, saw the hostility fade from the faces of the others and their smiles return. They wished him well, their lilting voices following him as he kneed the weary bay into a trot.

To the rear of No. 4 Battery, when he came in sight of it, he noticed that a number of extra tents had been erected and from O'Leary, who had evidently been on the lookout for him, he learnt that one of these had been set up as a naval officers' mess.

"Captain Heath left word for you to dine with him there, sorr," his orderly added, taking the horse from him, after assisting him to dismount.

"Thanks, O'Leary." Phillip, unable to get his injured leg to the ground, had to cling to his stirrup-leather to hold himself upright, carefully flexing the bruised and swollen muscles. "My . . . my compliments to the Commander and say that I am more than grateful for his invitation. But I have to report to Sir Colin Campbell first . . . do you know where he's to be found?"

"His Honor came back ten minutes before you, sorr, and I fancy 'twas Lord Lucan with him, by the cut of his jib and all the officers in fine cavalry uniforms trailing after him." O'Leary waved a big hand in the direction of the derelict farmhouse, which Sir Colin used as his staff headquarters. "That's where

they went, sorr. But . . ." The orderly regarded Phillip with concern. "You look just about fit to drop, Mr Hazard, so you do.
Would it not be a wise precaution, now, if you were to let a surgeon dress that leg for you? 'Tis not a bit of good trying to do
more than you're able for, is it, sorr? And there's two or three
of our naval surgeons up here now, with the *Niger*'s party and
twiddling their thumbs, the lot of them, with nothing else to
do, so they say."

Phillip released the stirrup-leather balancing himself with
difficulty. "I'm all right," he said thickly. "But the Admiral's
horse is quite done up. See what you can do for him in the way
of food and a rub down, O'Leary, if you please, because I shall
need him tomorrow. And then you can dismiss. Get some sleep
yourself. I'll want a call at first light, I expect."

"Aye, aye, sir," O'Leary acknowledged resignedly, but he was
muttering to himself as he led the tired bay horse away.

On entering the farmhouse, Phillip found it full of officers—
cavalry officers, for the most part, as O'Leary had said—and,
spotting Lawrence Shadwell among them, he limped across the
crowded room to ask him what was going on. Sir Colin Campbell's senior aide-de-camp expelled his breath in a brief sigh. "It
would seem that a Russian attack on Balaclava is imminent,
Hazard," he answered flatly. "One of Rustem Pasha's spies has
just come in with the most alarming intelligence yet. Sir Colin,
Lord Lucan, and the Pasha are questioning the fellow now, to
make quite certain he's telling the truth as regards the enemy's
movements and intentions, for we don't want another false
alarm. But if he's right, then I imagine we shall be on stand-to
throughout the night."

"Do you think he's right?"

"Well, he seems to know what he's talking about," Shadwell
admitted. He supplied terse details, and then added, "If I were
you, I should get a meal and what rest you can, while you have
the chance. I will see that you are sent for if you're needed and,
if you've any message for Sir Colin from Admiral Lyons, I'll see

that he receives it. You can do no good waiting here at the moment, I assure you."

Phillip accepted his offer gratefully, and, having passed on his message, started to make his way to the naval encampment. Hobbling painfully along in the swiftly fading light, he was surprised to hear a familiar voice call him by name and, stifling an exclamation, looked up to see the portly figure of Surgeon Fraser blocking his path. They exchanged greetings and Phillip said, his tone faintly cynical, "Don't tell me, Doctor, that *you* have also been transferred from *Trojan*?"

"Temporarily, Mr Hazard. There was a call for volunteers from my branch to do duty ashore and"—Angus Fraser shrugged his ample shoulders—"I answered it. A trifle foolish of me at my age, I fear, but I am a Scotsman, as you are aware and, since Sir Colin Campbell is a countryman of mine and in command of the Highland Brigade . . . och, well, here I am! Ah . . ." He hesitated, eyeing Phillip searchingly. "I observe that you are limping. Is that old wound of yours giving you trouble?"

"I had a fall and bruised it, Doctor. But it's nothing, I—"

"Should I not judge whether that is the case, Mr Hazard?" the Surgeon put in. "Come . . . our field hospital is but a step from here and there's been no call on my professional services since I landed early this morning, so let me take a wee peek at that leg of yours, will you not? 'Twill give me something to occupy my time and you'll be needing the dressing changed, in any event." He smiled, a hand on Phillip's arm urging him forward. "This way."

It would have been a waste of breath to argue with him, so Phillip suffered himself to be led to the field hospital noticing, not altogether to his surprise, that Able-Seaman O'Leary was grooming his horse with a great show of energy nearby, although his orderly was at pains to avoid his gaze.

Angus Fraser took his time, subjecting the leg to careful examination when he had cut away the dressing.

"It is not too bad, Mr Hazard," he stated at last. "Whoever

cared for this knew his business . . . the wound is clean and would heal fine if you were to lie up with it a day or so. But I fear it is little use my suggesting that you return to your ship, is it?"

Phillip shook his head. "No, Dr Fraser, none at all."

"So I thought. Mind, I could order you to go sick . . . you are not my commander now, Mr Hazard, and this wound could give you a great deal of trouble, if you don't rest it. However . . ." The doctor was smiling, already busying himself with a fresh dressing. "I will pad the leg well for you and offer you the advice, for what that is worth, to use it as little as circumstances permit. Horseback riding is *not* the exercise I should prescribe for you, but at least riding is better for you than walking. And a tot of rum might help to ward off fatigue, while I am applying this bandage." He called and an elderly pensioner, who was on duty as orderly, brought the rum, which Phillip swallowed gratefully.

"How are things aboard the *Trojan?*" he asked.

"Well enough, Mr Hazard. Our new commander might be considered a taut hand by some but he is just and a fine seaman, by all accounts. His health is not of the best, though . . . he has not permitted me to make a proper examination of him, but he has sought my aid for a mild digestive malaise. Like yourself, Mr Hazard, he is anxious not to miss a chance of action. There is a rumour that some of the steam frigate squadron may be ordered to Eupatoria, the *Trojan* among them, but we have heard nothing definite. There . . ." He completed the dressing, regarding his handiwork with pardonable approval. "Although I do say it myself, I am not a bad hand at bandaging. This should protect the wound from inadvertent injury and enable you to perform your duties adequately. But the leg is very badly bruised and a good deal swollen—I cannot promise that you will be free of discomfort for the next few days, I'm afraid."

Phillip sat up. "Thank you, Doctor, it feels very much easier now."

"I've done nothing but renew the dressing," Angus Fraser assured him. "You owe the fact that you can walk at all to whoever treated it for you yesterday. Was it a military surgeon?"

"No. It was a woman—a young woman in the camp of the 93rd, as it happens. My horse took a tumble over one of the tent-ropes, due entirely, I'm afraid, to my lack of attention," Phillip confessed.

"A young woman, eh? Do you know her name, by any chance? We could make use of the services of so excellent a nurse here, should the expected Russian attack take place."

"Well . . ." Phillip hesitated, frowning. "She told me that her name was Catriona Lamont, Doctor, but when I called at the camp half an hour ago, the other women denied her existence. It was odd, really . . . Miss Lamont, was obviously a young lady of education and breeding, not the type usually to be found among the soldiers' women, and I'd be prepared to swear that not only did she exist, she also tended my leg. But . . ." He shrugged. "The others told me I was light-headed and must have imagined her! A sergeant's wife, a Mistress MacCorkill—according to them—was my good Samaritan."

"Odd indeed, Mr Hazard," Surgeon Fraser agreed. He helped his patient to rise. "If there is time, I will try to solve the mystery for you by calling at the camp myself. But you, I think, should get yourself a meal and as much rest as your duties will permit . . . not that you will get a hot meal anywhere in camp, I fear. Sir Colin will have no fires lit, I'm told. I requested coffee when I first reached here but the orderly said that there was no boiling water and, in any case, the coffee beans supplied to the army are green! Imagine sending green coffee beans to an army in the field . . . it beats all, does it not?"

It seemed to be typical of the British Army's muddled commissariat arrangements, Phillip thought. He thanked Surgeon Fraser and, acting on his advice, went to the naval mess tent, where he was served with an unappetizing meal of cold salt pork and ship's biscuit. Commander Heath was not there but he learnt from *Niger*'s First Lieutenant that Lord Lucan's son, Lord Bingham—who acted as his aide-de-camp—had been sent to Lord Raglan's headquarters on the plateau, with a warning of the impending attack on Balaclava.

"It seems that the Turkish spy's report is being accepted as accurate," Lieutenant Dunn told him. "And that we shall be attacked at first light by at least twenty-five thousand Russians. I am ordered to man my guns throughout the night and I believe the 93rd are sleeping again in their battle lines, each man with his musket beside him, and the sentries doubled. Well . . ." He yawned resignedly. "I must relieve my commander. Let us hope, Hazard, that young Bingham's mission is successful and that Lord Raglan will send us reinforcements from the Upland before first light!"

Phillip paid a visit to Sir Colin Campbell's farmhouse head-quarters before retiring but the Brigade Major, Colonel Sterling, told him that Lord Bingham had not yet returned from the Upland.

"Sir Colin is making his nightly inspection of the 93rd's lines and Lord Lucan is with him, Mr Hazard . . . they will probably have met and talked to Admiral Lyons when he was on his way back to his ship." He added kindly, as Captain Shadwell had done, "Rest that leg of yours, won't you? You will be sent for if you are needed."

Conscious that this was good advice, Phillip took it. Lying on the bare ground, in his tent, he slept from sheer exhaustion the instant he closed his eyes. . . .

CHAPTER FIVE

1

The morning of October 25—the anniversary of the Battle of Agincourt, although few of the defenders of Balaclava remembered this—dawned obscurely. A heavy autumnal mist lay over the Heights and the Upland, reducing visibility to a few feet and extending over the Valley of the Tchernaya and, from the head of Sebastopol Harbour to the gorge of Balaclava. From thence it spread eastward across the Plain, over which it hung like a thick, impenetrable pall.

Under cover of this all-enveloping curtain of vapour, Cossack *vedettes* were early astir, boldly crossing the river at several points. From there they advanced unchallenged to reconnoiter yet again the positions of Lord Lucan's Cavalry Division, General Bosquet's *Corps d'Observation* on the Sapouné Ridge, which they studied with field glasses from a respectful distance, and finally that of Sir Colin Campbell's Brigade of Turkish auxiliaries and the lines occupied by the 93rd in front of Kadi-Koi. They returned to report "an ostentatious weakness" in the two last and added the surprising information that the high ground at Kamara, overlooking Canrobert's Hill, was destitute alike of guns and pickets.

Prince Menschikoff, the Russian supreme commander, had given Lieutenant-General Liprandi instructions to advance from the Tchernaya Valley and attack the British line in flank and rear as soon as the opportunity afforded and this, it seemed to his subordinate commander, was the opportunity for which he had been impatiently waiting. Menschikoff had made it clear to him that Balaclava was to be taken at all hazards and the stores and shipping in the harbour forthwith destroyed. Having achieved his primary objective, he was then to remain in occupation of both harbour and gorge, holding his forces in readiness to link up with a two-pronged attack, which would—as soon as he was in position and the British supply line cut—be launched from Sebastopol by General Luders and from Bakshi-Serai by Prince Menschikoff himself.

Liprandi had under his command 25 battalions of infantry, 34 squadrons of cavalry—including Hussars and Lancers, as well as Cossacks of the Don—and some 78 field guns, a force amounting in all to a total of over 24,000 well-trained fighting men.

Opposed to him, and apparently forming an outer and—according to the Cossack patrols' reports—unsupported first line of defense, were a thousand Turco-Tunisian auxiliaries placed, with a few guns, in four redoubts on Canrobert's Hill and the Causeway Heights, which covered, somewhat inadequately, the Woronzoff Road. Over a mile to their rear, his Cossack commanders had informed him, at the head of the gorge at Kadi-Koi, were positioned a single British regiment of between five and six hundred men—armed, not with Minié rifles but muskets—some Turkish battalions and two small gun batteries. All seemingly lacked defensive trenches, and one gun position, manned by seamen, had only been set up in the last 24 hours. Between a thousand and fifteen hundred seamen and Marines manned the Balaclava Heights behind them but—if the Cossacks were to be believed—these were spread out in a widely extended line to the east of the gorge, with 32-pounder gun emplacements and howitzer batteries also at widely spaced intervals, and they, like the Turks, were unsupported.

The harbour itself, congested with shipping, was in too chaotic a state, a reliable Greek spy had informed him, to permit the entry of any naval vessels save, perhaps one or two small steam frigates, most of which were denuded of their guns.

General Liprandi ordered an advance from Tchergoun

towards the Woronzoff Road, under cover of the misty darkness. He halted at the mouth of the Baidar Valley, resting his right wing on the hills in the vicinity of Tchergoun. In spite of the reports of his patrols, he found it hard to believe that the British line could be as lightly held as it appeared to be and, suspecting that some deception had been practiced in order to lead him into a trap, he was at first reluctant to commit his whole force to an attack on the Causeway. On the advice of his cavalry commander, he had discounted the British Cavalry Division in his assessment of the position. For one thing, his own cavalry outnumbered them by almost three to one and, for another, Prince Narishkin had assured him, they were ineptly led and had never previously attempted to try conclusions with the Cossacks.

Nevertheless, experienced campaigner that he was, the Russian General was aware of the reputation of Sir Colin Campbell, and he decided to proceed cautiously and thus avoid the trap he feared. He accordingly detached four battalions of infantry from his left wing, under Major-General Sémiakine and, with the Regiment of Azov, commanded by Colonel de Krudener, in the van, sent them forward to occupy the high ground at Kamara. Supported by cavalry and preceded by Cossack skirmishers in open order, this body crossed to the south of the Woronzoff Road and, unnoticed by the Turks, advanced on Kamara. Here they waited, keeping the Turkish position in No. 1 Redoubt on Canrobert's Hill under observation, as far as the swirling mist would allow. An aide galloped back to General Liprandi with the encouraging news that they had, so far, met with no opposition.

As the mist began slowly to disperse, Prince Andrei Narishkin, who had been sitting his horse in obvious discomfort at the head of his own regiment of Chasseurs of Odessa, rode back to where General Liprandi waited with his staff. They made way for him, in deference to his rank and because, as a member of Prince Menschikoff's staff and an Imperial aide-de-camp, he enjoyed a privileged position which entitled him to confer with—and even to advise—their own commander.

"We shall lose the advantage of surprise, General," he pointed out, "if we delay our attack for much longer. Perhaps you would like me to probe the position with some squadrons of cavalry?"

The General turned to glance at him, thinking, not for the first time, how desperately ill he looked. He had lost an arm at the Alma and the other wounds he had sustained in that disastrous battle were not yet fully healed. Reason enough, most people would have supposed, for him to remain at Bakshi-Serai with the two young Grand Dukes, Nicolai and Mikail, who fumed and fretted for action but who, nevertheless, had not been permitted to join the troops in the field and had had to content themselves with reviews and parades. Why, Liprandi wondered—again not for the first time—had their Supreme Commander yielded to the Prince Narishkin's pleas and sent him, a sick man, to lead the cavalry here today? Why, for that matter, had Narishkin requested the command? He had had his wife with him, on the last occasion that the General himself had visited Prince Menschikoffs' headquarters—a young and beautiful girl and a niece of the Emperor —with whom he had been comfortably, even luxuriously accommodated in one of the best houses in town. They had been married for only a few months—yet another reason, in his own view, at all events, for the prince to stay where he was.

However, this was no time to ask questions, and he respected his young cavalry commander's ability as much as he admired his courage, so answered courteously, "Do not worry, Highness, it is not my intention to delay the attack for an instant longer than I must. But I shall use General Rykoff's Cossack cavalry . . . yours will be needed, for the attack on Balaclava." Motioning to his chief of staff, Liprandi issued his orders. The main body was to advance in five columns, flanked by Cossacks and with thirty field guns, preparatory to launching a frontal attack on the Turkish-held redoubts, as soon as General Sémi-akine should send word that he had taken Canrobert's Hill from the rear. . . .

2

At 6:30 a.m. the Turkish colonel in No. 1 Redoubt glimpsed the approaching enemy dimly through the mist and, realizing that he was surrounded, ordered the distress signal to be hoisted to the top of the flagstaff. His three 12-pounder guns opened a hesitant fire on the Cossack skirmishers to their front, while his riflemen hastily flung up gabions to protect the rear of their position and, grouped behind these, poured a volley of musketry into the ranks of the Regiment of Azov. The Russian infantry took cover and two batteries of their horse artillery galloped up to their support, unlimbered and loaded. . . .

The British Cavalry Division had turned out, as usual, an hour before daybreak, to enable Lord Lucan to make his customary inspection. This over, the men were dismissed to water their horses. Lucan, with his staff and accompanied by General Scarlett and Lord George Paget—upon whom, in the absence of Lord Cardigan who slept aboard his yacht, command of the Light Cavalry Brigade had devolved—started to ride in the direction of Canrobert's Hill.

It was Lord George who first observed the Turks' distress signal. Reining in his horse, he pointed to the flagstaff and said, in puzzled tones, "Hullo—there are two flags flying, are there not? What does that mean?"

"Surely, my lord," one of the Earl of Lucan's aides suggested, "it means that the enemy is approaching?"

"Are you certain—" Lord George began, only to break off as his question was dramatically answered when a gun in the redoubt opened fire. It was met by a thunderous cannonade from the high ground to the right and a round shot came hurtling down towards the little group of mounted officers, scattering them and passing between the legs of Lord George Paget's horse.

Lord Lucan swiftly took in the situation and started to shout his orders. An aide was sent galloping across the valley to warn Sir Colin Campbell, a second despatched to Lord Raglan's headquarters on the Upland, nearly six miles away, to request immediate infantry support. Turning to his Brigade commanders, he said, having to shout still louder to make himself heard above the now continuous roar of gunfire, "Since Lord Raglan failed to act upon the communication sent to him yesterday evening by Sir Colin Campbell and myself, and since he has left us here altogether without support, I consider it our first duty to defend the approach to the town of Balaclava and the harbour. The Turks will have to do the best they can—we are in no position to help them. The defense of the harbour will depend chiefly on my cavalry, so that I shall be compelled to reserve them for that purpose. But"—he shrugged—"I will see whether we can accomplish anything by means of a feint. We may, at least, delay them. Lord George—"

"At your service, my lord."

"I am placing the Light Brigade in reserve," Lucan told him and, cutting short his protests, turned to the Heavy Brigade commander. "General Scarlett, you will mount your Brigade at once, if you please. I shall require one regiment to escort Captain Maude's troop of Horse Artillery, as soon as you can get them mounted."

Both Brigade commanders set spurs to their horses and dashed off, at breakneck speed, to carry out these instructions.

The Battle of Balaclava had begun.

3

It seemed to Phillip that he had slept only a few minutes when a hand grasped his shoulder and shook it none too gently.

"Mr Hazard, sorr, 'tis time you were waking." He recognized O'Leary's strong, unmistakable brogue and, still more than half asleep, made an effort to sit up.

"What is it, O'Leary?" he demanded.

"Drink this, sorr," the seaman urged, thrusting a pannikin into his hand. "'Twill put fresh heart into ye, so it will, and drive the stiffness from your leg. 'Tis a drop of the good stuff, sorr. I'll have your horse saddled and waiting by the time you have the last drop swallowed. The pity is I've not any more to be giving that horse of yours, too, for in truth, sorr, the poor crater's in a worse state than you are yourself."

Still dazed with sleep, Phillip thanked him. He gulped down the potent mixture of rum and lime juice in the pannikin and this had the effect his orderly had promised it would—probably, he thought gratefully, because O'Leary had added his own grog ration to it. Fully dressed, as he had lain down, save for his cap and pilot jacket, he donned these and limped to the entrance of the tent aware, as he drew back the flap, that it was daylight but that a thick, impenetrable mist hid even his own outstretched hand from his sight. He had shaved, after a fashion, the previous evening but, passing his fingers over his chin and feeling the night's growth of stubble on it, he sighed, and reached for his razor again. Shaving with cold water was by no means easy and he found himself wishing, as he scraped at his chin, that the Navy might be granted official permission to grow full beards, in addition to the permitted side and chinwhiskers, particularly in conditions such as these.

His shave finished, he again donned his cap and stepped out into the grey dimness, to look about him in bleary-eyed bewilderment. Only O'Leary's shouted, "Over here, sorr!" enabled him to grope his way to his horse. "Sure, you can't see a thing," the big Irishman said, with irrepressible cheerfulness. "But they say Sir Colin Campbell's about to ride to the Scotchmen's position, so I took the liberty of waking ye, for I thought you'd be wanting to go with him. They're over yonder . . ." He waved vaguely into the damp curtain of mist. "If you'll get up, sorr, I'll take ye to them."

"Can you find them, in this?" Phillip asked.

O'Leary assisted him into the saddle. "I've a fine bump of locality . . . I'll find 'em. And if you're back here in a couple of hours, sorr"—he lowered his voice to a confidential whisper— "the naval cooks have rigged some kind of an oven contraption and they say they'll give us all a hot meal without another soul being the wiser. Sure, a man can't lay a gun properly on an empty belly, can he, sorr? And with your permission, Mr Hazard, I've volunteered to lay one of the *Vesuvius*' guns in Number Four Battery, seeing the gunlayer's down with the cholera."

He was a good man, Phillip thought, for all his reputation as a "Queen's hard bargain" and a rebel, and, in any case, most of the trouble he had got himself into aboard the *Trojan* had been a direct result of the late Captain North's persecution of him. In a situation like this, Able-Seaman Joseph O'Leary was worth his weight in gold.

"Certainly you can have my permission, O'Leary," he agreed, as the horse moved hesitantly forward. "That's what you came ashore for, is it not?"

"It is, sorr . . ." The mist hid his grin but it was there. "Now, if you'll steer a mite to port, I believe you'll find the other gentlemen getting mounted. Good luck, sorr!"

"And to you, O'Leary," Phillip answered warmly. He steered the required course and duly found himself among Sir Colin Campbell's staff, sitting their horses patiently, as they waited for the mist to disperse. But Sir Colin, he realized, was not with them.

"Sir Colin has gone ahead," a young lieutenant of the 93rd informed him, "guided by one of my platoon sergeants on foot. I've never seen him so impatient. It's as if he feels it in his bones that an attack is coming and, although he ordered the rest of us to wait until we could see where we're going, *he* had to be there. But you can see nothing in this infernal mist, can you? I only hope my fellow doesn't contrive to lose his way because that *would* be a disaster!"

With the first lightening of the eastern sky, the mounted officers moved forward to the rising ground occupied by the 93rd, where—to their relief—the shadowy figure of their Brigade commander could be seen pacing slowly up and down between the Highlanders' ranks. To a diffident enquiry from Colonel Sterling as to whether he wished to ride on to the Cavalry Division Camp, which was his usual practice at this hour, Sir Colin shook his head.

"No, no . . . I'll stay here. Something is wrong, I can sense it but—" he was interrupted by the dull echo of a single gun, fired from his right front, and Phillip heard him stifle an exclamation as he turned to an immensely tall officer who stood close by. "That," he asserted positively, "came from Canrobert's Hill."

A moment later, as if in confirmation of his words, came the crackle of musketry and the deep roar of heavy gunfire from the same direction and when, with a suddenness that was startling, the mist receded, an aide-de-camp could be seen approaching at full gallop, leaning low over his horse's neck.

"And that," a deep voice observed gravely, "means trouble, I fancy, Sir Colin." Phillip recognized the tall officer in green cavalry uniform, who stood at Sir Colin Campbell's side, as Colonel Beatson, the Bashi-Bazook commander of whom Alex Sheridan had spoken the previous day. His voice, although grave, was without a tremor and he added quietly, "The Turks, it seems, are being attacked on two sides."

"Pray God they hold, Colonel," Sir Colin answered.

"Pray God that Lord Lucan is able to give them some support, sir. Judging by the volume of that gunfire, they are being attacked by a large force and"—Beatson's heavy brows met in a frown as, head on one side, he listened—"I fear they are only replying with musketry at present. Well, sir, if you will permit me to do so, I think I had better rejoin my brigade. It is possible that General Scarlett may have need of me, in the circumstances."

Sir Colin held out his hand and the two men took leave of each other with a mutual respect and liking that, Phillip thought, watching them, was very evident. Then, as a dragoon orderly led the Colonel's horse up, Sir Colin turned and resumed his measured pacing of the Highlanders' ranks, pausing here and there to address the men, his voice raised so that they might all hear him.

"Remember, 93rd, there's no retreat from here . . ." His accent was rich and strong. "Ye maun die where ye stand, if need be."

"Aye, Sir Colin, we'll dae that, never fear," one of the sergeants assured him and, from man to man and rank to rank, the Highlanders responded in similar heartening fashion to his stern injunction. "We'll hae nane but Hie'land bonnets here!" a young grenadier company subaltern shouted, and the men about him grinned and raised a subdued cheer. They stood to their arms on the crest of the hill and, with two Turkish battalions on the right flank and a company of a hundred invalids—lately returned from hospital at Scutari—in support, awaited the arrival of the galloping cavalry aide. As they did so, Phillip saw one of the invalids, a tall, fair-haired Regimental Sergeant-Major of the 42nd, suddenly break ranks and approach Colonel Ainslie, limping perceptibly.

"Sir!" The 93rd's commanding officer turned to face him and he saluted, standing smartly to attention. "Will you grant me permission, sir, to join the 93rd? My place is with them, sir."

He smiled and added, echoing the young ensign who had quoted Sir Colin Campbell, "Amang the Hie'land bonnets, where I belong and where I had the honour to be at the Alma. My regiment is not here but I doubt, sir, if that's their fault or their wish."

The Colonel eyed him approvingly. "I doubt very much if it is. What is your name, Sergeant-Major?"

"Menzies, sir—Peter Menzies."

Colonel Ainslie gave the required permission. "We shall be proud to have you with us, Sergeant-Major Menzies."

"Thank you very much, sir." Phillip watched him go, a tall, determined figure in his fine Highland bonnet and patched scarlet jacket and saw him, a few minutes later—his limp hardly noticeable now—place himself in the front rank of the Grenadier Company of the 93rd . . . just as Lord Lucan's aide jerked his panting horse to a standstill beside Sir Colin Campbell and breathlessly delivered his message.

"The Turks in Number 1 Redoubt on Canrobert's Hill are under attack, sir, from the direction of Kamara as well as to their front. Lord Lucan has instructed me to tell you that the Russians are advancing in very large numbers, supported by cavalry and field guns, from the direction of Tchergoun and the Baidar Valley, having crossed the river. They appear to be about to attack the Causeway Heights, sir, and the Turkish redoubts guarding the road."

"Have you any estimate of their numbers?" Sir Colin asked.

The young officer shook his head. "I can only tell you that they are in very considerable strength, sir. His lordship has sent word of the attack to Lord Raglan and has requested immediate infantry support. He has ordered out the Cavalry Division, together with a troop of Horse Artillery, and they are mounting now."

"Does Lord Lucan intend to support the Turks?" was Sir Colin's next question and, once again, the A.D.C. could only shake his head. "I am instructed to inform you that his lordship will take the first opportunity that occurs to confer with you, sir. In the meantime he will send you what news of the enemy's movements he is able to obtain, sir."

Sir Colin thanked and dismissed him, with a composed, "Assure his lordship, if you please, that I shall be here, whenever he is at liberty to confer with me. And tell him that I will send Captain Barker's battery to aid him in his endeavour to support the Turks." He added, to no one in particular, as his own staff gathered about him, "Let us say that it will take forty minutes for Lord Lucan's request for support to reach Lord Raglan. Then a further two or three hours for one of the infantry divisions to march down from the plateau . . . even if the order is given at once, which may not be the case. That means, gentlemen, that we must hold on here for the next three hours at least, with the force we have now and such support as the Cavalry Division is able to provide. Well, I suppose it must be done and every minute the Turks can delay the enemy's advance will be in our favour. But I should like more information concerning the enemy's movements and numbers—and General Bosquet must be told, of course."

He gave his orders with calm confidence. An alert Captain Barker was instructed to support the Cavalry Division; three mounted officers were sent forward to report the position on Canrobert's Hill and the Causeway, and another to the French First Division on the Sapouné Ridge, with orders to bring back a report of all that could be seen from General Bosquet's command post. Sir Colin then despatched Captain Shadwell in search of the Turkish commander, Rustem Pasha, and, turning to Phillip, began, "Mr Hazard, it would be as well if you were to arrange to have a message transmitted to Admiral Lyons. Inform him that—" with a murmured apology, Colonel Sterling interrupted him, "A galloper is here with a dispatch from Colonel Hurdle on the Marine Heights, sir. He says that it is urgent."

Sir Colin read the dispatch, a grim little smile playing about his lips. "It would seem," he told his staff, "that our Turkish spy brought us a most exact estimate of the enemy's strength and intentions last night. Colonel Hurdle tells me that Liprandi appears to be about to launch a full-scale attack on our forward position. His main body is moving forward in five columns from the river, with a very large force of cavalry, which he estimates at over thirty squadrons, and they are escorting more than this number of field guns. The Turks will be overwhelmed . . ." he added a few technical details and then told Phillip, "Your Admiral has signalled that he is coming ashore at once. He expects to join us here within the next hour or—" again he was interrupted, this time by Colonel Ainslie, who rode over to announce that Lord Lucan had his cavalry mounted and formed up in front of their camp.

"And look, Sir Colin," the 93rd's commanding officer went on, "are those not the Greys advancing now to the support of the Turks?" He pointed and, following the direction he had indicated, Phillip saw that some squadrons of the Greys were crossing the South Valley and making for Canrobert's Hill. Easily distinguished, even at that distance, by their tall bearskins and fine grey horses, they were galloping resolutely across the open ground, a troop of Horse Artillery with them and Barker's a little way behind, spurring after them. As the watchers gathered about Sir Colin Campbell held their breath, the first troop unlimbered and, turning their six-pounder guns on a tightly packed column of Russian infantry advancing from Kamara, opened a rapid and determined fire. The Russian column halted and, when the second troop caught up with and unlimbered to the right of the first, the whole enemy column was seen to be withdrawing out of range.

The British Horse Artillery's success was, however, short lived. As the column of infantry fell back, a Russian battery, escorted by Cossacks, advanced to take their place, followed by two others, which opened up unexpectedly from the southeastern slopes of the Causeway Heights. Their fire was accurate and deadly, and the British six- and nine-pounders were no match for the Russian twelve's. Under a withering cannonade, the British gunners received the signal to retire, but, as they started to limber up a shell burst in their midst, killing a number of men and horses and—as Phillip learnt later—severely wounding the able and gallant battery commander, Captain Maude. They were too far away for those watching from the 93rd's position to see clearly what was happening and the whole area was clouded with gunsmoke, but one of Sir Colin Campbell's aides came dashing back at that moment, with the alarming intelligence that the Tunisian auxiliaries in No. 1 Redoubt were no longer returning the enemy's fire.

"They've suffered very heavy casualties, sir," the A.D.C. said breathlessly. "And are being attacked on two sides by Russian field guns. I don't believe they'll hold for much longer, they—" He pointed despairingly. "Look, sir, they're running!"

He was right, Phillip saw. The Turkish auxiliaries in No. 1 Redoubt, evidently fearing that, with the withdrawal of the British cavalry and artillery, they were about to be left to their fate, had given up all attempts at resistance. Although the remnants of Maude's battery joined Barker's and again unlimbered and opened fire, covered by two squadrons of the Greys, it was too late. Led by a mounted officer, the Tunisians came scrambling down the slope to the rear of Canrobert's Hill in wild disorder, flinging down their muskets and accoutrement as they ran. They screamed their terror aloud when some of the Cossack skirmishers spurred after them, to halt their flight with ruthless barbarity, riding down the wounded and using their lances and pistols on the others.

A large, massed force of Russian infantry, the pale early morning sunlight glinting on their bayonets, started to move towards the abandoned redoubt, their assault preceded by a prolonged cannonade. Then several Cossacks leapt their wiry little horses over its ramparts and the redoubt was carried, the infantry making a bayonet charge on the heroic handful of defenders who remained. Evidently, Phillip decided, watching through his Dollond, the retreat had been too precipitate to allow time for the three naval twelve-pounder guns to be spiked since, a little later, these were again firing . . . only this time their fire was directed against the second redoubt, on the south side of the Woronzoff Road.

The terrified Tunisian gunners fired a single ragged volley of musketry from behind their low parapet, and then, as the Russian shells started to fall among them, they fled from No. 2 Redoubt in the same hopeless confusion as their comrades had displayed earlier, making no attempt to cover their retreat. Again the Cossacks galloped after them and few escaped their merciless pursuit. Some made for No. 3 Redoubt, hoping to find shelter there; one or two, bolder than their fellows, turned on their pursuers, seeking to unhorse them before the lances could strike home, but the majority ran shrieking at the pitch of their lungs towards the 93rd's lines, leaving the plain below them littered with their dead.

"They must be stopped," Sir Colin Campbell said, still not raising his voice. "Lawrence, ask Rustem Pasha, if you please, to send some of his officers to meet and rally them. They can form up with his regiments on our right."

"Sir," Colonel Sterling put in, "the cavalry are falling back and Captain Barker's troop is returning."

The Heavy Cavalry Brigade was now, Phillip saw, positioned below and to the left of Canrobert's Hill, the Light Brigade some distance to their rear, below No's 3 and 4 Redoubts, both of which were still putting up a brave show of resistance. But when the Scots Greys, covering Maude's troop, rejoined General Scarlett, the whole Brigade—menaced by a large body of Russian cavalry and under fire from Canrobert's Hill and the eastern end of the Causeway—withdrew still further, the Turco-Tunisians in No. 3 Redoubt followed the example of their fellows and fled.

Those in No. 4 continued to hold out, delivering a well-directed fire into No. 3 as the Russians made to take possession

of it and, from the Sapouné Ridge above them, General Bosquet's mortars put an end to the Cossacks' slaughter. As a result,
when the time came for them to seek safety in flight, many of
the defenders in No. 4—having spiked their guns—deservedly
succeeded in reaching the 93rd's lines.

The Cavalry Division was forced to fall back still further
and their withdrawal brought them into the 93rd's line of fire
and that of Captain Barker's Battery of nine-pounders which,
having received a fresh supply of ammunition, was endeavouring to cover the Turk's retreat. Observing this, Sir Colin
Campbell said, "I will, I think, ride over to confer with Lord
Lucan, gentlemen, and suggest that his lordship places his Division so as to guard our left flank. The Turks have gained us an
hour and a half . . . let us use this to the best advantage we
can. Colonel Ainslie!"

"Yes, Sir Colin?" The 93rd's commanding officer was at his
side.

"The Russians on Canrobert's Hill will have our range very
soon. To avoid unnecessary casualties among your men, order
them to retire a few paces and lie down behind the crest of the
hill. Our turn is coming next, I fancy, but while we are waiting, I don't doubt that our naval gunners and the Marine
Artillery on the Heights will make good practice. Eh, Mr Hazard?" He turned to Phillip, a faint smile curving his lips.

"They will indeed, sir," Phillip agreed, admiring his stoic
calm. "Have you any orders for me, sir?"

His movements deliberately unhurried, Sir Colin consulted
his watch, a battered silver timepiece, which he pulled from the
breast pocket of his blue frock coat. "Your Admiral should, by
this time, be on his way up here, should he not? He will no
doubt wish to have a first-hand account of the situation here,
so perhaps, Mr Hazard, you will be so good as to meet him and
deliver your account? Return to me here as soon as you can,
with any information Sir Edmund is able to give me as to the
situation in the port."

"Aye, aye, sir." Phillip obediently turned his horse's head in the direction of the defile that led to Balaclava. He was exceedingly reluctant to absent himself from his post at this moment but, to his relief, his absence was in the end less prolonged than he had feared it might be. Ten minutes at a reckless gallop past the village of Kadi-Koi and down the rutted track brought him the welcoming sight of Sir Edmund Lyons and his staff approaching, and he was able to make his report as he rode back with the Admiral to the head of the gorge.

Sir Edmund listened to all he had to tell in frowning concentration, for his recital was punctuated and, at times, almost drowned by the ominous rumble of gunfire echoing across the South Valley. Several of the Marine Artillery batteries on the Heights to their right were firing almost continuously but, judging by the volume and direction of the sound, the naval guns to the left of Kadi-Koi had not yet opened . . . which meant, Phillip decided, that the enemy's advance had so far been contained by Sir Colin Campbell's judicious positioning of the Cavalry Division. He mentioned this and the Admiral nodded.

"Sir Colin knows his business. But our Marine Artillery will be in need of more ammunition at the rate they are using it," he observed. "Supplies are being sent up but, all the same, it will do no harm to expedite them . . ." He despatched a midshipman on this errand. "Commander Heath is in our Number Four Battery at Kadi-Koi, is he not?"

"I understand that he and Commander Powell are both there, sir," Phillip answered.

"Then we'll head in that direction, Phillip. I will have a word with him before I go on to Lord Raglan's headquarters."

As the small party neared Kadi-Koi, skirting the tents of the 93rd, Lord Cardigan thundered past them, his aides on sweating horses, and the Light Brigade commander in such a fever to join his command that he galloped past without greeting or apology . . . and probably, Phillip thought, without realizing of whom the party in the dust cloud behind him consisted. Admiral Lyons looked after the tall figure in the theatrically resplendent uniform, mounted on the magnificent chestnut thoroughbred but, mopping the dust from his face, forbore from comment. Instead he instructed Phillip to inform Sir Colin Campbell that all the warships in Balaclava Harbour had men standing to their guns.

"The *Sanspareil* is off the port with steam up and Captain Dacres will bring her in, should this be necessary," the Admiral went on. "That will be *your* responsibility, Phillip . . . and you must not hesitate, should the enemy carry Sir Colin's position and threaten the harbour to ride at once to Captain Tatham—he knows exactly what will be required, I have discussed the situation with him fully since I landed this morning. In fast . . ." He shrugged. "An order was received from General Airey, addressed on Lord Raglan's behalf to Captain Tatham, requiring him to load the transports and send them outside the harbour. This was delivered aboard the *Simoom* just as I was leaving, and I confirmed it . . . it is a wise precaution and, in any event, will enable *Sanspareil* to enter without delay. But we are not going to yield Balaclava to the Russians, Phillip."

"No, sir. But you say that Lord Raglan . . ." Phillip hesitated, conscious of the Admiral's eyes on his face. "I mean, sir, that his lordship . . . well, his lordship must have despatched that order *before* the Turks were driven from the Causeway Redoubts, sir, and—"

"I know what you mean," Admiral Lyons put in. "His lordship has timid counsellors, perhaps. Captain Tatham will hold the head of the harbour with the steam frigates anchored there now. I've had guns placed aboard the *Diamond* and, if necessary, men are standing by to reinforce our seamen and Marines on the Heights. *Wasp* and *Diamond* are in position— the other steamers will join them, after towing out the transports and . . ." The roar of heavy and prolonged gunfire drowned his next few words and he broke off, gesturing ahead of him to where No. 4 Battery had opened with all its seven 32-pounder guns. "I shall be with Lord Raglan," he added, when there was a brief lull in the firing. "Probably throughout the day."

"Very good, sir." Phillip waited for his dismissal but it did not come at once. The Admiral reined in, his glass to his eye, ranging it this way and that and asking occasional questions but, from where he had halted, there was little to be seen, so after a while he snapped the telescope shut and laid a hand on Phillip's arm.

"Return to Sir Colin Campbell, Phillip, and do not leave your post unless it should be necessary to signal the *Sanspareil* to undertake the defense of the harbour. Then, as I said before, you must not hesitate, you understand? Everything may depend on the speed with which she is brought in."

"I understand, sir."

"Good—then back to your post. If there should be heavy casualties among our own men or the 93rd, send for extra stretcher parties from the *Diamond* to evacuate them . . . they, too, will be standing by. And you may need a galloper." The Admiral glanced over his shoulder to give a crisp order to Cowper Coles, his Flag Lieutenant, who was riding behind him. "I'll leave you one of the mounted orderlies the cavalry have so kindly provided me with." He smiled, with wry humor. "Don't forget that you are here to observe, not to fight."

"Aye, aye, sir." Phillip saluted and, as the Admiral's party took the left-hand track towards the village of Kadi-Koi, he trotted off to rejoin the 93rd. Passing their tents, he saw that most of the women had gathered in a silent group on the far side, from whence they were anxiously watching all that was going on. So absorbed were they that they neither saw nor, apparently, heard him ride past, his newly acquired galloper—a trooper of the 8th Hussars—cantering at his heels.

Not one of the women looked round, and, although he searched for her among their number, he could not be sure that the slim figure with the dark proudly held head, whom he imagined he recognized as Catriona Lamont was, in fact, she. . . .

CHAPTER SIX

When *he reached* the rear of the 93rd's position, Phillip realized that several changes had taken place during his short absence and, his Dollond to his eye, he looked about him, frowning.

The Highlanders were still lying down behind the crest of the hill in their two lines, each man with his musket at his side, alert and watchful. But to their right he noticed that the Turco-Tunisian battalions—although well out of range of the enemy's guns—were moving about restlessly as if, he thought shocked, they were again contemplating flight.

Then, with an even greater sense of shock, he observed that the Cavalry Division had withdrawn from the strategically well-chosen position Sir Colin Campbell had earlier advised them to occupy. Instead of being formed up between Kadi-Koi and their own camp in the South Valley, where they'd covered the 93rd's vulnerable left flank, they were proceeding across the Plain of Balaclava in a north-westerly direction. Which meant, Phillip realized, his heart sinking, that if Sir Colin Campbell's Highlanders should fail to repel the expected Russian attack then— apart from such resistance as the naval guns and the Marines on the Heights behind them could offer—the way to Balaclava Harbour would be open. And the *Sanspareil* was still at anchor outside the harbour entrance, with no prospect of being able to enter until a passage had been cleared for her. . . .

He watched, in silent dismay, as the two brilliantly uniformed British Cavalry Brigades executed their withdrawal by alternate regiments and with parade ground precision, led by the Light Brigade. Reaching the western extremity of the South Valley, they halted immediately below the Sapouné Ridge, to form up in line of brigades, facing east. Even at that distance, they made a splendid, colourful spectacle, the sunlight striking bright reflections from lance-tips and drawn sabres and glinting on brass dragoon helmets and gold-frogged hussar jackets . . . yet the line of captured or abandoned redoubts on the Causeway Heights must, Phillip thought, have mocked them, and he turned away, lowering his glass.

Sir Colin Campbell, he saw, had returned—seemingly unperturbed—from his conference with Lord Lucan, and was again pacing slowly up and down between the ranks of the 93rd, on foot, his groom holding his horse nearby. To the obediently prostrate Highlanders, their commander was repeating his earlier reminder that there could now be no retreat and, as they had before, the men responded with shouted promises and subdued cheers, most of these drowned by the thunder of the guns. To their right front, Captain Barker's nine-pounder battery was firing almost continuously, as, too, were the naval guns to their left and on the Heights behind them. Occasionally, through the drifting smoke, it was possible to glimpse the enemy guns with which they were engaged, and now and then a shell burst overhead or a round shot ricocheted between the ranks of crouching, red-coated soldiers.

A young officer of the 93rd, when Phillip questioned him concerning the withdrawal of the Cavalry Division, shrugged disgustedly. "They are, I have been given to understand, sir, obeying an order from Lord Raglan, which has just reached them—to take ground to the left in support of the Turks, who are wavering. They most certainly are wavering, as you can see . . ." His gesture, in the direction of the Turkish troops, was contemptuous. "But they are, alas, now with *us* and not, as his lordship seems to imagine, in the redoubts on the Woronzoff Road, where they should be! And from whence, I was told, sir, they pillaged the Cavalry Division's camp during their inglorious retreat. I refer to those placed in the westernmost of the redoubts—the others were intent only on saving their skins. But judging by their previous behavior, these gentry will waver all the way to the harbour if we are attacked and it would, I'm afraid, take more than our Cavalry Division to stop them!"

His words proved unhappily to be prophetic. The Russians had brought up more field guns, under cover of the smoke and, although their infantry remained on the Tchernaya side of the Causeway Heights, these guns, escorted by Cossacks, concentrated a fierce fire on the Tunisian and Turkish battalions posted to the right of the 93rd. As if it had only needed this to decide them, the Tunisian auxiliaries broke and fled for the second time that day, their high-pitched screams of "Ship, Johnny, ship!" echoing back from the rocky heights towards which their panic-stricken flight was directed. In a matter of as many minutes—although a few held fast—two battalions had abandoned their arms and their allies and were hurling themselves in a yelling, jostling mob through the Highlanders' camp, intent on making for the harbour and the ships they hoped were waiting there to take them to safety.

Because his attention was wholly taken up by what was happening on his immediate front, Phillip did not see the reception accorded them by the Highlanders' womenfolk, and he did not witness the cowardly attempts to loot and pillage made by some of the fleeing Arabs. Afterwards, however, he listened with grim satisfaction to the story of how some of the indignant soldiers' wives had set upon and belaboured the intruders with any weapon that came to hand, from tent-props to smoothing irons, until, compelled to drop their spoils and with the derisive cries of the women in their ears, the wretched mob had continued their inglorious retreat to Balaclava, a mile below them . . . only to be met by Captain Tatham and a party of resolute seamen, who had ordered them unceremoniously back to their posts.

"Dogs!" the officer whom Phillip had questioned exploded

wrathfully. "Miserable curs! What could Lord Raglan have been thinking of, to give us such miserable scum to fight with, while retaining the rest of our brigade to do trench duty with the Guards? If the defense had been entrusted to the Highland Brigade alone, Balaclava would have been secure, but as it is . . ." He broke off, pointing ahead through the wreathing, greyish-yellow cloud of gunsmoke and there was a faint tremor in his voice as he said, "My God, look, sir . . . over there! The Russian cavalry are advancing across the Causeway Heights!"

Conscious of a quickening of his pulse and a sudden dryness in his throat, Phillip allowed his gaze to follow the direction of the ensign's pointing finger. Dimly, through the smoke, he could discern a great mass of Russian horsemen, moving slowly but with confidence along the lower slopes of the Causeway having, apparently, crossed the Woronzoff Road from the North Valley. It was impossible accurately to judge their number but, at a guess, he put this at something in the region of two thousand, although there could have been more. There was, however, no doubt at all of their intentions and he drew a quick, startled breath. They were the elite of the Russian cavalry, the blue of Hussar and Lancer uniforms and the dark green of Chasseurs' tunics mingled with the grey greatcoats of the ubiquitous Cossacks, and they were led, he saw, by a regiment of splendidly horsed Chasseurs, whose commanding officer rode along, some distance ahead of the leading squadron.

Although at extreme range, Barker's nine-pounder battery—loading, on an order from Sir Colin Campbell, with round shot—did swift but momentary execution among their packed ranks. This, however, while it caused them to change direction by wheeling obliquely, did not halt their advance, and their own field guns, ranged on the 93rd's position, afforded them cover until they vanished into the swirling gunsmoke. Phillip saw that Sir Colin was returning for his horse, and he seized the opportunity to deliver Admiral Lyons's message to his aide-de-camp, Lawrence Shadwell, who was with him. Shadwell passed this on to his chief as he mounted and Sir Colin beckoned Phillip to his side.

"Do nothing to disrupt the Admiral's present arrangements for the defense of the harbour, Mr Hazard, without an order from me," the Highland Brigade commander told him. "Unless you see me fall, in which event you will have to refer to Colonel Ainslie. But if you . . ." He stifled an exclamation, peering ahead of him into the smoke to where some squadrons at the rear of the Russian mass—amounting to between five and six hundred men—detached themselves and made for the 93rd's position. As they did so, a company of the 93rd, which had evidently seen the advancing enemy cavalry, rose as one man to their feet and, with bayonets fixed, moved forward towards the crest of the hill to meet them.

"Shadwell!" thundered Sir Colin, "Those men must hold their ground!" Without giving his aide-de-camp time to deliver this order for him, he set spurs to his horse and, thrusting past the offenders, turned in his saddle to wave them back reprovingly. "93rd, 93rd . . . damn all this eagerness! Keep your lines!"

The men, hearing him or, at any rate, comprehending the meaning of his raised arm, stiffened and at once re-formed in disciplined obedience. All the Highlanders were, by now, on their feet but still concealed from the enemy by the brow of the hill behind which they had lain for so long and their officers, repeating their commander's order, proceeded to dress them meticulously.

They were in two lines, extended to cover as much ground as their depleted numbers would allow. A party of the Guards— a fatigue party, Phillip judged, by the look of them, on their way to Balaclava—under two young officers, having sought Colonel Ainslie's permission to do so, ranged themselves on the 93rd's right flank, in an attempt to fill the gap left there by the defection of the Tunisians. Here they were joined by the invalids' company, and a Turkish battalion, consisting mainly of those Arab auxiliaries who had rallied, was posted on the extreme right of the position under the command of Rustem Pasha himself, who could be seen fiercely exhorting his men to stand firm.

As the main body of Russian cavalry went on its chosen way without haste, riding in a shallow trough which, running parallel to the Woronzoff Road, concealed their presence from the British Cavalry Division at the opposite end of the Causeway, the smaller, detached force quickened its pace, coming rapidly nearer. A strange hush fell at that moment, the silence oppressive and curiously ominous, as the supporting guns ceased fire to enable their own men to approach the 93rd's position. In the silence, it was possible to hear the champing of bits and the clink of sabers as the cavalrymen rose in their saddles, advancing without attempt at concealment. They must have witnessed the precipitate flight of the Tunisians, Phillip supposed, and having deduced from this that Kadi-Koi and the head of the Balaclava gorge were now virtually undefended, they were expecting to meet with no opposition. They advanced at a brisk trot, without scouts or skirmishers and, as they started to breast the lower side of the slope some eight hundred yards from where the 93rd waited with growing impatience, Sir Colin Campbell at last gave the order to advance and open fire on the enemy when they came within musket range.

Needing no urging, the 93rd moved to the crest of the hill, two thin, widely extended lines of red-coated, kilted Scottish soldiers—seeming, to the surprised Russians, to have materialized from out of the ground. There, as their commander had ordered, they waited for the enemy to come within range of their muskets. Their steadiness was so impressive, their bearing so resolute, that the Russians did not suspect that they were unsupported—all, in fact, save for the Marines and naval guns on the Heights behind them, that stood between Balaclava and capture—and the leading squadron hesitated. Then, as the first volley of musket fire rang out in almost perfect unison, they halted.

There were few casualties among them but, in spite of this, they checked their advance and seemed on the point of retreating when, in response to a shouted order from the officer at their head, the leading squadron wheeled to the left. Followed by the second and third, the whole force swiftly gathered speed and thundered once more into the attack, with the object of turning the weakened right flank of the 93rd. Faced by a less experienced commander or by less courageous and well-disciplined troops, they might have succeeded, Phillip realized, watching them, his heart suddenly quickening its beat.

Sir Colin Campbell's demeanor was, however, magnificently calm. "Shadwell," he observed to his aide, his tone admiring, "that man understands his business. Order up the Grenadier Company to cover our right." His quick appreciation of his opponents' intentions and the decisive manner in which he twice reorganized his line so as to meet and counter the Russian attack, undoubtedly saved Balaclava for, faced by "the thin red line tipped with steel," the Russian cavalry did not charge.

Under their company commander, Captain Ross, the Grenadier Company poured a well-aimed volley into the first two squadrons at a range of less than four hundred yards, and although the Russians made a third attempt to carry the 93rd's position, it was a half-hearted one, made at a trot, and when it failed, the enemy withdrew, discomfited. The Highlanders fired another volley into their retreating backs, Barker's battery and the naval guns in No. 4 and on the Heights opened up again and, as they galloped out of range, the 93rd—once more sternly prevented from charging after them by Sir Colin—cheered lustily and threw their bonnets in the air.

But while the way to Balaclava Harbour had been barred to them, the Russian cavalry had not been defeated. The main body's leisurely advance along the Causeway Heights had brought them, at last, almost within sight of the British Cavalry. Lord Lucan's Division was drawn up below the Sapouné Ridge at the western extremity of the South Valley, where Lord Rag-

lan's last order had placed them, to await the support of the
First and Fourth Infantry Divisions. These, with Bosquet's First
Division, were now on their way down from the Upland. The
British Commander-in-Chief had established his battle headquarters on the crest of the Sapouné Ridge, where General
Canrobert shortly joined him. It was an ideal command post.
Looking down from his six-hundred-foot high eminence, Lord
Raglan could see the whole Plain of Balaclava spread out before
him, his view of the enemy movements in the North Valley as
clear to him as those of his own troops in the South Valley since,
from that height, the low hills of the Causeway running between
them offered no obstruction. Unhappily, he failed to realize—
until it was much too late—that the view of his subordinate
commanders at Kadi-Koi, and elsewhere on the Plain itself, was
completely obscured by the dividing hills.

While Sir Colin Campbell had glimpsed the first large body
of Russian cavalry briefly through the gunsmoke, as they
crossed to the south side of the Causeway Heights, he had since
lost sight of them, and Lord Lucan was unable to see them at
all. The regrouping of the Russian troops in the North Valley and
the advance of the Russian cavalry along the north side of the
Causeway, although visible to those on the Sapouné Ridge, could
be seen by no one on the battlefield itself . . . least of all by Lord
Lucan, against whom the Russian cavalry were advancing.

From Admiral Lyons, who remained with Lord Raglan
throughout the day, Phillip later heard the full story of the day's
tragic and—to those who took part in the battle for Balaclava—
inexplicable errors. At the time, in common with everyone else
under Sir Colin Campbell's command, he was mystified by what
followed the 93rd's successful repulse of the Russian cavalry.
Lord Raglan, whose orders were taking fully half an hour to
reach those for whom they were intended, had seen the
Tunisians abandon the redoubt on Canrobert's Hill, and he
despatched what became known as "the second order" to Lord
Lucan when he saw the remaining redoubts meet with a simi-

lar fate. In this he commanded Lucan *"to detach eight squadrons of Heavy Dragoons in the direction of Balaclava to support the Turks, who,"* the order concluded, *"are wavering."*

Lord Lucan, from where his Division was positioned, had not seen the cavalry attack on the 93rd and although he had watched the Turks flee in fear of their lives from the redoubts on the Causeway, he was not yet aware that those he was now commanded to support had long since retreated to the harbour. Anxious, however, to do all in his power to assist Sir Colin Campbell in the defense of Balaclava, he went in person to General Scarlett of the Heavy Cavalry Brigade. To the delight of the whole brigade, Lucan instructed him to detach eight of his squadrons and move them as rapidly as he could towards Kadi-Koi, in support of Sir Colin's Turks. General Scarlett obeyed the order with alacrity and himself led off the selected squadrons—two each from the 5th Dragoon Guards, the Scots Greys, the Inniskillings, and the 4th Dragoons. Accompanied by Colonel William Beatson, his two aides, Captain Alexander Sheridan and Lieutenant Alexander Elliott, his orderly, and the brigade trumpeter, he made for Kadi-Koi.

Being quite unable to see them, he had, of course, not the slightest idea that, separated from his small detachment by little more than the width of the Woronzoff Road and the Causeway which carried it, the main body of General Liprandi's cavalry—consisting of about three thousand men—was proceeding towards him from his left. Neither force could see the other; the Russians had the advantage both of overwhelming numbers and an elevated position, whereas Scarlett and his five hundred dragoons had the disadvantage of having to pass through their own divisional camp and a vineyard situated beside it, which considerably impeded his rear squadrons. Neither he nor the Russian cavalry commander had troubled to send out scouts or post look-outs and each proceeded on his way in ignorance of the other's presence.

From the crest of the hill they had so gallantly and suc-

cessfully defended, Sir Colin Campbell and his staff, with the
93rd and their supporting troops, as well as the Marine and
naval gunners on the Heights above and behind them, had a
grandstand view—second only to Lord Raglan's—of the epic cavalry engagement which took place shortly after their own. They
saw General Scarlett's two aides—the first of whom, by reason
of his distinctive Indian Army uniform and magnificent Arab
horse, Phillip recognized as Alex Sheridan—hold a brief con-
sultation with Colonel Beatson, and then all three cantered up
the southern slope of the Causeway Heights. There, evidently
catching their first shocked glimpse of the advancing Russians,
they paused momentarily before wheeling round to gallop back
at breakneck speed to bring the alarming news of the enemy's
close proximity to their commander.

Sir Colin ordered Captain Barker's troop forward but, powerless to offer him any further assistance, stood watching in
grim silence as General Scarlett formed up his outnumbered
force to receive, as best he might, what now seemed the inevitable attack. His fellow brigade commander's calm matched
his own if, indeed, in that supremely testing moment, it did not
excel his stoic deliberation.

While Colonel Beatson cantered up the slope again to keep
the enemy under observation and his two aides dashed hither
and thither with his orders, General Scarlett wheeled his leading squadrons to face the enemy. They consisted of a scant
three hundred men of the Scots Greys, the Inniskillings and the
5th Dragoons—the Green Horse—and in response to his orders,
the officers rode out in front of their men to form them into
line, their own backs turned heroically towards the menacing
mass of horsemen they were preparing to meet.

Phillip, watching through his Dollond, saw Lord Lucan come
hastening up, presumably with the order, which Scarlett had
already anticipated, to charge the enemy. Somewhere on the
far side of their camp, the Light Brigade had been posted in
reserve, beyond the watcher's line of vision, and the remaining

squadrons of the Heavy Brigade were also forming up. They, like the two squadrons of the 4th Dragoons, which had originally been detached, were greatly impeded by vine trees, tent-ropes, and picket lines and were compelled to take ground to the left, so as avoid these obstacles. The Greys, too, on the left of the line, found themselves among tents and tethered horses but the anxiously watching Highlanders raised a cheer when, at last, the gay scarlet jackets and tall bearskins began to assume some semblance of alignment. Even so, to all those who watched it, the precise, parade ground movements and the careful wheeling into line seemed unbearably prolonged.

The Russians, however, Phillip noticed, when he turned his glass on them, were also re-forming. They had been trotting downhill but now they halted, five hundred yards from the British and, to the sound of successive trumpet calls, closed up into a tightly-packed square, from which two powerful wings were flung out to widen their front and, he supposed, probably with the object of out-flanking Scarlett's line. Their numerical superiority was so immense, their strategic position apparently so unassailable that their hesitation was, it seemed to Phillip, arrogant and born more of confidence than caution. The grey-clad horsemen sat motionless in their saddles, observing what was going on below them, their demeanour almost contemptuously indifferent—as well it might be, despite all the wheeling and dressing of the British Heavy Brigade, since in previous encounters and even on more equal terms, no British cavalry unit had ever charged them. It was evident that they did not expect Scarlett's puny handful of dragoons to charge them now—least of all uphill—and they waited, delaying their own charge, as a cat might wait for a mouse to venture too close.

"He must move," Sir Colin Campbell muttered, his voice low and strained, and obviously referring to General Scarlett who, although he had now placed himself facing his first line, was still not satisfied with their dressing, for he restrained them with his raised saber. "He cannot receive a charge, such as the enemy will make, unless his line is in motion, even if—" The Highland brigade commander broke off, a sudden gleam in his eyes, as General Scarlett turned to face the enemy at last. With his aides, his orderly, and his trumpeter, he rode without haste to the precise center of his line and the thin, clear notes of the British trumpeter sounding the Charge, echoed and re-echoed from the enclosing hills.

The instant it had sounded, Scarlett set spurs to his horse and made straight for the dark square of Russian horsemen poised on the hill-top above him, his tiny escort of four men at his heels . . . and all five at a headlong gallop. British cavalry drill, Phillip was aware, called for series of successive orders, sounded first by the brigade trumpeter and then repeated by each of the regimental trumpeters, by means of which the line was directed first to walk-march, then to trot, to canter, to gallop, and finally to charge. With the enemy barely five hundred yards away and the brigade trumpeter sounding only the Charge, the leading squadrons, although no less eager than their commander to obey the order, had, perforce, to keep to their alignment and therefore begin their advance at a slower pace than his. Their pace quickened rapidly, as the Greys cleared the last of the tent-ropes and the whole line gained momentum, but by the time it broke into a gallop, Scarlett and his staff were fifty yards ahead of the Greys and Inniskillings, riding knee to knee, as they had ridden into the Charge under Lord Uxbridge at Waterloo. Reaching the great, packed, motionless square of Russian cavalry, they saw their brigade commander, his aides still close at his back, hurl himself against it and then vanish, swallowed up by the grey tide. The Russian cavalry commander, who attempted to bar their way, fell with Lieutenant Elliott's saber buried in his chest.

The first line of Greys and Inniskillings—the former conspicuous by reason of their splendidly matched grey horses—

struck the enemy center a minute or two later, meeting the front rank of Hussars with an impact that sent them staggering. Their battle cries—the wild Irish yell of the Inniskillings and the fierce, moaning wail of the Greys—could be heard quite distinctly by those grouped about Lord Raglan on the Sapouné Ridge, six hundred feet above them and, across the length of the valley, at Kadi-Koi. Muted by distance, the spine-chilling sound rang in the ears of the 93rd like a death-knell and, hearing it, the Highlanders tensed uneasily—several, Phillip noticed, standing with heads bowed momentarily in prayer. Although under arms, Sir Colin Campbell's men were mere spectators now, their duty to continue to guard the approaches to Balaclava and, in consequence, no more able to go to the aid of General Scarlett and his gallant dragoons than were Lord Raglan and his staff, perched high on the plateau at the far end of the South Valley. Aware of where their duty lay, the Highlanders could only wait in apprehensive silence for whatever should be the outcome of the British heavy cavalry's valiant attack.

Few of those who watched dared hope that it would be successful or even that the Heavies would survive. Such a charge, forced upon them by circumstances, was contrary to every tried and tested concept of cavalry tactics and must therefore, however heroically it was carried out, be doomed to failure. Scarlett was hopelessly outnumbered, his tiny force compelled to charge uphill, with an ever-increasing distance between his lines, and part of his brigade still entangled amongst vines and tent-ropes so that, to most of the horrified spectators, it seemed that he was leading his whole brigade to certain death. This conviction grew as the Greys and Inniskillings of the leading squadrons attempted to hack and thrust a way through the great mass of enemy horsemen which closed about them. So few were they and so numerous the Russians that only here and there could a scarlet jacket be seen, only occasionally a grey horse or a burnished helmet be glimpsed in the struggling mêlée of combatants.

To add to the nightmare quality, the scene was not obscured, as other engagements had been, by cannonsmoke. No guns fired; every detail of the struggle could be seen with hideous clarity and the only sounds were the thunder of galloping hooves, the rattle of accoutrements, and the thud and clash of furious, hand-to-hand battle. The Russians were, however, Phillip saw through his glass, packed too densely to permit of proper swordplay and, for this reason, the Cossacks were precluded from using their lances and pistols. As a result, the British suffered fewer casualties than they might otherwise have done, and the sheer audacity and resolution with which they had charged gained them an unexpected advantage. Sabers flashed in the bright, pitiless sunlight, horses fell with shrill screams of agony, and their riders were flung from their saddles and trampled underfoot but . . . incredibly, some of the scarlet jackets had already fought their way through. Some were turning back into the battle again when the second line of Inniskillings and 5th Dragoons struck the Russian center with even greater impact than that of the first. They drove a perceptible wedge in the packed ranks of grey-clad Cossacks but, as they did so, the two wings on either flank, consisting mainly of Hussars and Lancers, started to wheel inwards, with the evident intention of taking their attackers in the rear.

This plan might well have succeeded, had it not been for the remaining squadrons of the Heavy Brigade, whose delay was to prove providential. They had formed up in their separate regiments—the 4th Dragoons were on the right, Phillip saw, the Royals a little way behind them, in the center, and General Scarlett's old regiment, the 5th, with a squadron of the Inniskillings on the right. Each regiment charged on its own, without waiting for orders, two on the Russian right flank, one in the center, the final charge being made, with devastating effect, on the enemy's left flank by the 4th. The Russians, who had wheeled round in their extended wings to encircle and crush the Greys were, instead, taken in the rear and, as some of the Greys contrived to turn about in order to give them battle, they found themselves caught in their own trap, without room in which to maneuver. The 4th Dragoons cut right through and routed them.

Already wavering and forced to give ground, the rest of the huge square of Cossacks were steadily driven back, reeling and thrown into confusion by the fury and disciplined courage of each succeeding British charge. Unable to withstand the pressure from their front, some of the rear files broke ranks and fled. Others followed their example and, with startling suddenness, the seemingly impenetrable enemy formation began to disintegrate, losing both unity and menace, as column after column broke away and scattered, to seek refuge in ignominious flight.

On the crest of their hill at Kadi-Koi, the men of the 93rd watched in stunned disbelief as they saw the unmistakable figure of General Scarlett, in blue frock coat and battered dragoon helmet, with three of his staff beside him, emerge from the struggling welter of men and horses.

Their amazement turned swiftly to excitement when he was followed by a knot of Greys and Inniskillings, still miraculously keeping together in some semblance of their original line. Within a few minutes the whole great enemy force was in headlong retreat, re-ascending the ridge of the Causeway Heights in complete disorder, pursued by a few red-coated British dragoons. A troop of Horse Artillery spurred after them, to unlimber their guns when they reached the Woronzoff Road.

The cheer that went up from the Highlanders was one of pride, mingled with heartfelt relief. They were aware, Phillip thought—as possibly, in the first flush of their victory, the combatants were not—of how incredible that victory had been, with such odds against them. He heard Sir Colin Campbell, who was scanning the Causeway with his glass, put his own thoughts into words, in an aside to Colonel Sterling, and then was startled to hear him say, with a puzzled exclamation, "The Light

Brigade has not moved! But surely Lord Lucan must have ordered it in pursuit?"

"That would not appear to be the case, Sir Colin," the colonel returned, frowning. "And now"—as the thin notes of a cavalry trumpet call sounded faintly across the intervening distance— "General Scarlett is recalling his brave Heavies, I believe. Wisely in the circumstances, I don't doubt, but it means an end to the pursuit."

"Aye, so it would seem," Sir Colin sounded surprised and upset. "And the cup of victory dashed from their lips! I was expecting Lord Cardigan to attack the enemy on the flank—he had a unique opportunity after the 4th Dragoons made their charge. But one can only suppose that he had his orders and was reluctant to go against them, although for a man of his fire, I should have imagined that . . ." He broke off, biting back the words he had been about to say and expelling his breath in a deep sigh. "I will ride over," he added, a little later, after another prolonged inspection of the scene of the battle with the aid of his field glass. "I should like to offer my congratulations in person to the Scots Greys. Well, Mr Hazard"—as he observed Phillip—"you have been privileged to witness what, I feel certain, will one day be recorded in the military history books as one of the greatest feats ever performed by cavalry. I have never seen it equalled in all my years of army service and I can tell you, only British cavalry would have had the spirit and discipline to do what General Scarlett's gallant fellows did today. Perhaps you would care to ride across with me to tell them so?"

"Indeed, sir, I should," Phillip assented eagerly. "If you have no other orders for me."

Sir Colin smiled faintly. "We do not yet need the *Sanspareil*, Mr Hazard—thanks be to God! And let us hope that we shall not need the help of your naval stretcher parties either."

The butcher's bill, Phillip thought, unable to suppress a shudder of apprehension. When, however, with Sir Colin Campbell and other members of his staff, he reached the Heavy

Brigade's lines, he was amazed to learn that the casualties had been—in the circumstances—comparatively light. Less than eighty had been killed and wounded, according to the first count, of whom less than a dozen had, it seemed, lost their lives. General Scarlett himself, his Indian Army adviser, Colonel Beatson, and his aide-de-camp, Lieutenant Elliott, had suffered saber cuts and Lieutenant-Colonel Henry Griffiths, the Greys' commanding officer, had been shot in the head, but only Elliott was severely wounded. Captain Sheridan, Scarlett's other aide, his giant orderly, Shegog, and the brigade trumpeter, who had followed him throughout the charge with selfless heroism, had emerged from it virtually unscathed and, from Alex Sheridan, Phillip heard a first-hand account of the Heavy Brigade's magnificent feat, couched in a few modest words.

No one, in his hearing at all events, said very much about the Light Brigade's failure to support the charge, but it was evident, from the glum faces of both officers and men when the Light Cavalry were permitted a brief stand-down, that feelings on the subject ran high among them. The majority, Alex Sheridan told him, in reply to his diffident question, blamed Lord Cardigan for too rigid an interpretation of his divisional commander's orders.

"I saw them pleading with him," the tall aide-de-camp confided, tight-lipped. "Captain Morris, who is commanding the 17th Lancers, apparently begged to be permitted to lead his regiment alone in pursuit of the flying enemy, but his lordship would not have it. The poor Light Cavalry!" He sighed, displaying a keenly felt regret he made no attempt to hide. "The whole of this campaign has been nothing but frustration for them, I fear, through no fault of their own, Mr Hazard. They are the cream of the British army but . . ." He shook his head despondently and then forced a smile. "Perhaps their hour may yet come and they will be given a chance to wipe out the memory of this last humiliation, at least."

"Let us hope that it may," Phillip agreed, little knowing how soon that hour was to come for the Light Brigade or with what tragic finality the humiliation was to be erased from the memory of all who were to witness it. Alex Sheridan repeated his sigh.

"You may wonder," he said quietly, "why I should feel so strongly concerning the Light Cavalry, Mr Hazard. I once held a commission in the 11th Hussars and Lord Cardigan was my commander officer, so . . . I have reason, perhaps. I still feel that I am one of them."

"That is understandable," Phillip assured him sympathetically, thinking of his own feelings for the *Trojan*.

"There are some bonds which are not easily broken, Captain Sheridan. No doubt your loyalty to Lord Cardigan—"

"I hold no brief for his lordship," Alex Sheridan interrupted, his tone harsh. "But cowardice is not one of his faults, you may take my word for that. Well"—he excused himself, reddening perceptibly beneath the tan of his cheeks —"I will go and have a word with my old comrades, if you'll forgive me, Mr Hazard. In any case, I believe that Sir Colin is about to pay a visit to the Greys, is he not? And I see that Colonel Griffiths is now out of the surgeon's hands."

Phillip rode over to the Greys' lines with Sir Colin. They were re-forming, so that the roll might be called and their commanding officer, whose head was heavily bandaged, called them to attention. He made to salute but Sir Colin forestalled him. "No, Colonel," he said, and doffed the Highland bonnet he had worn since the Battle of the Alma. "If you will permit me . . ." Sitting his horse bareheaded, he addressed the men with visible emotion. "Greys, gallant Greys . . ." his voice carried from rank to rank, despite the tremor in it. "I am sixty-one years of age but, if I were young again, I should have been proud this day to serve in your ranks!"

The Greys, as deeply moved as he, cheered him to the echo, and their colonel wrung his hand. Sir Colin took his leave of them and, after a second brief conference with Lord Lucan, returned to the 93rd's position at Kadi-Koi.

CHAPTER SEVEN

1

T**he end of the** Battle of Balaclava was approaching and with it the disastrous charge of the Light Cavalry Brigade, which—although it was to result in failure and a hideous loss of life—was nevertheless to eclipse, in the hearts and memories of the British people, the brilliantly successful charge made earlier by the Heavy Brigade.

Phillip, who had been privileged to see so much during that long, eventful day on shore, did not witness the last act in the drama. From Kadi-Koi little could be seen, save the galloping of aides-de-camps from the Sapouné Ridge to the Plain. Having, with the spirited aid of the naval and Marine batteries and Captain Barker's troop of Horse Artillery, beaten back an attempt by the enemy to turn the right flank of the Balaclava defenses by an advance from Kamara, the 93rd were permitted to stand easy. They waited, grumbling a little, but nothing else of moment occurred within sight of their position.

From his lofty vantage point on the Sapouné Ridge, Lord Raglan, however, saw much more. He watched through his glass as the routed Russian cavalry re-grouped in columns across the eastern end of the North Valley, a line of field guns in front of them and their infantry massed at the mouth of the gorge behind them. They occupied what appeared to be an impregnable position; field guns and infantry held the ridge of the Fedioukine Hills and cavalry the lower slopes to their right, whilst the captured Turkish redoubts on the Causeway Heights —now occupied by the eleven battalions of infantry which had initially stormed them—covered their left front.

The main body of the enemy offered no immediate threat to Balaclava from their present position and, indeed, seemed to the British Commander-in-Chief and his staff, to be expecting an attack, rather than planning to launch one. His most urgent task was, therefore, Lord Raglan decided, to recover the Causeway redoubts which, since these commanded the Woronzoff Road, must constitute a serious threat to his lines of communication with Balaclava Harbour for as long as they remained in Russian hands. Although strongly held, it occurred to him that—being without support—the enemy might well abandon the redoubts if resolutely attacked, and he now had two infantry divisions approaching a position from which such an attack could be delivered, in addition to the Cavalry Division and the promised aid from General Canrobert.

The French First Division and eight squadrons of the Chasseurs d'Afrique had already reached the Plain, although the British First and Fourth Infantry Divisions—ordered down two hours before—were taking considerably longer to complete their descent than Lord Raglan had anticipated. Seeking to hasten them, he despatched an order to Sir George Cathcart, who was in command of the Fourth Division, instructing him to *"advance immediately and recapture the Turkish redoubts."* The Duke of Cambridge was ordered to support Cathcart's attack with the Guards Brigade and the two regiments of Sir Colin Campbell's Highland Brigade—the 42nd and the 79th—still with his division.

These orders were duly delivered but Sir George Cathcart—whose men had been all night on trench duty—appeared in no hurry to carry them out. Exasperated by the delay and more anxious than ever to recover the lost redoubts, the British Commander-in-Chief sent a written order to Lord Lucan, which read: *"Cavalry to advance and take advantage of any opportunity to recover the Heights. They will be supported by the infantry, which have been ordered to advance on two fronts."*

Once again Lord Raglan failed to take into account the fact that the troop movements, so clear to him from the Sapouné Ridge, could not be seen by his subordinate commanders on the battlefield itself. Since the Heavy Brigade's magnificent charge had effectively cleared the South Valley of all enemy cavalry, Lucan had lost sight of them, as well as of the main body of their infantry, and he was unable to see either of the two British infantry divisions plodding—in the case of the Fourth—wearily down from the plateau. He interpreted Lord Raglan's order, reasonably enough in the circumstances, to mean that he was to advance and attempt to recapture the Causeway Heights as soon as he received the infantry support which—the order suggested—was on its way to assist him in this endeavour.

Accordingly he mounted his division, ordered the Light Brigade to cross the Woronzoff Road and take up a position at the western end of the Causeway Heights, drawing up the Heavy Brigade behind them and to their right. From here they were facing down the trough of the North Valley and the enemy could at last be seen, both cavalry and infantry massed behind the line of guns at the opposite end of the valley. After subjecting their position to a prolonged and careful scrutiny, Lord Lucan also decided that this was impregnable, and, as he believed that Lord Raglan had commanded him to, he waited, with ever increasing impatience, for some sign of the expected infantry support, so that he might advance against the redoubts. After a quarter of an hour had passed without any evidence whatsoever of an infantry attack, he gave permission for the officers and men of both his brigades to dismount and stand easy. They waited, eating what scanty provisions they had with them, for another thirty minutes, without moving from their position. The appearance of the Cavalry Division, despite its inactivity, caused the Russians to abandon the two westernmost of the Turkish redoubts, both of which were, in any case, destitute of guns.

When, at long last, the Fourth Division reached the Plain, Sir George Cathcart made a show of carrying out his Commander-in-Chief's instructions. He marched past the scene of the Heavy Brigade's charge, taking his time and with skirmishers preceding his main body, and eventually occupied the two deserted redoubts, with infantry and nine-pounder guns, opening a desultory fire, at extreme range, on those held by the enemy. He then, as Lucan had done, ordered his division to halt and await the progress of events, making no attempt to advance. The threat of his presence, with that of the Cavalry Division was, however, sufficient to alarm the Russians and, from the Sapouné Ridge, teams of artillery horses with hauling tackle trailing behind them, could be seen cantering up to the redoubts. Their purpose was clear to all who saw them. They were about to remove the captured British naval guns, no doubt with the ultimate intention of despatching them, as proof of victory, to the Tsar, after they had been paraded triumphantly through Sebastopol. . . .

For Lord Raglan, educated in the stern military traditions of the Great Duke, to permit the enemy to take away British guns unchallenged was more than he could stomach. He gazed down, glass to his eye, his face losing, for once, its accustomed expression of unruffled composure, as those about him were quick to notice. He was aware that, at all costs, he must regain possession of the captured guns before the Russians had had time to drag them away from the redoubts but . . . Sir George Cathcart's division was immobile, that of the Duke of Cambridge still too far away to be called into action, and he dared not move the 93rd from Kadi-Koi, lest the enemy attempt another advance from Kamara.

There remained the cavalry, of course—the cavalry, which had already won a superb victory against overwhelming odds only an hour or so before. There remained, in particular, the Light Cavalry Brigade, smarting under the humiliation they had suffered because they had been allowed no part in the Heavy

Brigade's triumph, every man eager—or so Lord Raglan had been informed by A.D.C.'s who had visited their position—to wipe out the memory of what, for them, had been a fiasco. The fact that the Russians were removing the captured naval guns suggested that they were preparing to retreat from the Causeway Heights, so as to rejoin their main body before darkness fell. That they might do so at once if charged by the cavalry, seemed to the British Commander-in-Chief a distinct possibility, if not almost a certainty . . . and if the cavalry went into action, Sir George Cathcart would have to give them his support. The Guards might even be able to storm Canrobert's Hill, which was inaccessible to cavalry . . . Lord Raglan lowered his telescope, his mind made up. In his normal, courteous voice he requested General Airey to write another order to Lord Lucan and the Quartermaster-General came to his side, an open message-pad resting on his sabretache.

"Lord Raglan wishes the cavalry to advance rapidly to the front, follow the enemy, and try to prevent the enemy from carrying away the guns," the Commander-in-Chief dictated, choosing his words with care. Anxious though he was that his order should be understood and acted upon at once, he was still unaware that Lord Lucan's view of the Turkish redoubts was cut off by the undulating ridge of the Causeway Heights and he considered it unnecessary, in the light of his previous order, to specify which guns he meant or on which front he wished the cavalry to advance. He did, however, realize that the Russians had some thirty field pieces of their own, in addition to the captured naval guns, with which to defend the Heights and added, *"Troop of Horse Artillery may accompany."* Then, when Airey read this back to him, he remembered the three hundred Chasseurs d'Afrique sent to his assistance by General Canrobert and ended, *"French cavalry is on your left. Mark the order 'immediate.'"*

The Cavalry Division's inexplicable delay in carrying out his first order still irked him and, after General Airey had written as he dictated and appended his signature to the flimsy sheet of paper on which his instructions were pencilled, he hesitated. Finally he called after the aide-de-camp who had claimed the privilege of delivering the order, Captain Edward Nolan of the 15th Hussars, who was on Airey's staff, "Tell Lord Lucan that the cavalry are to attack immediately!"

Nolan saluted and swung himself on to his horse. Disdaining the safer but longer and more circuitous track his fellow A.D.C.'s had used to descend to the Plain, he displayed his consummate horsemanship by making his own descent straight down the precipitous escarpment, risking life and limb to do so but driven by a sense of urgency that brooked no delay. Despite his youth and the junior rank he held, Edward Lewis Nolan had written a book on cavalry tactics and was an acknowledged authority on the subject—and his faith in the invincibility of British cavalry had been rekindled by the success of the Heavy Brigade that morning. It had always been his contention that cavalry—and above all, light cavalry—when properly led, could achieve anything. He considered that the British cavalry had been deplorably led up to now but the order he bore was, it seemed to him, the chance for which the Light Brigade had been waiting and longing ever since they had landed in the Crimea. This order was their chance of glory, their opportunity to prove, beyond all shadow of doubt, that they were the best in the world. Even Lord Lucan, to whom he himself had given the derisive nickname of "Lord Look-on," could not deprive his magnificent light cavalry of their chance now, Nolan thought grimly, as he spurred his frightened horse to the foot of the escarpment and reached in his pouch for the order.

That order and the arrogant manner in which the young aide-de-camp delivered it to Lord Lucan, together with their Commander-in-Chief's verbal instructions, was to send 673 men into the "valley of death," from which only 195 were to return. Yet neither Lord Raglan nor his Quartermaster-General could have foreseen the tragic consequences since it had not, for a moment, occurred to either that the written order was obscure or capable of being misunderstood. Still less had they imagined that Edward Nolan might be responsible for the misunderstanding or Lord Lucan in any doubt as to which guns he was prepared to capture.

To Nolan, however, the guns which mattered were not the British naval twelve-pounders, now being dragged from the Causeway redoubts in some haste—they were the enemy guns at the far end of the North Valley a mile away, behind whose protection the Russian cavalry had sought shelter after their rout by the British Heavy Brigade. When Lucan, bewildered by the written order and by the verbal command to attack that accompanied it, asked resentfully, "Attack, sir . . . attack what? *What* guns, sir?" Nolan savoured this moment of heady triumph to the full.

He flung out his arm in a dramatic gesture that embraced the North Valley and answered, with a provocative scorn he made not the smallest effort to conceal, "There, my lord, is your enemy! *There* are your guns!"

The order was madness but . . . it had come from Lord Raglan, had been delivered by one of the Quartermaster-General's own A.D.C.'s, and therefore must be obeyed. And obeyed at once, it seemed, without waiting for infantry support . . . with bleak resignation, Lord Lucan in his turn dictated a written order and sent it, by one of his staff, to Lord Cardigan, directing him to lead the charge with the Light Brigade.

For cavalry to attack field guns in battery without infantry support was, as he well knew, contrary to every rule of warfare. To do so between flanking hills, which were the site of other gun batteries and which gave concealment to battalions of riflemen was, as he was also unhappily aware, to invite disaster; yet, when the Light Brigade commander rode over in person to point this out to him with a dismayed bewilderment that matched his own, Lucan could only answer bitterly, "I know it—but Lord Raglan will have it. We have no choice but to obey."

Icily Cardigan made acknowledgment, lowering the point of

his sword in formal salute and disdaining further protest. He and Lucan were brothers-in-law but they had scarcely spoken a civil word to each other for thirty years. They could not break their silence now, could not forget the habit of years, even for long enough to enable them to discuss an order which both recognized as likely to result in the annihilation of the Light Brigade—and, perhaps, of the entire British Cavalry Division—if it were carried out with the immediacy Lord Raglan had apparently demanded. The mutual dislike and rivalry which had always marred their relationship raised an insuperable barrier between them at this moment and each stood implacably on his dignity, the memory of past quarrels too bitter to be assuaged.

"Advance very steadily," Lord Lucan instructed. "And keep your men well in hand."

There was the same coldly formal acknowledgement. Murmuring cynically to himself, "Well, here goes the last of the Brudenells!" the Earl of Cardigan wheeled his great chestnut charger and went back to mount his men, his orders given with admirable calm and obeyed as calmly.

The five splendid regiments of the Light Cavalry Brigade rode, with unparalleled gallantry, to their doom, in three lines, their commander at their head and, with poetic justice, the first to meet his death in the terrible, mile-long charge was Edward Nolan, riding with the 17th Lancers. . . .

2

Phillip was watching the headlong descent of General Airey's aide-de-camp through his Dollond when a galloper—who had taken the more usual route from the Sapouné Ridge—pulled his sweating horse to a standstill and gave a written despatch to one of Sir Colin Campbell's aides. Sir Colin read it, frowning, and then motioned Phillip to his side.

"The time has come for you to request the Captain of the *Sanspareil* to bring her into the harbour, Mr Hazard," he said. "I should be obliged if you would do so. This"—he indicated the message he had just read—"is from your Admiral. He tells me, in confidence, that there is . . . how shall I put it? A risk that more heed may, perhaps, be paid to panic counsels than the situation here warrants. Should these have reached the commander of the harbour—Captain Tatham, is it not?—the Admiral considers it advisable that they should be firmly contradicted, from whatever source or in whatever form they may have reached him. This will be your task . . . do you understand?"

"I think so, sir. That is . . ." Phillip hesitated, puzzled by the manner in which his instructions had been given. Sir Colin did not, as a rule, mince words; he issued his instructions clearly and precisely, without prevarication. But of course, if orders had been sent to Captain Tatham from Lord Raglan's headquarters, neither Admiral Lyons nor Sir Colin Campbell could countermand them, however little they might approve of the measures which had been ordered. Panic counsels suggested that an order to abandon Balaclava Harbour might have been issued and, aware that the Admiral was as determined to hold the harbour as the commander of Balaclava's defenses, Phillip smiled suddenly. He understood now what was required of him and why, with his usual foresight, Admiral Lyons had sent him ashore to act as naval liaison officer. "You mean, sir, that I am to contradict any such—such rumours firmly?"

"But with discretion, Mr Hazard," Sir Colin qualified. "You can testify to the fact that the position here is still secure and, I believe, likely for the present to remain so."

"Yes, indeed sir," Phillip answered readily.

Sir Colin echoed his smile, a gleam in his tired eyes. "And the harbour will not be abandoned, if I can prevent it—your Admiral and I are of one mind in this matter. The remaining regiments of my Highland Brigade will soon reach the Plain. I imagine that the aide-de-camp we have just seen, descending in such haste from Lord Raglan's command post, bears orders for an attack aimed at the recovery of our lost redoubts. Should this be successful and if I am permitted to keep all three Highland regiments here, then I am confident that panic measures, so far as the harbour is concerned, would be a grave error at this time."

"I understand, sir. Am I at liberty to repeat what you have told me to Captain Tatham?"

"As a chance remark you overheard—certainly, Mr Hazard, if you find it necessary. But"—the Highland Brigade commander's smile widened—"not, perhaps, as my official opinion. Although you have, of course, your Admiral's authority, as well as mine, to order the *Sanspareil* into harbour as soon as a passage can be cleared for her—before nightfall, if possible. Leave your galloper here, in case I require to make contact with you before your return."

"Aye, aye, sir," Phillip acknowledged. He did not spare the Admiral's bay and, although occasionally impeded by ammunition parties, made remarkably good time on his journey back to the harbour. Here he found, as Sir Colin's instructions had led him to expect, that frantic efforts were being made to clear the harbour of shipping. When he ran Captain Tatham to earth on the Ordnance Wharf, his news was greeted with relief. An aide-de-camp had brought an order signed by General Airey, the Captain of the *Simoom* told him, soon after the fleeing Turkish auxiliaries had reached Balaclava, clamoring to be taken aboard ship and conveyed to the safety of Constantinople.

"*They* told us the battle was lost and that the Russians would be upon us within half an hour," Tatham said. "I'm afraid, however, that we dealt with them somewhat unsympathetically. I lined up a party of bluejackets and threatened to shoot them like dogs if they did not return to their posts. The mid. in charge was a proper young fire-eater and he put the fear of God into the lot of them!" He chuckled reminiscently and then sighed. "But when General Airey's aide made his appearance, with orders to load what stores and ammunition I could and get the transports to sea, I began to fear that the Turks might have been right, after all. Tell me—what is happening, Hazard? We've been starved of reliable news down here. All we've heard are wild rumours and almost incessant gunfire."

Phillip gave him a brief account of the progress of the battle and then returned to the subject of the *Sanspareil.*

"Well, it's an ill wind that blows nobody any good," Captain Tatham returned wryly. "I'll send a boat out to her at once. Within the next hour or so—thanks to General Airey—we shall have the harbour clear enough for her to steam straight into her anchorage. And no one will welcome her more warmly than I shall, I can tell you! Captain Dacres will, of course, become senior officer and assume *my* responsibilities and he cannot do so too soon to please me." He paused, eyeing Phillip searchingly, and then asked, "Do you wish to go out in the boat, Mr Hazard?"

"I think not, sir. My orders are to attend Sir Colin Campbell. When I left the 93rd's position, there appeared to be a possibility that the Duke of Cambridge's division was about to make a counterattack on the Causeway Heights. I am anxious to see whether it has succeeded."

"You are lucky devils, you amateur soldiers!" Captain Tatham asserted, with mock envy. "Judging by the volume of gunfire, the attack is probably already taking place . . . though it sounds more distant than it did earlier and our Marine guns are silent."

He was right, Phillip thought, as they both listened for a moment or two to the far-off thunder of guns. But he offered no comment and, after asking a few more questions concerning the battle, Captain Tatham held out his hand.

"Well, I won't detain you from your grandstand seat any longer. I can understand your eagerness to return to it and, were I in your place, I should feel as you do, I expect. In any case, I'm grateful to you for saving me a great deal of unnecessary work. I can now concentrate on supplying the seemingly insatiable demands of the ammunition parties, instead of loading all the shot and shell they need into ships and sending them out to sea—which, I must confess, Hazard, has gone sorely against the grain. But in the light of my orders . . ." He shrugged and passed a hand wearily across his sweat-damp brow. "I was keeping our steam frigates here, with guns manned, as I expect you noticed, so as to make a fight of it, if we had to."

"Yes, sir." Phillip permitted himself a faint smile. "I had noticed that."

The *Simoom*'s commander repeated his sigh. "And *they* have adequate reserves of ammunition, perhaps needless to add. Admiral Lyons, when I spoke to him earlier this morning, seemed quite determined that we should *not* abandon Balaclava but, I imagine, if Lord Raglan—" He hesitated, looking enquiringly at Phillip and plainly seeking reassurance. "What of Sir Colin Campbell, Hazard?"

"Sir Colin, judging by a conversation I overheard before I left Kadi-Koi, is of precisely the same mind as the Admiral, sir," Phillip told him. "And he endorsed the order to bring in the *Sanspareil*. In fact, sir, he said—" He was interrupted by the sound of galloping hooves and a voice calling his name. "Sir! Lieutenant Hazard, sir!" He turned, startled, as the young 8th Hussars trooper whom, on Sir Colin Campbell's instructions, he had left at Kadi-Koi, jerked his horse to a standstill beside him, almost bringing the lathered animal to its knees as he flung himself from the saddle. The man was white-faced, so distressed and agitated that the first words he blurted out were well nigh incomprehensible.

"Steady, lad!" Phillip put out a hand to grip his arm. "What are you trying to tell me?"

"The naval stretcher parties, sir . . . I was sent to tell you, they—they're needed urgently, sir, at the Cavalry Division camp." He drew a choked breath. "The Light Brigade—my regiment, sir, they—they've been wiped out."

"Wiped out?" Phillip echoed, shocked and bewildered. "What do you mean?"

"It looks," Captain Tatham put in grimly, "as if the attack on the Causeway Heights has failed, Mr Hazard. The cavalry—"

"No, sir," the young trooper interrupted, tears streaming unashamedly down his cheeks. "The cavalry did not attack the Causeway, they . . . they charged the guns, sir, the Russian guns at the end of the North Valley. The Light Brigade, sir, they charged the guns and—"

"But in heaven's name!" Captain Tatham exclaimed. "There must be some mistake—"

"No, sir." The 8th Hussars trooper shook his head wretchedly. "There's no mistake, sir. That's what they did. A galloper brought word from Lord Raglan himself and . . . I've seen them, sir, those that got back. Just a handful and all of them wounded. They say the French Chasseurs went in to aid them and that the Heavies tried to cover their retreat, other-wise none of them would have got out alive. My regiment, sir . . ." His teeth closed over his trembling lower lip, as he made a brave effort to control himself. "All that's left of them is the half squadron in attendance on Lord Raglan, my troop and B troop, sir. The rest . . ." He could not go on.

Phillip and Captain Tatham exchanged horrified glances. The North Valley, Phillip thought, why had the Light Brigade charged the Russian guns in the North Valley? Surely not on Lord Raglan's orders, alone and unsupported? He wondered whether Lord Cardigan had led them, whether he, too, was dead but, when he asked his galloper, the man did not know. He had, it appeared, seen only a few of the survivors, desperately wounded men on lamed and mutilated horses, who had some-how managed to escape the dreadful carnage and drag themselves back to the South Valley. Some were being cared for by their own surgeons in the Cavalry Division's field hospital but this, already crowded with wounded from the Heavy Brigade, was hard pressed and badly in need of help.

"I will send the stretcher parties up," Captain Tatham said. "They are standing by and I'll try to get some wagons. Go ahead of them to Kadi-Koi, Mr Hazard, so that you can direct them to where they are most needed."

"Aye, aye, sir," Phillip acknowledged. He mounted his horse and, the trooper in stunned silence at his heels, returned to Kadi-Koi.

When the naval stretcher parties reported to him, he worked with them, as he had done at the Alma, sickened and heartbroken by what he saw. The scenes he witnessed in the field hospitals and dressing stations would, he knew, never be erased from his memory for as long as he lived. Hour after weary hour the surgeons toiled, amputating shattered limbs, patching up broken bodies, performing their ghastly work to the sound of agonized screams, for there was little they could do to alleviate the suffering of the wounded men, to many of whom death came as a relief. Chaplains knelt beside the dying, offering their prayers, giving what comfort faith could provide, now holding a flask of water to parched lips, now giving absolution to men who pleaded for it mutely from pain-dimmed eyes, unable to speak.

On one journey, with a loaded wagon, to the hospital above the harbour, Phillip saw Lord Cardigan ride past, bare-headed, several members of his staff with him and one, apparently, badly wounded, for two of his brother officers had to support him to keep him from falling from his horse. The Light Brigade commander did not speak, did not glance into the wagon or the stretchers borne by the naval party; he rode past, his glittering uniform covered with dust, his face devoid of expression, as if he were lost in thought and oblivious to his surroundings. A wounded sergeant of the 11th Hussars called out to him from his stretcher but he seemingly did not hear and, as the mounted party vanished from sight, the sergeant murmured wryly, "Well, his lordship made history today, like a real hero. That was all I wanted to tell him. He led us all the way and was the first to reach the guns—a real hero."

Thinking to console him, Phillip, who was leading his horse, paused beside the stretcher. "His lordship did not hear you, Sergeant, but he'd be glad, I feel sure, to know your opinion of his conduct."

"It's the truth," the wounded man said. "I never saw him flinch, not once, and the shells were bursting all round him. The only time he raised his voice was when Captain Nolan tried to ride past him—then his lordship hollered out, ordering him back into line. I think, myself, sir, that the Captain was trying to stop us—he brought the order from Lord Raglan, you see, and I reckon it was a mistake. We were never meant to charge those guns, it was madness, sending us in alone like that without the infantry. But a shell struck Captain Nolan in the chest. Funny thing . . ." The sergeant glanced up at Phillip, an odd little smile playing about his lips. "Even after that, he didn't fall from his horse. Rode back right through us, he did, with his right arm held high above his head and a terrible sort of shrieking sound coming from him. I saw him and I heard the scream he gave. It was like nothing human, that scream." He drew a laboured, sighing breath and closed his eyes, as if suddenly at the limit of his endurance. Before the stretcher reached its destination, he was dead. . . .

3

By nightfall, the naval party had done all that was required of them and Phillip dismissed them. He made his way back to Kadi-Koi in the swiftly gathering darkness, feeling unutterably weary and his injured leg starting to ache again. Food and a chance of a few hours' rest were what he craved but the *Sans-pareil* had been entering harbour when he had made his last journey down to Balaclava and he was anxious to inform Sir Colin Campbell of the battleship's reassuring presence there before asking permission to go off duty. Lights gleamed from the farmhouse in which the commander of the Highland Brigade had established his headquarters but, on reaching it, one of the staff officers on duty told him that Sir Colin was with the 79th.

"The Brigade is complete once more, Mr Hazard," he added, with satisfaction. "The Guards are to return to the plateau but both the 42nd and the 79th are to remain here with us, heaven be praised! Sir Colin has gone to inspect our reorganized defenses, with Colonel Sterling, if you want to see him—but I can send a message to him, if you wish. You look as if you've worked yourself to a standstill."

Conscious that he had, Phillip accepted his offer gratefully. He was on his way to his tent when a tall, kilted figure stepped out of the shadows to block his path.

"Sir!" The Highlander saluted and Phillip recognized him, by his voice rather than by his appearance in the dimness, as Sergeant MacCorkill of the 93rd, with whose wife Catriona Lamont had found shelter. He reined in.

"Sergeant MacCorkill, is it not? What can I do for you, Sergeant?"

The Sergeant laid a big hand on his horse's bridle. He said respectfully, "With your permission, sir, I will be taking you to our camp. There is someone who is wanting to see you urgently, in order to ask you to do her a favour. You'll be wearied, I don't doubt, but 'twould not be taking you very long and, if you have not eaten, my wife would gladly be heating a bowl of gruel for you. Her gruel is fine, nourishing stuff, sir."

Phillip had to make an effort to force his exhausted brain to take in what the man was saying. Someone wanted to ask a favour of him . . . was not that what he had said, before extolling the merits of his wife's gruel? Certainly there was someone in the Highlanders' camp to whom he owed a favour, a lady who . . . he smothered a yawn. In the circumstances, he could hardly refuse the tall Sergeant's request, so he inclined his head.

"Very well, Sergeant. But tell me, you are taking me to Miss Lamont, are you not—Miss Catriona Lamont? She is, I presume, the 'someone' to whom you refer so guardedly?"

"Aye, sir." The Sergeant started to lead his horse in the direction of the 93rd's encampment. "That is—" He hesitated, glancing back as if uncertain, even now, of how far Phillip could be trusted. "I am taking you to the young lady you know as Mistress Lamont, sir."

Phillip stared at him, searching his face in the dim light but learning little from it. "Is Lamont not her name, then?"

"It was her mother's name," Sergeant MacCorkill admitted. "We—my wife and I, sir—we were agreeing that it would be best if the young lady were to use her mother's name whilst she was with us. There are reasons, you will understand and—"

"No," Phillip objected, with some irritation. "I do *not* understand. Nor can I be expected to understand, unless you tell me the reasons for all this mystery."

"Mystery, sir? There is no mystery. It is just that—"

"Is there not? Then why, pray, when I called at your camp yesterday and inquired for Mistress Lamont, did your wife and the other women deny her very existence? They even attempted to convince me that I had imagined my meeting with her! Why, Sergeant?"

"That will be for Mistress Catriona to tell you herself, sir," the Sergeant returned woodenly.

"I can only assume that you are endeavouring to conceal her presence in your camp from the military authorities," Phillip accused, determined to force the man to give him an explanation. "Is there some good reason for that?"

"Aye, sir, there is."

"Then what is it? Well"—when the Highlander remained obstinately silent—"if you are afraid that I might betray her, why are you taking me to her now?"

"I have no fear that you will betray her, sir. Certainly not when you have heard how she comes to be here."

Phillip lost patience with him. He reined in. "I shall accompany you no further unless you tell me for what reason she has sought refuge in your camp, Sergeant. I am entitled to know that, at least."

"It would be coming better from Mistress Catriona herself," Sergeant MacCorkill demurred. "I have not the words and am not knowing the whole story. But if you insist, sir—"

"I must insist, Sergeant," Phillip said firmly. "I respect your loyalty and I am, as you know, indebted to both Mistress Catriona and your wife for the timely assistance they rendered me after my fall. However if I am to be asked a favour—which, because of my indebtedness, I should find it difficult to refuse— then I must know by whom and why this favour is required, before committing myself. Is that too much to ask?"

"No, sir, it is not," the Highlander conceded. He had halted, relinquishing his grasp of the bay's rein so that he might turn to face its rider. "I will tell you what I can, sir. But you will please to respect my confidence. You understand, I—"

"Of course," Phillip assured him. "You have my word that I shall repeat nothing you tell me, Sergeant MacCorkill."

"Thank you, Mr Hazard." The Sergeant resumed his slow, long-striding walk, his hand once more on the rein, urging Phillip's tired horse to follow him. "You were asking why Mistress Catriona sought refuge in our camp well, the answer is simple enough. We are all Sutherland men in the 93rd, sir, known to each other by clan and name all our lives, and our women too. Our ties are family ties and very close. Before I was taking the Queen's shilling, sir, I was employed as a ghillie in the service of Mistress Catriona's grandfather—old Sir Alastair Moray of Guise—and my wife, Morag, was nursemaid to the family. So from whom else would Mistress Catriona seek help, when she was in need of it? 'Twas Morag who was caring for her—and her twin brother also, sir—after their mother died in giving them birth. They were like her own bairns to Morag, the two of them, for all she was herself just a young lassie when they were first given into her charge, and she was loving them as if they had been her own. And small wonder—they were a bonnie pair, as I can well remember." The gruff voice softened momentarily. "Their father was going abroad, you see, after he was losing his wife. The family is old but few Highland families are wealthy, so that the Morays of Guise are usually needing to seek their fortunes overseas, if they are not serving in the army—or in the navy, sir, like yourself. Captain Ninian Moray—Mistress Catriona's father—was a military engineer."

"In the British Army?" Phillip questioned. He was faintly puzzled, for the name Moray was one to which he could attach no particular significance and he wondered why Catriona had been at such pains to conceal it.

"No, sir." The Sergeant shook his head. "As a young man, the Captain was serving in India with the Company's Army of Bengal, but his health broke down due to the climate, and he could not return there. After his wife's death, he came out to Russia, to take service under the Tsar and . . ." He hesitated. "He was associated with a Colonel Upton and his son, sir, in the building of the naval dockyard here in Sebastopol, Mistress Catriona was telling me. You will be knowing about Mr Upton, I don't doubt, sir?"

Phillip was about to deny it when he recalled having heard that the cavalry had captured Mr Upton with his wife and four small daughters, in a farmhouse outside Balaclava, at the end of the flank march . . . he frowned. Upton had claimed to be a British civilian but his wife had been Russian and, on General Airey's orders, he had been placed under arrest on suspicion of being, in fact, an enemy spy. His wife, at her own request, had been sent back to Sebastopol with the children, as far as he could remember—or else to Constantinople—and, again on Airey's orders, the farmhouse had been searched for evidence of Upton's duplicity, and a plan of Sebastopol found hidden there. If Catriona's father had been associated with him, then that suggested . . . Phillip drew in his breath sharply.

"Yes," he said, "I have heard of Mr Upton, Sergeant. He is being held under house arrest in Balaclava, is he not, in the belief that he came here to spy on us?"

"That is so, sir," Sergeant MacCorkill agreed and lapsed into a moody silence. Phillip waited for him to continue his narrative, his interest in Catriona's story now thoroughly aroused but, when the Highlander failed to do so, he asked curiously, "How did Mistress Catriona make her way here in the first place, Sergeant? I presume she came in search of her father but—did your wife and the other women smuggle her aboard one of the troop transports? Is that why they are hiding her in your camp?"

"No, sir." The Sergeant roused himself. "Mistress Catriona was reaching Balaclava a day or so after we took it. As to how she made her way here, why"—there was a note of pride in the deep, lilting Highland voice—"she came on foot, sir, dressed in peasant clothing to enable her to pass unmolested through the Russian lines. She is a very courageous and spirited young lady, and she was not wishing to remain in Sebastopol, when her own kith and kin were laying siege to the place. She was waiting her opportunity and then she was making her escape—alone, sir. She was not travelling with Mr Upton and his family but, hearing of his fate and fearing that she might share it, she sought refuge with us. 'Twas quite by chance that she found Morag— my wife, sir—for she had no idea that either of us would be here, but she knew, of course, that the women of the regiment would help her. We deemed it prudent to conceal her presence in our camp lest, by some misunderstanding, she were to be sent back to Sebastopol, as they were sending Mistress Upton."

"You mean," Phillip said, astonished, "that she was in Sebastopol when our troops landed? But for how long had she been there, MacCorkill?"

"Well, sir . . ." Sergeant MacCorkill gave vent to a sigh.

"She had been there for close on two years, I am thinking— aye, it would be that, at least. As a child, Mistress Catriona formed a strong attachment to her father and he was promising that, as soon as she should be old enough, he would send for her to keep house for him. The Captain was a man of his word and, when she was seventeen, he was sending for her. I was from home by then, sir, but I mind Morag telling me of it. 'Twas as if the lass had been granted her heart's desire when she was receiving her father's letter . . ." He shrugged resignedly. "One cannot see into the future, of course and, although no one was wanting her to go, least of all old Sir Alastair, there was no stopping Mistress Catriona! She was travelling out to Constantinople, in the care of friends of the family, and her father was meeting her there and taking her back with him to Sebastopol. 'Twas the last we saw of her, until now."

"And what of her father?" Phillip pursued. "Is he still in Sebastopol, do you know?"

"Captain Moray is dead, sir," the Sergeant answered flatly. "He was taken ill within a few months of Mistress Catriona's arrival, it seems, and he died soon after war was declared, leaving her alone and without the means of returning home. There was not much money and so she was having to take employment as governess, with the family of a Russian nobleman. She was with them until she made her escape, sir, and she was telling us—my wife and me, sir—that they were very good to her. All the same, in the circumstances, Mistress Catriona was feeling that she could not stay in Sebastopol, Mr Hazard. In her place, I'd have felt the same, sir."

As indeed, he would himself, Phillip thought. His interest now keenly aroused, he asked a number of other questions, but Sergeant MacCorkill was unable to tell him any more.

"You will need to ask Mistress Catriona herself, sir," he declared woodenly. "I have told you all that I am knowing, Mr Hazard. More, perhaps, than she would have wished."

"But the favour she intends to ask of me?" Phillip insisted. "Don't you know what that is, Sergeant?"

"You'll be knowing yourself, sir, very soon," the tall Sergeant assured him. He gestured ahead of them to where the flickering glow of bivouac fires lit the darkness—the first that Sir Colin Campbell had permitted. "Our camp is here." Still with a guiding hand on the bay's bridle, he led the way to his wife's tent. There was another horse tethered outside it and, even in the dim light, Phillip recognized it as the splendid Arab charger Alex Sheridan rode and which, he had confided, came from the stable of Omar Pasha, the Turkish Commander-in-Chief. Sheridan had ridden the beautiful animal at the heels of General Scarlett, he recalled, when the Heavy Brigade had made their brilliant charge earlier in the day but, when he attempted to question Sergeant MacCorkill as to the whereabouts of the Arab's owner, he could only shake his head.

"I cannot say, sir. The horse was one of those in the Light cavalry charge and, by a miracle, is unhurt. But I know of no Captain Sheridan. As you will be aware, the Light Cavalry Brigade were almost wiped out."

He was painfully aware of this, Phillip thought, recalling the wounded and dying men he and his party of bluejackets had carried from the battlefield but he said no more, and the Sergeant assisted him to dismount.

"If you will be going in, sir," the man invited, holding back the tent-flap. "I will see that both of the horses are fed and watered. Yours, I am thinking, would be the better for a rubdown."

Phillip thanked him and entered the tent. It was lit by a single oil lantern and, at first, after the darkness outside, he could see little save the shadowy outline of two women, both of whom were kneeling beside a prostrate figure wrapped in a Highlander's plaid. Hearing his voice, the nearer of the two, Catriona Moray, rose to her feet, handing the horn drinking vessel, from which she had been attempting to spoon some liquid into her patient's mouth, to her companion.

"He is very severely wounded," she offered, in explanation, as she drew Phillip to one side. "Thank you for coming so promptly, Mr Hazard."

"I'm at your service, Miss—er—Miss Moray."

"So Sergeant MacCorkill has told you who I am. Has he also told you how I come to be here?" Her question was softly voiced and Phillip inclined his head. "I insisted on his telling me. It's not his fault—I refused to come, until he did."

Catriona Moray's fine brows rose in a faintly surprised curve. "I do not mind your knowing, Mr Hazard. I should have told you myself, had there been an opportunity, for it was not my wish to deceive you. What else did the Sergeant tell you?"

"Only that you had a favour to ask of me." Phillip hesitated, regarding her uncertainly. She looked pale and exhausted, he saw, and there were ominous stains on the front of the apron she had donned to cover her dress. As if in answer to his unspoken question, Catriona said quietly, "We have been to the battlefield, I and the other women, doing what we could. What tragically little we could . . ." She caught her breath and Phillip saw pain in her lovely, smoke-blue eyes, a pain that no words could assuage. "There were so many, Mr Hazard."

"I know," Phillip returned gently, "I was also there." He laid a hand on her arm. "What can I do for you, Miss Moray?" When she was silent, fighting to control the tears which had come, unbidden, to her eyes, he added, "I recognized the horse outside, the grey Arab. It belongs to one of General Scarlett's aides, Captain Sheridan of the Indian Army. Is he perhaps the man you—" but Catriona interrupted him, her voice husky.

"No. There was an Indian Army captain being treated by the surgeons when I left. They—they were amputating his arm. He was with the wounded of the 11th Hussars and . . . you know, I expect, what they—what happened to them?"

"Yes."

"Did you"—her eyes lifted to his, still full of tears, searching his face—"did you see the charge they made, Mr Hazard?"

"No, I did not see it."

"They charged the Russian guns," Catriona whispered brokenly. "They charged straight for them, Mr Hazard. Surely that was madness, to pit men and horses against guns? Yet they are saying that Lord Raglan ordered it!" Her voice shook but she managed to steady it as she went on, "I did not see the charge either but I was told what happened, I—my brother was there, with the Scots Greys. Thank God, he was one of those who came back unscathed. I—I could not believe my eyes when I saw him. He was leading the grey horse you saw outside, Captain Sheridan's horse, with a wounded trooper in the saddle who . . . was dead, when Alastair brought him back. He did not know, he was too stunned and shocked to . . . realize. The Greys did not charge, you know—Lord Lucan held them in reserve, to cover the Light Brigade's retreat, he said. But it was strange. In my dream it was Alastair I found, I . . ." She broke off, biting fiercely at her lower lip, a vain attempt to still its quivering. She had momentarily forgotten the favour she wanted to ask of him, Phillip realized and, for the time being at least, had also forgotten the wounded man at the other end of the tent. Feeling her tremble, he put both arms round her, holding her tenderly, as he might have held a frightened child.

"What dream?" he asked, thinking to distract her.

Catriona shivered. "A dream that . . . has haunted me, ever since this war began," she said. "It was because of the dream that I could not stay in Sebastopol, Mr Hazard. It was always the same dream. I . . . was walking along a—a narrow valley with some other woman and all about us were wounded men, crying out to us to help them, to give them water, to tend their wounds. Just as they did this evening, except that the cries were more piteous and their wounds more . . . more hideous than in my dream."

Phillip felt her tremble again and his arms tightened instinctively about her slim, shaking body. "Do not speak of it if it is painful for you, Catriona," he begged, but she shook her head.

"No, I—I want to speak of it. It is so strange." Once again, with a great effort, she contrived to steady her voice. "Everything happened as it happened in my dream, save only for the last part. In my dream, there was a man lying alone, with blood on his face and soaking his uniform. He—he was dying and he called out to me by name, asking me to come to him. I knelt beside him and wiped the blood from his face and it . . . it was my brother, it was Alastair, who thanked me for . . . for coming to him. He had been afraid, he told me in the dream, afraid to die alone. I . . . perhaps you think it foolish, to set so much store by a dream but, in the Highlands, we do set much store by dreams. And Alastair is my twin, you see. Twins, identical twins, have a special sort of relationship, a special closeness. Each knows what is happening to the other, even when they are apart and, if one is hurt, the other feels his pain."

"I have heard that," Phillip observed, when she again lapsed into silence. "But it was not your brother you found, was it? You told me that he was unhurt."

"Yes, that's true," she admitted.

"Well, then?" Phillip urged, still as if he were endeavouring to offer consolation to a child. "The dream differed from the reality, did it not? It was wrong."

Catriona stared at him, clearly shocked by his scepticism. "Oh, no!" she exclaimed, "The dream wasn't wrong. The—the man was lying there, just as I had seen him a hundred times before, and he called out to me. He asked me to help him. It was already dark and we had only a few lanterns between us. Morag was carrying one and I took it from her as I went to kneel beside the poor wounded man and . . . and wipe the blood from his face. He was lying somewhat apart from the others, alone. I think he must have lain there for a long time unnoticed, on the hillside up which the Greys and the rest of the Heavy Cavalry Brigade charged this morning. Or perhaps, when they were searching for wounded, they believed him dead, because they brought many Russian wounded to the field hospitals. I saw them there, being cared for with our own men."

"*Russians?*" Phillip echoed, startled. He glanced over to where the wounded man was lying, with Morag MacCorkill still patiently attempting to force a few drops of liquid between his tightly closed lips. "But . . ." His eyes had grown accustomed to the lantern-light now and he noticed that a gold-laced green cavalry jacket had been spread across the all-enveloping plaid by which the injured man was covered.

There was something familiar about the be-frogged uniform and about the gold *aiguilette* which, though stained and all but hacked in two, still hung by one of its tarnished cords from the shoulder of the jacket. The uniform was patently not British and the *aiguilette* denoted a high ranking officer in the Russian Army, an imperial aide-de-camp, and Phillip felt himself stiffen, unwilling to believe the evidence of his own eyes, his mind rejecting the possibility of so fantastic a coincidence as he turned to face Catriona once more.

"He is a Russian officer, is he not?" he demanded, his tone harsh.

"Yes," she admitted, offering no explanation.

"And you brought him here! In heaven's name, why? Surely, in the circumstances, you—"

"He is dying," Catriona put in, a catch in her voice. "Cannot you see that, Mr Hazard? Would you have had me fail to show mercy and compassion to a fallen enemy?"

Remembering the compassion with which the Governor of Odessa had treated him, following his own capture, Phillip was compelled to shake his head. "No, Miss Moray. But would it not have been wiser to have taken him to one of the field hospitals where they—"

Again she interrupted him. "Where they have no cure, save amputation? His left leg is gangrenous—the surgeons would have insisted on taking it off. And to what purpose? That would not save or prolong his life, it would not. In any case, the field hospitals are overwhelmed with casualties, as you must have seen for yourself. The surgeons are desperately hard pressed— they have no time to spare for the dying, Mr Hazard, and no means of alleviating their suffering. One of them, a cavalry sur-

geon, told me as much"—she spoke with controlled bitterness—
"when I sought his help. It was on his advice that I—that I acted
so unwisely in bringing this officer here. But here, at least, he
can die in peace."

"You are sure that he's dying, Miss Moray?"

Catriona freed herself from Phillip's protective embrace.
"The surgeon said so," she confirmed. "He has a saber wound
in the chest—it is very deep and has penetrated the lung. No
man could live for more than a few hours with such a wound."
She shrugged helplessly. "You have only to look at him, if you
doubt my word. We have done all we can but he is sinking fast."

Phillip glanced reluctantly at the wounded Russian. The
man's face was a white, unrecognizable blur but he did not go
closer, did not attempt to identify him, since there was no need
for him to do so. Fantastic though the coincidence was, he knew
who lay there—knew and shrank from the recognition for this
time, it was evident, he could not send Mademoiselle Sophie's
husband back to her. The man she had married barely six
months before, in the great domed Cathedral at Odessa—the
arrogant young princeling, whom he had hated, envied, and
despised because Mademoiselle Sophie had married him—was
dying. Dying here, in this small lamplit tent, from a British dragoon's saber-cut, received during the fierce mêlée on the slopes
of the Causeway Heights this morning.

This morning . . . he drew in his breath sharply. What had
Catriona Moray said, about the leg wound being gangrenous? It
was too soon, surely, for gangrene to have set in but—Narishkin
had lost an arm and been wounded in the leg at the Alma, which
suggested . . . Phillip's throat was suddenly tight. It suggested
that Prince Andrei Stepanovitch Narishkin, Colonel of the Chasseurs of Odessa, must today have gone into action with his
wounds imperfectly healed and an empty sleeve, where his
sword-arm had been. Enemy or not, this was courage of a very
high order; the selfless, calculated heroism of a man who had
known what it meant to fall on the field of battle and, as such,

deserving of his respect, even of his admiration. As if she had guessed the trend of his thoughts, Catriona observed softly, "The brave men are not exclusively ours, are they, Mr Hazard? In any war, both sides have their heroes. The pity of it is that so many of them must die."

And their widows weep for them, Phillip reflected, thinking of Mademoiselle Sophie. He inclined his head unable, for a moment, to speak. Then, the words less a question than a statement, he said, "You know who he is, Miss Moray?"

"I know only too well," she admitted, without hesitation. "He is the Prince Narishkin."

"Then you have met him before?"

"I have *seen* him before," Catriona corrected. "He was a frequent visitor to the house in which I was employed as governess, after my father died. My employer was his aunt—I was governess to his two young cousins, who live in Sebastopol." She smiled faintly. "In Imperial Russia, a governess is seen but never heard. All the same, I once spoke to the Prince Narishkin. He was gracious and kind. His aunt and the rest of the family were kindness itself to me, Mr Hazard, and this I—I cannot forget." Once again, Phillip saw, her eyes were misted with tears and this time she did not seek to hide them. "One should not shed tears for the enemy, should one? Yet for Prince Andrei, I . . ." She glanced up at him sadly. "But you know him, do you not? He was asking for you, saying your name again and again, begging me, if I could, to bring you to him. He said he had something to tell you—that was why I sent for you, Mr Hazard. But now that you have come, he is unconscious, he does not realize that you are here."

"I can wait," Phillip offered, "at any rate until dawn, in case he should recover consciousness."

"Thank you," Catriona Moray acknowledged, as if he had done her a service. "But you are tired, are you not, and I do not suppose you have eaten since this morning. Be seated, please, and rest. I will watch over our—our fallen enemy, while Morag prepares some food for you. We haven't much but you are welcome to share what we have."

Phillip did as she bade him. There were a great many questions he wanted to ask her concerning Narishkin's family and, in particular, concerning Mademoiselle Sophie but, in spite of this, within a few minutes of seating himself with his back against the tent-pole, his head slumped forward onto his chest and he slept.

CHAPTER EIGHT

1

"*Lieutenant Hazard!*" Please to bestir yourself, sir." The whispered voice was that of Sergeant MacCorkill's wife, Morag. Accustomed, when at sea, to being turned out of his hammock—often after only a few hours' sleep—Phillip was instantly alert. He sat up, stretching his cramped limbs, stiff from a night spent on the hard ground.

"I am awake, Mistress MacCorkill," he said. "What is it?"

"'Tis this, sir." Morag MacCorkill thrust a steaming bowl into his hands and offered him a horn spoon, a smile briefly lighting her gaunt face. "I am sorry indeed to have to disturb you, and you sleeping like a babe, sir," she told him. "But 'tis wanting scarcely an hour to dawn and you have not yet eaten. You will be needing food more than you are needing your sleep now, I am thinking."

A pleasantly savory smell rose from the bowl and, as he inhaled it, Phillip thanked her. It seemed a long time since he had eaten any sort of meal, least of all a hot one that smelt as appetizing as this did, and he was about to fall hungrily upon the contents of the bowl when, with full wakefulness, memory returned. He glanced uneasily across to the opposite side of the tent, his conscience pricking him. He had slept, as Morag MacCorkill had put it, like a baby, while Mademoiselle Sophie's husband lay dying, a few feet from him. Perhaps he was already dead but . . . his first quick glance reassured him. Prince Andrei Narishkin lay as he had lain the previous evening, still swathed in the folds of the borrowed Highland plaid, with Catriona Moray kneeling at his side.

Sensing Phillip's eyes on her, she looked up from the cloth she was in the act of moistening and shook her head wordlessly, before she laid the freshly wrung cloth on the wounded man's brow. Narishkin stirred and cried out something in a high pitched, agonized voice which shattered the prevailing silence but, again meeting Phillip's gaze, the girl repeated her head-shake. A few minutes later Morag MacCorkill took her place beside the wounded Russian and Catriona moved across to join Phillip in his corner, also carrying a bowl of steaming broth. He made room for her, holding her bowl until she had seated herself.

"How is he, Miss Moray?"

"He is delirious and in a high fever," she answered despairingly. "Much as he has been throughout the night. I would have wakened you, had he recovered consciousness and asked for you, Mr Hazard. But he did not and"—she brushed a lock of unruly hair from her damp brow wearily—"he is sinking fast, I am afraid."

"Perhaps, by this time, the surgeons are not all so hard pressed—" Phillip began, thinking of Surgeon Fraser. But she cut him short. "I sent Morag for one of the 93rd's surgeons during the night. He administered an opiate, to lessen the pain but that, it seems, is all anyone can do for him now. Except"—she sighed—"except set his mind at rest, if only one knew how and I, alas, do not."

"What do you mean?"

"You heard him cry out, just now?" Catriona asked. "Well, he keeps saying a name I cannot catch, the same name, over and over again, at times quite frantically, as if it meant a great deal to him. He has talked, in his delirium, and I believe that is a woman's name but I cannot be certain and—"

"Was the name Sophie?" Phillip put in quietly. "Or Sophia?"

Catriona looked up at him, her eyes widening in surprise. "Yes, I fancy it might have been. But what leads you to suppose that it was and . . . who is Sophie?"

"She is his wife." He said it without a qualm, his voice expressionless. "They were married in Odessa when I was a prisoner of war there, following the loss of the *Tiger.*"

"But did not Prince Andrei marry a niece of the Emperor?" Catriona demurred. "I am sure I heard the Paveloffs speak of it. He was betrothed to one of the grand duchesses, whose name was . . ." She frowned, in an effort to remember. "The Grand Duchess Olga Caterina Mihailovna, was it not?"

"Olga Caterina Sophia Mihailovna," Phillip amended. He added wryly, the old, all-too-familiar knife twisting in his heart as it always did when he permitted himself to think of her. "Whom I knew as Mademoiselle Sophie."

"As *Mademoiselle Sophie?* But—were you actually acquainted with her? Was this in Odessa, Mr Hazard?"

"No, it was before that. You see, we brought her out with us from England in the steam frigate *Trojan,* just before war was declared. She was accompanied by her *duenna,* a rather fearsome Austrian baroness called von Mauthner." He explained the circumstances, and went on, "We had, of course, no idea who she was—her identity was revealed to our Captain in sealed orders from the Admiralty, to be opened only after we had sailed. Captain North did not confide in any of us. In common with the rest of the ship's company, I was instructed to refer to our passenger as Mademoiselle Sophie so, naturally, I did so. There was some speculation as to her nationality but she spoke French, German, and English fluently and, her companion being Austrian—"

"You suspected nothing?" Catriona put in.

Phillip smiled faintly, as the bittersweet memories came flooding into his mind. "Towards the end of the voyage we did—when our Mademoiselle Sophie was received by Lord Stratford de Redcliffe in person and when we learnt that her ultimate destination was Odessa. But at the time, our orders bound us not to talk of the matter."

"You are at liberty to talk of it now, surely?"

He shrugged. "Yes, I suppose so. But—"

"What was she like?" Catriona asked eagerly. "Tell me about her, will you not, Mr Hazard?"

Reluctantly at first, Phillip found himself telling her of the voyage and of *Trojan's* two mysterious female passengers. After a while, however, as they sat side by side sipping their broth, it became almost a relief to confide in her and to talk of Mademoiselle Sophie to an understanding and sympathetic listener. He chose his words with care, at pains to give no hint of the feelings he had secretly cherished for the lovely, dark haired girl, with whose urgent delivery to Constantinople his late commander had been entrusted, unaware that even the tone of his voice when he spoke of her was a betrayal.

Catriona listened for the most part in silence, only occasionally prompting him gently, and he went on to tell her of his imprisonment in the residence of the Governor of Odessa, of the wound he had suffered when the *Tiger* had been shelled and set on fire, and finally of Mademoiselle Sophie's daily visits to his sickroom.

"I can't be sure, looking back now, whether she did come or whether I imagined her presence," he confessed. "I fear I imagined it for, like that poor fellow over there, I was delirious and almost out of my mind. Yet it seemed to me, that she kept vigil at my bedside and even prayed for my recovery."

"Why doubt what you want to believe, Mr Hazard?"

"How can I help it?" Phillip protested. "It would scarcely have been fitting for a Russian Grand Duchess to visit a British prisoner of war, surely? Even if his prison were the Governor's palace and his physicians the Governor's own as, in fact, mine were. The Russians treated us well, all of us, not only our wounded . . . although it is tantamount to a court martial offense to mention this now in the British Fleet! But both officers and seamen were given the freedom of the town, entertained and made welcome in their homes by the townsfolk, the sick given the best of care, so that we felt more like guests than prisoners. And this was in Odessa, a town which our combined fleets had recently bombarded and left in flames! It is strangely at variance with the terrible tales one hears of Russian atrocities, committed on the battlefield, is it not?"

"The atrocities are committed by the common soldiers," Catriona said. "For whom there is, perhaps, some excuse. They are ignorant peasants, taught to expect no mercy at the hands of the enemy. In consequence they show none, either during or after a battle . . . and the Cossacks are the worst! I expect you saw them today?"

"I saw them, Miss Moray," Phillip confirmed grimly.

Catriona avoided his gaze. "I, too, was treated with the greatest possible kindness and generosity during my stay in Sebastopol, Mr Hazard. The Russian nobility are chivalrous, almost to a fault—or so I found, and I lived amongst them for two years, my father for much longer. Many of them were our friends. That is why . . ." She hesitated, looking up at him now and searching his face gravely. "Mr Hazard, do not be offended but . . . if she held you in particular esteem or if there was a— a sentimental attachment between you, I believe that even a Russian Grand Duchess might have defied convention and ignored what was fitting."

Taken off his guard by the unexpectedness of her suggestion and all that this implied, Phillip reddened in confusion. "I do not think that Mademoiselle—that Her Imperial Highness held me in particular esteem, Miss Moray. And as to a sentimental attachment, I—" He had been about to deny it vehemently but the denial froze on his lips as, in memory, he heard again Mademoiselle Sophie's sweet, gentle voice and the words with which she had—or he had imagined she had—taken leave of him.

"We shall not meet again, Phillip but . . . to know that you are living, somewhere in the world, will comfort me. The heart does not forget . . . and, when peace comes, I shall see you with the eyes of the heart, as you set your course for England." His hands clenched

convulsively at his sides, the palms clammy despite the early
morning chill pervading the tent. She had bent over him then,
he remembered, and her lips had brushed his cheek. *"May God
be with you, now and always, my dear English sailor . . ."* Had he
imagined those words, he asked himself, the words and the
farewell kiss? Had the whole episode been a dream, born of
pain and delirium, of despair and frustrated longing? It was possible, it was quite likely; he might very easily have deluded
himself, for was not the wish father to the thought and every
dream an illusion? Yet the words were printed indelibly in his
memory, never, it seemed, to be forgotten whether Mademoiselle Sophie had said or he himself invented them when his
mind was wandering in that strange limbo, which lies between
waking and sleeping and, sometimes, between living and dying.

His gaze went involuntarily to the still form of Prince Andrei
Narishkin and then, almost guiltily, to the small, pale face of
Catriona Moray, upturned to his, its expression full of concern.
She, too, had dreamed, he reminded himself and, with her Highland ancestry, set much store by the dream, on her own
admission; what dreams, what delusions were haunting poor
Narishkin now, as he stirred restlessly beneath the plaid which
covered his broken body? Catriona had said that she wanted to
set his mind at rest . . . could this be the purpose for which
they had all three been brought together? Was the coincidence,
which he had thought so fantastic, the strange working of a
divine providence, intentional, rather than blind chance?

Phillip drew a long, uneven breath. "The sentimental attachment was on my part," he said aloud, "not on hers. Her Imperial
Highness was very young, a child, fresh from the schoolroom,
and with a child's trusting innocence. If she honored me with
her friendship, she likewise honored several of my brother officers and we all—because we had met no one like her—expressed
our life-long devotion to her when she left the *Trojan*. Our personal devotion for, of course, in the circumstances and with
our two countries at war, it could be no more than that but in

token of friendship, she entrusted me—as First Lieutenant of the *Trojan*—with a ring. It was an emerald ring, of considerable value, with the arms of Her Imperial Highness's family cut into the face of the stone. I had it on my person when I was taken to Odessa and—"

"*This* ring, Lieutenant Hazard?" The interruption came from the shadows on the far side of the tent. The voice, although faint, was perfectly lucid and it was Narishkin's. Phillip lapsed into a startled silence but quicker than he to realize what had happened, Catriona whispered urgently, "He is conscious at last—go to him, please, Mr Hazard. He . . . may not have long."

Obediently Phillip went to kneel by the wounded man, and Morag MacCorkill slipped unobtrusively away, leaving the three of them together. The ring, with its double-headed eagle crest, lay in the Russian's outstretched palm, the magnificent stone gleaming in the lantern light and Phillip felt an odd tightening of the muscles of his throat as he recognized it. He made, however, no move to take it and Narishkin let the ring fall on to the tartan plaid and roll slowly towards him.

"Please," he invited, "my wife would have wished you to keep her gift, on behalf of your brother officers of Her Britannic Majesty's frigate *Trojan*. Take it, will you not, Mr Hazard, for this time the gift comes also from myself." The bloodless lips curved briefly upwards, in a smile of singular warmth. "The case is in my pocket, if you need it."

Phillip took the ring and started to stammer his thanks but Andrei Narishkin weakly motioned him to silence. "I am in *your* debt and it is a threefold debt, my friend, if—from the threshold of eternity—I may be permitted thus to address you?" His English was fluent and accentless but the words were a trifle slurred, as if each one cost him an effort.

"A threefold debt, sir?" Phillip bent closer. "I can recall only one occasion when I might have merited your Highness's gratitude and even then, I—"

"I will refresh your memory," Prince Narishkin offered.

"Firstly, I am indebted to you for having delivered my bride to me with that—that childlike, trusting innocence, of which you spoke just now, completely unimpaired. Secondly—and this, no doubt, is the occasion you *do* recall—for having saved my life, after the bloody battle in which we engaged at the Alma. Thirdly . . ." His smile returned, lighting the wan face and rekindling in the pain-dimmed eyes something of their old, arrogant mockery. "Thirdly for allowing me to die in such good company as your own and that of the young woman who caused me to be brought here. I should be obliged if you would convey my thanks to her, for she has been more than kind. I have no ring to give her but there is a cross about my neck, which is of some value, if she would accept it."

"Miss Moray is here, sir," Phillip told him. "If you would care to speak to her."

"Is she? Alas, I cannot see her . . . it is dark, is it not? I can scarcely see your face and I should like to. Have you a lamp, by any chance?" Phillip was about to move the lantern but Catriona forestalled him with a swift headshake and a finger to her lips. He apologized awkwardly. "You haven't one? Well, no matter, the darkness is not unpleasant, and so long as my benefactress is aware that I am grateful . . ." Narishkin sighed. "It is good to have a woman's care, when one is in pain. Sophia was with me in Perekop and Simpheropol, you know, and would have remained with me in Bakshi-Serai in order to . . . fulfil her wifely duty and care for me. But"—his expression relaxed and his eyes no longer held even a hint of mockery—"she is to have my child, Mr Hazard, which rejoices us both."

Taken off his guard a second time, Phillip managed to control his voice. "Permit me to offer you my congratulations, sir," he said stiffly. He was conscious of Catriona's hand, resting lightly on his arm and added, with more warmth, "That is indeed wonderful news."

"I think it is," the Russian said. "At least my name will be carried on and my estates have an heir, God willing. Sophia is in Odessa now—as soon as I knew she was with child, I forbade her to . . . stay any longer with me. I sent her back to my mother's house, which is outside Odessa. She will be safe there, I trust, she and . . . the child. Your army, as well as your navy, will have . . . all they can do to reduce Sebastopol to . . . submission. Too much to . . . waste men and . . . ships on Odessa. The assault . . . was too long delayed, Mr Hazard. Your generals have . . . faint hearts, fainter than . . . the splendid soldiers they . . . command. It is . . . curious, is it not, that I . . . am in my . . . present predicament because Sophia's cousin, the . . . insufferable Nicolai . . . accused me of . . . cowardice. Very . . . curious and somehow . . . ironic . . ." His voice was gradually becoming fainter, the words more slurred and indistinct and, observing this, Catriona signed to Phillip to stand aside.

"His life is ebbing fast," she told him, with a pity she made no attempt to hide. "Already his sight is almost gone but—he has had his wish, he has talked to you and I believe that you have set his mind at rest. So leave him to me now, Mr Hazard, and I will do what is necessary. I do not think he feels any pain but, if he does, there is this draught the surgeon left me." She held a cup to Andrei Narishkin's lips and he gulped its contents thirstily as, deftly raising his head, she pillowed it against her breast. "We cannot summon a priest of his own faith but I will say a prayer for him, the same prayer that I have said for many soldiers since yesterday morning. Please God it may suffice . . ." Her voice was low and infinitely gentle. Phillip could not hear what she said but evidently the words of her prayer reached the dying man, for he emitted a deep sigh of relief.

"Sophie—Sophie beloved! Is it possible that you are here?" His voice was miraculously stronger and his left hand reached out to grasp Catriona's, the blind eyes lit with a glow that held neither mockery nor arrogance but only joy and a strange sort of contentment. He had spoken in French and Catriona answered him in the same language. "Yes, I am here. My place is with you, Andrei."

"With the arrogant, strutting *poseur* to whom you have the misfortune to be married, brought up—according to your cousin Nikita—by women?" Narishkin asked wryly. "With the soldier who, Nikita claims, has no taste for English steel?"

Catriona hesitated, clearly bewildered by the bitterly phrased questions and at a loss to know how best to answer them. She closed her eyes for a moment, as if seeking guidance in prayer, and then said quietly, "I am with my husband, Andrei —with the father of my unborn child and I—I am proud that it is so."

To Phillip, listening intently yet hearing only part of their whispered conversation, it was as if Mademoiselle Sophie herself were speaking. The answer was, he knew in his heart, the one that she would have given. He wanted to go but, an unwilling eavesdropper, was nevertheless incapable of taking the few steps which would have rendered their voices inaudible to him and, as he heard Andrei Narishkin refer again to the coming child, he was conscious of a sense of deep and irreparable loss. He held her ring in his hand, the man she had married was dying in front of his eyes but, for the first time since their parting, he faced and accepted the fact that the lovely, innocent child whom he had known as Mademoiselle Sophie had no existence, outside his memory. She had become, in the interim, the Princess Narishkin and, treasure it how he might, the memory was only a memory. The heart, as she told him, did not forget but . . . there was room in it for reality as well as dreams.

From outside the tent, Sergeant MacCorkill's voice broke into his thoughts. "'Tis dawn, Lieutenant Hazard, sir, and your galloper here with orders for you to report to Sir Colin Campbell at Number Four Battery in half an hour. Your horse is ready saddled for you and I have myself to report for duty, by your leave, sir."

"Thank you Sergeant," Phillip acknowledged. "Carry on— I'm coming immediately." He picked up his cap and then, on impulse, knelt and his lips brushed Catriona's tear-wet cheek.

He could not have said whether it was of the ghost of Mademoiselle Sophie he thus took leave, or of Catriona herself and she, instinctively aware of his inner conflict, did not lift her head or took at him, but he heard her catch her breath on a sob. Prince Narishkin, he saw, as he rose to leave the tent, lay very quietly, his dark head still pillowed on the girl's breast and a faint smile curving his mouth. Compassionately, Catriona drew the blood-stained tartan plaid closer about him but he did not stir.

2

Outside, the usual Crimean mist swirled this way and that, half obscuring the shadowy figures who waited there and it was not until he spoke that Phillip recognized his brother Graham, standing at Sergeant MacCorkill's side.

"Good morning, sir," Graham greeted him, with correct formality but a broad smile. Still smiling, he added in reply to his brother's startled question, "*Trojan* has been ordered into Balaclava Harbour to assist in its defense. We are moored just astern of the *Sanspareil* and I am assigned to a gun position on the Heights. But we haven't got our guns up yet, so I asked for an hour's leave of absence."

"I see." Phillip took his horse's rein from Sergeant MacCorkill and, after repeating his thanks, led the animal through the line of tents in the direction of No. 4 Gun Battery, Graham falling into step beside him. "You want to talk to me?"

"Yes . . . and the deuce of a job I had finding you! I'm not curious, Phillip, and your 93rd sergeant was the soul of discretion but what were you doing in the Highlanders' camp? All the sergeant would say was that you had come on an errand of mercy."

"I suppose one might describe it thus." Phillip sighed. "It is a long story, so perhaps we could defer explanations until a more opportune moment. You understand, I—"

"Of course," his brother assured him. "If I do not understand, at least I can wait for the explanation. In any case, there isn't much time, for you're wanted and I must return to my gun's crew. I sent your cavalry orderly to brigade headquarters, by the by, because I wanted an opportunity to speak with you alone. As naval liaison officer, there's something I fancy you may wish to tell Sir Colin Campbell."

"Oh—and what is that?"

Graham eyed him gravely. "Phillip, the last transport left harbour last night, with wounded for Scutari. She took every man who could be crammed aboard her, but the hospital is now filled to overflowing and, with every hour, more wounded are being brought down from the cavalry lines. Some, because there is no room for them in the hospital, have lain all night on the wharf, awaiting embarkation. They are without food, water, or medical attention apart from what they were given in the field hospitals . . ." He paused and Phillip stared at him in shocked and uncomprehending surprise.

"I don't think I follow you, Graham," he said. "What do you mean by the *last* transport? There are plenty of transports at anchor outside the harbour entrance—I saw them myself yesterday. They were only cleared to enable the *Sanspareil* to enter and permit her room to maneuver—"

"But they will remain at anchor outside Balaclava," Graham put in. "Captain Dacres, as senior officer, has taken command of the port. He has issued orders that no ships are to enter, for whatever purpose—and that includes for the purpose of evacuating the wounded, Phillip."

"What! You cannot mean that. Why—"

"Alas, I do. Evacuation of the wounded must take second place to the defense of Balaclava, unless and until we abandon it. There are strong rumours current that the harbour is to be abandoned"—Graham spoke with stark earnestness—"and I am not, I assure you, repeating gossip. It is widely believed that we are, in future, to share Kamiesch and Kazatch with the French, and that our seamen and marines, together with the *Sanspareil* and the remaining frigates in the harbour, are to fight a rear-guard action. We're to hold off the enemy for as long as we can and then retire on the ships of war, for evacuation. That means, of course, those who can walk—or run. The wounded will be left to the tender mercies of the Russians, while the Kadi-Koi defenders retire to the Upland."

"You say this is rumoured?" Phillip demanded.

"Yes. But Captain Dacres' order lends credence to the rumour. He, presumably, is acting on instructions from higher up, for he is normally a humane man."

"From higher up?" Phillip echoed, more shocked than ever. "Do you mean from Admiral Lyons?"

"You will know more about that than I, my dear Phillip," his brother evaded. "Since you delivered Admiral Lyons's instructions to the *Sanspareil* in person, did you not? You spoke to Dacres, surely?"

True, Phillip thought, he had but . . . his heart sank, as the full significance of his brother's words sank in. "That was two days ago, Graham!" he exclaimed. "Or three, I'm losing count of time. But the Admiral was determined that we should not abandon Balaclava then and, as recently as yesterday, he expressed the same determination. So, too, did Sir Colin Campbell . . ." He repeated brief details of his instructions from the two commanders. Graham listened, obviously unimpressed.

"Since then, the situation has undergone a drastic change," he stated, his tone clipped. "With yesterday's appalling disaster to the Light Cavalry Brigade, the number of wounded has increased fourfold, at least, and the decision whether or not to abandon Balaclava does not rest with either Admiral Lyons or Sir Colin Campbell, does it?"

"No, but—" recalling what Captain Tatham had told him the previous day, Phillip broke off abruptly. An aide-de-camp from

General Airey had come, bearing a signed order from Lord Raglan's headquarters and . . . what had the *Simoom*'s commander said? *"I began to fear that the Turks were right, after all, and the battle lost . . ."* And had not Sir Colin talked of the risk that "more heed might be paid to panic counsels than the situation here warrants" when he had read Sir Edmund Lyons's message?

"I see you now share my qualms," Graham observed dryly. "Which was why I sought you out to tell you of them. But I cannot absent myself from my post any longer, so"—he laid an affectionate hand on Phillip's shoulder—*"au revoir,* Phillip. Have a care for yourself, lad."

"And you, my dear fellow."

"Of course I shall. Oh, by the by, you won't find O'Leary on the *Vesuvius'* gun at Kadi-Koi. He has been ordered, with the rest of Commander Heath's guns' crews, to reinforce Captain Lushington's Brigade on the Upland." Graham smiled, without amusement. "Sebastopol must continue to be battered into submission, whatever losses we sustain at Balaclava. Commander Heath's party of over two hundred left last night, in darkness. The Highland Brigade, our Marines and seamen on the Heights, what is left of our cavalry and the Turks and, I was told, a French brigade under General Vinoy, remain to guard the approaches to Balaclava. Will they suffice, Phillip?"

This was the question Phillip asked himself as, having parted with his brother, he rode the short distance which separated him from No. 4 Battery. He found it manned by skeleton naval guns' crews and learned from Captain Shadwell that Sir Colin had insisted on spending the night there, constantly visiting outposts and showing himself to his men.

"If they loved him before, he won their hearts anew last night," the aide-de-camp said admiringly. "And he insisted of having Rustem Pasha with him, in order publicly to demonstrate that he still reposes confidence in the Turks. It's not a confidence the rest of us share but—" He shrugged. "It is

nonetheless typical of Sir Colin. He wants to see you, I understand, Mr Hazard. As a favour to me, though, do not keep him
any longer than you can help . . . he's had no sleep and has
not yet broken his fast. And he *is* human; his physical strength
isn't inexhaustible, as I endeavour to convince him when he
will listen! And he is the one man we cannot afford to lose at
his critical hour. You'll find him"—Shadwell's shrug was expres-
sive—"predictably, in our forward gun position. He's convinced
that another attack is coming."

Sir Colin, when Phillip found him, confirmed what his aide
had said, "If *I* were in command of Sebastopol, Mr Hazard, I
should most certainly order a sortie in force, within the next
few hours. To be followed, if successful, by a full scale attack
on the Balaclava defenses, from the high ground above
Kamara—our weakest point. Since I do not underestimate
Prince Menschikoff or his subordinate commanders, I am
preparing for the sortie as best I may. Now as to the harbour
defenses . . ." He went into details and Phillip, in response to
his questions, repeated what Graham had told him, as briefly
as he could, also mentioning his short but illuminating interview with Captain Tatham.

Sir Colin Campbell sighed. He looked exhausted but in his
tired eyes was kindled suddenly the unmistakable light of
battle. "This was what both I and your Admiral feared," he confessed. "The panic counsels, eh? Well, they shall not! Find Sir
Edmund, Hazard, find him and bring him here with all possible
speed, no matter what other plans he may have. Tell him the
matter is one of the utmost urgency and that . . ." He hesitated
for an instant and then smiled. "Tell him that I shall request Lord
Raglan to confer with us here . . . since the only way to combat
panic counsels is to offer those of a bolder kind. You'll find your
Admiral on shore, I believe—with Captain Lushington's Naval
Brigade, where he told me he intended to spend the night. And
hurry, my young friend—there's no time to be lost!"

"Aye, aye, sir," Philllp acknowledged and was on his way.

CHAPTER NINE

The momentous conference, which was to decide the fate of Balaclava, took place that morning. Waiting anxiously with his fellow aides, Phillip witnessed Lord Raglan's arrival, on horseback, accompanied by senior members of his staff and a cavalry escort, and he watched as Admiral Lyons and Sir Colin Campbell greeted the new arrivals and led them into the battery. He heard nothing of the deliberations that followed but, within less than an hour of their commencement, was sent post-haste to summon Captain Dacres from the harbour. He found the *Sanspareil*'s Captain in his cabin, laid low by an attack of fever but, when the urgency of the matter had been explained to him, the gallant Dacres swallowed a draught of quinine, was assisted into his uniform and managed, in stoical silence, to ride through the gorge to Kadi-Koi. By the time he arrived, the decision had been made. He received his orders and emerged, tight-lipped and deathly pale, in Lord Raglan's wake and leaning on the Admiral's arm and Sir Edmund himself accompanied him back to the harbour.

Phillip was given a written message to deliver to Commander Heath and would have departed on his errand in ignorance of the result of the conference, had not Sir Colin Campbell called him back.

"Balaclava is to be held at all costs, Mr Hazard," the Highland Brigade commander told him soberly. "I believe that we have made the right decision—indeed, I pray God we have. But you may rest assured that, whatever the outcome, the wounded will not be abandoned while any of us have breath in our bodies. And if we survive the attack which, I feel sure, must come either today or during the night, then I am hopeful that we shall retain possession of the port of Balaclava for as long as we are required to do so."

The attack Sir Colin had predicted came that afternoon and, as he had predicted, it was launched against the British right flank. A force of some four to five thousand Russian infantry, supported by field guns and some squadrons of Cossack, issued from Sebastopol soon after mid-day. Advancing under the cover afforded by the numerous deep gullies and ravines by which it was indented, this force, divided into eight separate columns, ascended the six-hundred-foot high plateau known as Mount Inkerman unobserved. Reaching the northern end of the plateau, they flung out skirmishers and advanced at a rapid pace across the rough, stony ground in an attempt to surprise and drive in the thinly held British outposts and pickets which were spread, at intervals, across the summit. The pickets put up a valiant resistance but were gradually forced to fall back, until three British nine-pounder field batteries were sent to their support. Galloping up, the gunners unlimbered and poured a rapid and accurate fire into the Russian columns, enabling the hard-pressed pickets to withdraw.

In the Second Division camp, situated a quarter of a mile south of the neck of land connecting the Inkerman Ridge with the Upland, bugles sounded the alarm and the startled troops hurriedly stood to arms. As a picket of the 49th, fighting every foot of the way, was finally driven back, the 1st Battalion of the Rifle Brigade—many of them in their shirtsleeves—launched a spirited counterattack, which succeeded in halting the Russian advance, and the Rifles hung on grimly, waiting for the arrival of the rest of their division.

Phillip, who had called on the commander of the Five-Gun Naval Battery after delivering his despatch to Commander Heath, unexpectedly found himself in the thick of the action.

He was standing with young "Bully" Hewitt, acting-mate of the *Beagle* and in command of the battery's rear Lancaster gun, when the sound of musket fire reached them, coming from the direction of Inkerman and rapidly increasing in intensity. It was still too distant to occasion them serious concern and both were standing on the gun platform, glasses to their eyes in an endeavour to make out what was going on, when a fierce hail of Minié balls showered down on the battery and sent the guns' crews diving for cover.

"Great Scott—I believe *we're* being attacked!" young Hewett exclaimed, his tone more astonished than alarmed. "Did you see where that volley came from, Mr Hazard?"

Phillip swung his glass in a wide are, equally puzzled. "No—" he began and broke off as a burst of musketry from the parallel immediately in front of the redoubt culminated in a high-pitched scream of agony. A soldier leapt from the trench, with blood streaming down his face, gesticulating wildly to his rear and shouting something which was lost in another prolonged burst of firing.

"The Careening Ravine!" Bully Hewett yelled, at the pitch of his lungs. "They're coming up the Careening Ridge—hundreds of 'em, by the sound of it!" With one accord, he and Phillip ran to the parapet. Below them and to their right lay the so-called Careening Ravine, a rocky cleft in the ground of considerable depth which, rising steeply, formed the precipitous western boundary of the Inkerman Ridge. Peering over the top of the parapet, with bullets whistling over his head, Phillip saw wave after wave of Russian infantrymen emerge from the ravine—part of the force, he afterwards learned, ordered to engage the Inkerman pickets. So cautious and stealthy had been their approach, and so excellent their concealment, that the first warning the forward observation posts had had of their presence had been when they opened fire.

Their shooting was accurate and the trench guards, taken by surprise, were swiftly overwhelmed, upon which the Russian commander, realizing that his force outnumbered its opponents, evidently decided to change the direction of his attack. Hewitt's Lancaster gun, a massive piece of 95 cwt., was trained on the Malakoff Tower—its usual daily target—and guarded by only the handful of seamen required to fire and serve it. Because of its greater range, the Lancaster was positioned to the right rear of the other four guns in the battery and some distance from them which meant, Phillip realized, that the advancing Russians could out-flank it with comparative ease once the opposition of the second line of trench guards was overcome.

On the other hand . . . he drew a quick, uneven breath, his mind racing, cutting corners. To capture and destroy a British gun position on the Upland would undoubtedly be a feather in the cap of any ambitious enemy commander. It might well seem to him of more importance than the mere execution of a successful out-flanking movement that would, at best, enable him to continue his advance along the ravine, in order to join in the attack on a few isolated pickets. He would be aware that the gun, trained as it was, offered no danger to a flank attack or one from the rear, and with the trench guards falling like flies under the sustained fire, from above, of his men's Minié rifles, would not the risk involved seem small, in comparison with the chance of glory?

Heedless of his own danger, Phillip vaulted on to the top of the parapet. From this vantage point, he saw that his assessment of the situation had not been far out. In the forward trenches and observation posts, not a scarlet jacket moved. In those nearest to the battery, British and Russian infantrymen were engaged in a furious, hand to hand struggle and, even as he watched this, he saw a fresh wave of Russians, with bayonets fixed, come charging down the slope from the head of the ravine. They came like madmen, to be followed by a second wave and then a third while, from the rocks to the right, those who had been firing into the battery started to move in closer, taking advantage of such cover as the ground afforded in an endeavour to conceal their intentions.

These were, however, clear enough. His heart pounding and his mouth suddenly dry, Phillip dropped down behind the protecting wall of the redoubt, the minute or so he had spent on its gabioned top seeming like an hour. He landed awkwardly on his injured leg and Hewett grabbed him, to demand reproachfully, "For pity's sake, sir, do you *want* to be killed? Surely you know better than to expose yourself to their fire like that? I was yelling myself hoarse but you—" Phillip cut him short. In a few brusque words, he described what he had seen and the tall young mate emitted a gasp of dismay.

"You mean they're going to try to take *this* gun? Over my dead body will any Russian do that!"

"Unless you can bring the gun to bear on them," Phillip told him. "It *will* be over your dead body, Mr Hewett."

"But . . ." Belying his own recent reproaches, Bully Hewett clambered on to the top of the parapet. He said breathlessly, as he jumped down a moment later, "You're right, sir. They're going to try to take us from flank and rear—a whole battalion of them. But they've some way to go yet and . . ." He was interrupted by an infantry officer, a captain, his gold laced scarlet uniform spattered with mud and blood and his right arm hanging limp at his side.

"We've lost the forward parallels. I . . . had to withdraw, they were coming at us from all sides and I'd less than a dozen men left unwounded. You can't hope to hold this redoubt. You'd better spike the gun and retire."

Hewett eyed him for an instant in frowning indecision and then, shouting in order to make himself heard above the crackle of musketry and the subdued rumble of cannon fire now echoing across from the Inkerman Ridge, he addressed his gun's crew. "I've had no orders from Captain Lushington to spike this gun or to retire, either. We don't leave the gun, boys—we'll bowse her round and give the enemy a taste of their own medicine! Look lively now, it's going to take all the hands we can muster. Bo'sun's mate, turn up reliefs and ammunition parties. The rest of you man those traversing tackles and haul for your lives!"

The seamen raised a ragged cheer and, in obedience to his shouted orders, set-to with a will, gallantly joined by a few soldiers who had staggered in, exhausted, from one of the forward outposts. Young Hewett climbed on to the top of the parapet again and, with his bare hands, started to wrench away fascines and gabions to clear a new embrasure for his gun. "This is the way she'll have to bear, lads. Put your backs into it and heave away there!"

The great gun came slowly round. Too slowly, Phillip began to fear, visualizing the approach of the enemy he could no longer see. A Minié ball buried itself in the churned-up ground at his feet and others whined overhead like a swarm of angry bees . . . at least, he thought, the Russians had not been able to bring any field guns up the Careening Ravine. However many of them there were, they were armed only with rifles and bayonets. Straining on the tackles with the rest, he found himself beside a giant gunner's mate, who grinned at him and then fell, as if pole-axed, knocking him off balance. As he picked himself up again, he saw a gaping hole in the big seaman's chest and felt, rather than saw, the warm blood from the wound with which his own face and jacket were now spattered.

"We need more hands," a despairing voice gasped, from somewhere behind him. "Volunteers, from the other guns . . . we'll never do it." The speaker was the midshipman with whom he had ridden up to Kadi-Koi. Recognizing him, Phillip clapped a hand on the boy's shoulder. "Go and ask for them, Mr Daniel. You know where to find them."

"Aye, aye, sir. I'll do that, sir." The small figure made off, running as if the devil were after him and, as Phillip took his place on the traversing tackle, he saw the lad reach the connecting trench and dive into it. Then Hewett yelled exultantly,

"One more heave, boys, and she's there! Heave . . . that's it, belay, she'll do. Stand by to secure and re-rig tackles. Break open that case of conical shells, Thompson, and muster your loading numbers. The rest of you, make this embrasure as shipshape as you can but keep under cover. Gunner's mate!"

"He's dead, sir." One of the men pointed.

"I'll lay her myself then." Hewett jumped down. He was in his element, cool and in full command of the situation—a boy who, in the space of a few minutes, had become a man—but he flashed Phillip an absurdly boyish smile as he said, lowering his voice, "Thank you, Mr Hazard, both for your suggestion and for lending a hand to carry it out. If I may ask one more service of you, will you take a party and cover our rear, sir? I spotted some of the enemy—about twenty or so of 'em—making their way round when I was up on the parapet, and it'd be a pity if they spoiled things for us now, wouldn't it? I only need a couple of minutes to bring my gun to bear on their main body and at a range of a few hundred yards"—his smile widened—"we can hardly miss, even with a Lancaster!"

"Right," Phillip promised, "you shall have your two minutes." The return of the youthful midshipman with the first of his volunteers solved his immediate problem. The men he had brought were all fresh and spoiling for a fight. Most were armed with cutlasses, half a dozen had muskets in addition and the soldiers, who had managed to withdraw to the redoubt from the forward trenches responded instantly to his call for more volunteers. With a party of some thirty men at his heels, Phillip led the way to the rear of the gun position and saw that Hewett's qualms concerning its vulnerability had been more than justified.

The Russians were massing for an attack but in far greater number than the mate had estimated. An advance party of about a score of riflemen, spread out in skirmishing order, were within a scant three hundred yards of the redoubt, where they had halted, presumably to wait for support. And this was coming, advancing steadily in two columns, each of company strength, from the right front of the redoubt . . . probably, Phillip decided, turning his glass on them as the sun glinted on the bayonets, those who had earlier taken the forward trenches and had now re-formed. Hewett could stop them, once he brought his Lancaster into action, and his own small force ought to be able to hold the skirmishers in check, should they attempt to attack from the rear.

He was about to lower his glass when he caught sight of a third group, to the right of the other two and nearer to where he now stood than either, gathered at the edge of the Careening Ravine, the curving lip of which had hitherto hidden them from both Hewett and himself. They were dragging a field gun up the steep, precipitous side of the ravine—a feat he had imagined impossible. But it had, at least, delayed them and, he fervently hoped, for too long; an attack on the rear of Hewett's battery, had it been launched at the moment when every available man had been hauling on the traversing tackles, might well have been fatal. It could still be fatal, if they brought their gun up and poured a hail of shells into the battery from above and behind. . . .

Phillip gave his orders with an outward calm he was far from feeling, posting the soldiers and the seamen with muskets behind the protection of the parapet, with Midshipman Daniel in command. He gave the boy his Dollond and indicated the group with the field gun.

"I'm going to try to work my way round to their flank with the rest of our men and drive them off the gun, because if they open up on us with that . . ." He did not complete his sentence but there was no need. The midshipman had seen the danger and he nodded, alert and eager.

"You want us to cover you, sir?"

"That's the idea, youngster. But your first responsibility is to hold off those skirmishers. Pick them off, if you can, but keep them pinned down, so that they can't interfere with us, understand? Those gunners are keeping well under cover behind the rocks. Don't waste ammunition on them until they get the gun up or we manage to flush them out. In either case, they'll have to show themselves and you can let 'em have it with everything you've got."

"Aye, aye, sir. You may rely on me, sir." The boy picked up a discarded rifle and offered it, smiling. "You might find that this will come in handy, sir."

Phillip took the weapon. He led his small party into the rear approach trench, giving a brief explanation of his hastily formed plan of action as they followed him.

"There's plenty of scrub, to give us cover, lads—use it and don't make any more noise than you can help. We'll get as close to that twelve-pounder as possible before we're spotted and then rush them. You understand, our object is to stop them bringing that gun into action against the battery. I don't care how we do it but we'll spike the gun if we can. So no splitting Russian heads until the gun's dealt with, unless they happen to get in the way, and the first man to reach the gun puts it out of action. Right? Keep well spread out, then, and pass the word back."

There was a murmur of approval and one of the men said, "More volunteers, sir—three of 'em, one with a Minié rifle. Permission to join, sir?" Before Phillip could signify his assent, a hand reached out to touch his shoulder and a familiar voice sounded close to his ear. "Will you be leaving me to spike the gun, sorr? I've a handspike with me and . . ." The rest of his words were lost as, with a reverberating crash, the Lancaster opened fire but Phillip, turning, recognized the grinning face of Able-Seaman O'Leary. He had no time to wonder how his ex-orderly had contrived to join the party or where he might have come from but he grinned back and then waved to the men to leave the trench. They did so, bent low, and were soon dodging across the scrub-grown, shell-scarred slope in the direction of the ravine, now running, now crawling, when they came to open ground, and well spread out to either side of him. A

second booming explosion from the Lancaster effectively covered any noise they might have made.

From behind him, Phillip heard the crackle of musketry, as
the party he had left behind in the redoubt opened up on the
enemy skirmishers. He could see very little as he inched his
way across a patch of broken ground, but venturing to raise his
head, took in the fact that the Russians grouped about the field
gun had ceased their efforts—temporarily, at any rate—to drag
it the last few feet. All their attention was rivetted on the results
of Hewett's shelling of the rest of their force on the lower lip
of the ravine. And small wonder, he thought grimly for, of the
two columns advancing so confidently to encompass the
destruction of what they had imagined to be a virtually defense-
less British gun emplacement, only one could be seen when
the smoke cleared. Of the other, a few fleeing figures were all
he was able to make out; the remainder were hidden from him
by a pall of grey gunsmoke, beneath which nothing moved.
Hewett's aim had been good and true, the leading column,
swinging round to commence their attack on his flank, had evidently presented a perfect target.

The second column had come to an abrupt halt and was
wavering, thrown into disorder as men broke ranks and ran for
cover . . . but they rallied when an officer dashed forward,
waving his sword, and continued their advance. British troops,
faced with a similar situation, would have spread out in open
order but the Russians, Phillip saw, as they had at the Alma,
retained their accustomed formation. The closely packed ranks
executed a right turn and fired a volley into the redoubt and—
whether as a result of this or by sheer ill-luck he could not
tell—Hewett's third shell overshot, smashing into the rock wall
to their left rear.

The officer commanding the field gunners, as if inspired by
this example, turned to shout a series of staccato orders at his
men, emphasizing them by bringing down the flat of his sword
on the backs of those standing nearest to him. Galvanized into

action, the gunners returned to their drag-ropes with renewed vigor and, after some frantic heaving, the twelve pounder lurched drunkenly over the edge of the ravine. It would take them only a matter of minutes to haul the gun on to level ground, load and train it on to Hewett's battery, Phillip's mind registered as, still crouching low, he instinctively quickened his pace. He and his small party still had about a hundred yards to cover but . . . it was now or never, he knew and, if he ordered his men to charge, this would, at all events, distract the gunners from their task. The chances were that two or three of his party would get through, even if the skirmishers caught them in an enfilading fire, and it only needed one man to spike the gun.

He halted and looked round, seeing O'Leary just behind him. "Here, lad . . ." He thrust his rifle into the seaman's hand. "Give me your hand-spike and you and the other man with a rifle leg it as fast as you can to those rocks on our right—see? Keep down and when you're under cover, open fire on them. Pick off the officer, if you can."

"Aye, aye, sorr." O'Leary did not hesitate. He relinquished his hand-spike and crouched down, smiling, the rifle, after a quick check that it was loaded, at the ready. "The Russian officer's as good as dead, sorr, don't worry. The best of luck to you and . . . have a care for yourself now, won't you? Joe . . . Lieutenant Hazard's orders, you're to come with me."

The two men set off and, the instant they were in position, Phillip got to his feet. "Right," he said to the others, "Out cutlasses and have at 'em, my lads! But remember, it's that gun we want. Keep well spread out and don't stop, even if the man beside you is wounded."

He never knew, after it was over, how he managed to reach the gun or even how long it took him to do so. All consciousness of time left him when he started to race towards it and he was as oblivious to the hitherto hampering pain of his stiff leg, as he was to any awareness of fear or expectation of failure.

The gun had to be spiked; his mind was blank, holding no other thought save this, no other desire or ambition. Minié balls whined overhead and spattered about him as he ran, riccocheting this way and that when he crossed a rocky outcrop and the skirmishers had him in their sights, but he did not deviate from his chosen path or slacken his pace. He did not look round, either, and had no idea whether or not any of his party had been hit although, hearing pounding footsteps behind him, he knew that some, at least, were close on his heels.

Then all other sounds were again drowned by the thunderous roar of Hewett's Lancaster. A moment or two later, he saw the Russian artillery officer fall, apparently without emitting a cry, despite the fact that his mouth was open and hideously gaping. The sword, which he had used so recently to belabour his reluctant men into the performance of their duty, flailed the air above his head in a macaber parody of the manner in which he had previously wielded it, and then the dead fingers opened to let the weapon slip from their grasp and their owner slumped forward to lie, very still, beside his gun.

O'Leary, Phillip thought, had carried out his orders admirably and, ever a hater of bullying officers, would, probably have enjoyed the grim pantomime had he been close enough to witness it. He himself did not, although he had given the order; but he recognized its necessity and knew that the odds against the success of his desperate little sortie were no longer as great as they had been. They might, indeed, have been halved for, as he had hoped, the loss of their commander threw the green-uniformed gunners into momentary panic. Some took to their heels and ran to the edge of the ravine for cover, from whence they kept up a desultory musket fire, too far away to be effective. The rest held their ground, making strenuous, efforts to lower the elevation of their gun and bring it to bear on the new and unexpected target presented by the charging sailors, who had seemingly sprung from nowhere. The blue-jackets—as was their wont when there was a prospect of coming to grips with the enemy—were cheering at the tops of their voices with a lusty exuberance that belied their scanty numbers and evidently convinced the Russians that others must be following in their wake.

Several more of their riflemen took refuge in flight but the gun's crew, after a valiant struggle, brought the muzzle of the twelve pounder round at last. Phillip found himself facing into it and, his brain suddenly ice-cold and all his perceptions sharpened, glimpsed a raised linstock, glowing redly above the dull metal of the gun-barrel. He yelled a warning to his party to fling themselves flat, aware that at point-blank range, this might be their only chance of survival. Round shot, striking rocky ground, could do more damage even than grape, as he had seen yesterday when Sir Colin Campbell had ordered Captain Barker's troop to load with it.

But . . . he had his pistol in his right hand, he realized, the hand-spike he had taken from O'Leary in his left. He came to a halt, breathing hard, forced himself to take careful aim at the man holding the linstock, and fired the pistol. Then, without waiting to see whether or not he had managed to hit his target, he hurled his body across the gun and rammed the hand-spike into the touch-hole with all his remaining strength, using both hands to drive it home. To be fully effective the spike had, of course, to be broken off but this was beyond him, Phillip knew, for he was surrounded by green uniforms.

A bayonet jabbed at him viciously; he eluded it, only to be met by another and then the butt of a Russian musket crashed down on the back of his head. The green uniforms vanished, swallowed up in the sea of pain which swept over him. The last thing he remembered was the sound of British cheers, coming from a vast distance, followed by a tremendous explosion which he imagined to have taken place within the confines of his own head.

After that he sank into the dark and frightening silence of a pit he knew instinctively was bottomless. . . .

CHAPTER TEN

1

When *Phillip returned* to partial consciousness, it was still quite dark and, on all sides of him, he could hear the groans of wounded men. Some asked for water, others begged for help, to enable them to change position and one, who was quite close by, asked again and again when the ship which was to evacuate them would arrive.

None received any answer that Phillip himself could hear, although he noticed a few dim figures carrying lanterns, who moved about in the distance and paused here and there, seemingly at random, in response to some sufferer's plea. He supposed that they must be medical orderlies or surgeons but, since he felt no more pain than usual from his bruised leg, he did not call out to them and, in any case, they did not come near enough for him to do so. He was neither anxious nor afraid and, beyond a vague desire to know how he came to be where he was, content to remain there, mute and uncomplaining. He was also very tired and, after a while, drifted back to sleep again, only occasionally disturbed when one of his fellows cried his agony aloud. Waking once, he heard and recognized the voice of a priest, administering the Last Rites to a man a few yards away and again, some time later, when another man prayed aloud, apparently alone.

It was daylight the next time he woke and a thin grey drizzle was falling for which, at first, he was grateful since it enabled him to assuage a thirst he had just begun to feel. After a time, however, when the drizzle became a downpour soaking through his clothing, he started to shiver and, as his discomfort increased, his acceptance of his situation became less passive. Where, he asked himself, had they brought him, and why? Presumably he had been wounded, although he had no recollection of anything of the kind but, if this were the case, why was he not in one of the field hospitals, or dressing stations, receiving attention? Had he, perhaps, been taken prisoner and was this the way the Russians treated their wounded prisoners?

Phillip attempted to sit up, hoping to identify his surroundings but found the effort beyond his strength. Even the mere raising of his head caused a feeling of nausea and an alarming dizziness so, after waiting until both these unpleasant sensations had subsided, he leaned cautiously over on his side, intending to question the man lying next to him . . . only to recoil in horror when he realized that the man was dead. An infantry soldier, in British uniform, he had evidently died of cholera within a short time of offering up his lonely prayer in the darkness and, reminded all too vividly of North, Phillip felt beads of sweat break out on his brow. He had seen many men die since coming to the Crimea but, for all its ghastly familiarity, death from cholera still shocked him and it was a considerable time before he could bring himself to lean over to his other side. His other neighbour was, to his relief, alive—a slim young trooper of the 11th Hussars, whose theatrically magnificent uniform was so stained and filthy that it was scarcely recognizable. He turned a gaunt, unshaven face in Phillip's direction when he spoke and said, in reply to his question, that they were on the Hospital Wharf at Balaclava.

"We're waiting for a ship to take us to Scutari, or so they told us. But no ship has come and I have been here since they carried me down from the Cavalry Camp. Our regimental surgeon took my foot off and patched me up and then he said he'd send me down to Balaclava, to the hospital, where I'd have better care. Instead they dumped me here . . . to rot, I suppose."

"But surely—" Phillip began, bewildered by the despair in the young trooper's voice.

"To rot," the boy repeated, with stark bitterness. "No food, no shelter . . . nothing but a sip of water from one of the Highlanders' women, who came down during the night." He raised himself on one elbow to study Phillip's uniform with resentful blue eyes. "You're a naval officer, are you not . . . sir? Can *you* not tell me why there are no ships?"

"There will be ships, lad. There are plenty of transports available to convey wounded to Scutari. Do not lose heart."

"You haven't heard the rumours, then," the young cavalryman returned. "Balaclava is to be abandoned and all of us with it. The ships have gone to the French anchorage, save for those over there—" he gestured towards the harbour Phillip could not see and then, turning his face away, lapsed into a brooding silence from which he refused to be roused.

Phillip stared dazedly at his uncompromising back, wondering what in the world he had meant. Memory slowly returned. Had not his brother Graham told him of the rumour that Balaclava was to be abandoned? He had said that Captain Dacres, after bringing the *Sanspareil* into harbour, had issued orders that no other ships were to be permitted entry, for whatever purpose . . . and that this included evacuation of the wounded. But . . . he frowned, in an effort to remember. Since then surely there had been a conference between Lord Raglan, Sir Colin Campbell and . . . yes, of course, Admiral Lyons, to which he himself had been sent to summon Captain Dacres. One of them, he could not recall which, had assured him that neither Balaclava nor the wounded waiting there for evacuation would be abandoned and, indeed, had added, *"So long as any of us have breath in our bodies."* If he told the young Hussar this, perhaps . . . unwisely, Phillip sat up. He glimpsed the masts and spars of the *Sanspareil* in the distance, bare of canvas, and those of another ship, a frigate, which were much more familiar to him, and then everything whirled about him in crazy circles. He fell back, striking his head and felt himself sinking once more into the dark and bottomless pit from which he had only lately returned.

This time, however, he was not alone for Catriona Moray was with him, holding his hand in both her own. Her voice, with its remembered lilting charm, told him quietly and confidently that he was going to get well and that she would care for him.

"Narishkin?" he asked, remembering. "Is he still with you?"

"He is dead," Catriona answered. "He died soon after you left and they buried him, with the dead of the 93rd. I do not believe that he would be ashamed to lie in their company."

No, Phillip thought, he would not. Strangely, with Catriona beside him, he did not think of Mademoiselle Sophie save, fleetingly, as Narishkin's widow.

"What of the battle?" he asked. "Did we hold off the attack?"

"You mean yesterday? Oh, yes, the Russians were driven back with heavy losses—four hundred killed, I have heard. Many of them retreated from the Inkerman Ridge into a ravine—the one they call the Careening Ravine, I think—and one of our Lancasters had their range. They say that our guns won the day—the Horse Artillery did splendid work, Sergeant MacCorkill told me, in support of the Second Division, and the Guards, although they were standing by, did not have to go into action at all. But . . ." she sighed. "War is a terrible thing. One cannot glory in any victory, when one sees, as I am seeing now, the cost of it . . . here on this wharf. These poor, suffering men, left here without food or water, I—we, that is to say, all the women—have been here most of the night. That is how I came to find you."

"Thank God you did!" Phillip whispered.

A gentle hand came out to touch his head. "This dressing should be changed, Mr Hazard. I will see to it and bring you food, as soon as I can. But it will mean leaving you for a little while, because I have used up all the dressings I had."

He did not want her to leave him, did not want to relinquish the small hand he had been holding in his but, with a murmured apology, she disengaged it. "I must go, Mr Hazard. There is so much to be done. Only two surgeons are working here . . . I am going to ask for more. These poor men cannot embark in a ship for Scutari without having received proper medical attention. Some have not even had their wounds dressed and . . ." Her voice broke suddenly on a sob and, to Phillip's distress, she was gone.

Following her departure, he lay for some time in a state of curiously dazed apathy, uncertain whether, in fact, he had seen and talked to her or whether—like Mademoiselle Sophie—Catriona Moray, too, was a figment of his own imagination, conjured up because he had need of her. After a while, the rain ceased and the sun came out and, bathed in its soporific warmth, he slept, less conscious now of the discomfort of his damp clothing and of the wooden boards on which he lay.

He wakened, feeling refreshed and almost himself again, to find that he was being carried on a stretcher across the wharf. Martin Fox was walking beside the stretcher and, seeing him open his eyes, gripped his shoulder with a warmth of affection and relief that pleased as much as it surprised him, for Fox was not given to displays of emotion.

"Phillip—thank heaven we found you!"

"Martin, my dear fellow, it's good to see you. But what are you doing here and—where are you taking me?"

Fox smiled at him. "Why to *Trojan,* of course," he said, answering the second question first. "She's here, in harbour, did you not know? As to what I was doing here—I was searching for you."

"For *me?*" Phillip echoed, puzzled.

"On the Admiral's orders," Martin Fox replied. "You were posted missing, believed killed or captured, apparently after yesterday's affair . . . concerning which there are numerous stories of your gallantry in capturing an enemy field gun, with a party of our Jacks, armed only with cutlasses. That's true, I take it?"

Phillip frowned, trying to remember but his mind was still blank where this episode was concerned, and he could only shake his head. "I simply don't remember, Martin."

"Well, everyone else does, I assure you. I . . . careful, there," Fox warned the stretcher bearers, as they reached the end of the wharf, where a boat was waiting. "Cox'un, lend a hand. Two of you take the foot of the stretcher and—"

"I can walk," Phillip protested and proved that this was no idle boast by stepping, unaided, into the boat. Familiar faces beamed at him in welcome and willing hands assisted him to the sternsheets, where Midshipman O'Hara, the boat commander, wrung his hand, stammering in his eagerness to express his own welcome.

"How," Phillip asked when, the greetings over and the boat under way, Martin Fox took his place beside him, "did you learn that I was neither killed nor captured? And how did you know where to look for me?"

"You can thank Seaman O'Leary for the information that you were still alive, Phillip. You had posted him, it appears, with a rifle to give your party covering fire. Well, when the gun was taken, O'Leary went in and dragged you out of the mêlée. According to his account"—Fox permitted himself a quick grin— "you were buried under a mountain of Russian bodies. Fifty, at least, though the number grows each time he repeats the story . . . he's aboard the *Trojan*, incidentally, suffering from a flesh wound in the leg. He came aboard this morning, at first light. He told us that he'd lost touch with you, when you were both taken to a field dressing station to have your wounds attended to, but he swore you were alive and not in enemy hands. So we started a search for you. You should have been taken to the *Diamond*, of course, or to the naval field hospital at Kadi-Koi. But that has been moved to the Upland, and our search there was both abortive and time wasting. We did find two seamen who had been in your party, though, and one told us that a military stretcher party had taken you to Balaclava. As you weren't aboard the *Diamond,* the embarkation wharf was the only other possibility. On our way there, we met a singularly beautiful young woman from the 93rd's camp, who said she had seen and spoken to you and told us exactly where to look."

Catriona Moray, Phillip thought gratefully. He had not, after all, imagined her visit and, as soon as he was physically able to drag himself up to the Highlander's camp, he would call on her to offer his thanks. His thanks and, perhaps . . . he sighed.

"What of the rest of my party, Martin?" he asked.

"The cutlass party—oh, most of them survived, I understand. A number were wounded but they're aboard the *Diamond.* If there are any of them on the wharf, I left orders with our stretcher party to transfer them to the *Diamond,* so don't worry about them, Phillip. Only military wounded are on the wharf and we're not permitted to interfere with the Army's arrangements for them." Fox shrugged his broad shoulders, an expression of mingled anger and concern on his face. "God help them, poor devils! The Army's arrangements appear to be pitifully inadequate, to put it mildly . . . as you know better than I."

Remembering the young Hussar and the man who had died of cholera beside him during the night, Phillip felt sickened. "And precisely what *are* the Army's arrangements for them, Martin?" he demanded, his throat tight.

Martin Fox repeated his shrug. "They await the arrival of a ship to evacuate them to Constantinople. But Captain Dacres, who is in command of the harbour defenses, as you probably know, has forbidden any ships to enter, except those required for its defense. This order is to remain in force until the Russian threat to Balaclava is removed."

"But in the name of humanity—" Phillip exploded.

Fox laid a hand on his arm. "Do not blame Dacres," he begged. "His responsibility is to hold the port against any attack the enemy may launch. The Army were informed of the order before it was issued but, in spite of this, they continue to send wounded down to the wharf, without making any provision to feed or shelter them. And there are only two surgeons—*two, Phillip*—to care for them! If it had not been for the Highlanders' women, including your beautiful Mistress Moray, and some of our off-duty Jacks, the mortality on that wharf would be twice what it is. It's bad enough, in all conscience as"—he reddened— "again, you know better than I. But at least we've got you safely away, thank God."

"Amen to that," Phillip responded, with deep sincerity. The boat was nearing *Trojan,* he saw, and at the sight of her, his heavy heart lifted. It would be good to be aboard *Trojan* again, even though his stay on board must, of necessity, be brief.

"How is Captain Crawford, Martin?" he asked.

Martin Fox avoided his gaze. "He went down with an attack of fever yesterday as, I understand, Captain Dacres did also. Both were ashore, dining at one of the army camps together and, I fear, must have picked up the infection there. Captain Crawford is one of the best commanders I have ever served under—the best, that is to say, with a single exception, my dear Phillip." He looked up then, to look Phillip full in the eye, and went on flatly, "But his health is far from robust and this has hit him hard."

"He's still aboard?"

"Yes—confined to his cabin. I'm temporarily in command." Fox hesitated, as Midshipman O'Hara brought the boat smartly alongside and the bowman secured his boathook to the chains. "Captain Dacres has asked to be relieved of his command."

"Of command of the *Sanspareil,* you mean?" Phillip stared at him.

Martin Fox nodded, "Of *Sanspareil* and the harbour defenses. It is rumoured that he is to be invalided. Commander Heath of the *Niger* is expected to succeed him . . . he went aboard *Sanspareil* this morning early, during the Middle Watch, I believe."

"I see," Phillip said, frowning.

"*Do* you, Phillip?"

"Yes, I think so. Admittedly my brain is not functioning particularly well at the moment but—"

"My dear chap, it's not functioning at all!" Martin Fox was regarding him with a delighted grin that almost split his face in two. "Why do you imagine the Admiral ordered an intensive search for you? Captain Crawford has also asked to be relieved and there is surely only one possible choice as *his* successor? *You,* Phillip, don't you understand? The only reason for your not being given your old command would be if you were too severely wounded to take it. For heaven's sake, I've been praying ever since I started to hunt for you that O'Leary was right and the worst you were suffering from would prove to be a concussion. And my prayers have been answered. You appear perfectly fit to assume command of this ship to me. Or at any rate, after a few hours' sleep, you will be. I'll call our assistant surgeon to look at you, of course, and I can fit you out with a frock coat and cocked hat, when you go to report to the Admiral."

"When," Phillip asked weakly, "am I supposed to report to the Admiral, Martin?"

"*Agamemnon* is expected to anchor outside the harbour entrance during the afternoon. You'll be summoned by signal . . . sir!"

Martin Fox offered his arm but Phillip, echoing his smile, refused the proffered assistance. He mounted the gangway and, apart from a barely perceptible limp, was walking quite steadily when he reached and saluted *Trojan*'s quarterdeck.

2

The Admiral's summons came during the First Dog Watch and Sir Edmund Lyons, who had come ashore from *Agamemnon,* received Phillip in the *Sanspareil*'s spacious day-cabin, where the unfortunate Captain Dacres lay, pale and obviously ill, stretched out in a cot which had been rigged there for him. Besides members of the Admiral's personal staff, Commander Heath and Colonel Hurdle, of the Royal Marines, were also present and a short conference, with a discussion of new plans for the Balaclava Harbour defenses, took place first and was swiftly concluded, to enable the commander of the all-important Marine Heights to return to his post.

When he had gone, Sir Edmund turned to Phillip.

"Captain Dacres and the commander of *Trojan*, Captain Crawford, have both requested to be relieved of their commands due to ill-health," he stated formally. "With the Commander-in-Chief's full knowledge and approval—although needless to tell you, with his and my deep regret—both these requests are to be granted. Captain Heath is to be appointed to command of the *Sanspareil* and of Balaclava Harbour . . . which leaves the command of the *Trojan* to be filled. It is a senior command, as you know, and in normal circumstances could not be offered to an officer of your rank, Mr Hazard. But I have an arduous and difficult task for this frigate to perform and you have previously served as her First Lieutenant and acting-commander, so . . . " He paused, eyeing Phillip searchingly. "If you are fit for duty, I intend to place you again in acting-command, with a temporary step in rank which, I trust, their Lordships will, on my recommendation, see fit to confirm. In the light of your gallant conduct during yesterday's attack on the Lancaster battery—which, of course, I shall bring to their notice—I anticipate that your promotion will be made permanent."

"Thank you, sir, I . . . thank you very much indeed, sir. I assure you"—in his borrowed frock coat and with a clean dressing on his head, Phillip faced his Chief confidently—"I am perfectly recovered, sir, and fit for duty."

"You received a blow on the head, did you not?" the Admiral enquired, still formally.

"Yes, sir. From a rifle butt—"

"Which did not succeed in splitting your skull? Amazing! Well"—dropping formality, Sir Edmund Lyons laughed—"I suppose there is something to be said for thick-headed commanders! Eh, Heath?"

"A great deal, sir." Leopold Heath was also laughing and even the tormented face of Captain Dacres wore the suspicion of a smile as he listened. The Admiral held out his hand. "Congratulations, Phillip. You have fulfilled the high expectations I had of you, my dear boy. And you will, I'm sure, be pleased to hear that young Hewett's conduct is also to be brought to their Lordships' notice."

"Indeed, sir, I am," Phillip answered, with sincerity. "No one deserves it more."

The Admiral asked him a few questions concerning Hewett's feat and then, smiling in Captain Dacres' direction, told him that both he and Captain Crawford were to be transferred to the *Banshee* as soon as they had recovered sufficiently to be sent to Constantinople. "Captain Dacres prefers to remain here but I have made arrangements for Captain Crawford to nurse his fever aboard my flagship, where we shall give him the best of care. A boat will be sent for him at once."

"At once, sir?" What, Phillip wondered, was the "arduous and difficult task?" that *Trojan* was to perform? He waited, in respectful silence, and Admiral Lyons went on, "Yes, at once, Commander Hazard. You will prepare your ship for sea immediately. I want you, if it is humanly possible, to get under way for Constantinople or, at all events, leave this harbour tonight, in darkness, so that your departure attracts no undue attention. The enemy is, in Sir Colin Campbell's opinion—for which I have the greatest respect—preparing for another attack on us. Yesterday's affair, although no doubt it seemed to you much more, was only a sortie in force, according to Sir Colin, intended to probe our defenses on the Inkerman Ridge . . . and that is where he believes the big attack will come. So you see, it's essential that we evacuate the wounded from here *before* it comes."

Light slowly dawned and Phillip was conscious of a feeling of intense relief and elation. "Do you mean, sir, that *Trojan* is to take them?"

"I do, Phillip." The Admiral spoke gravely. "You are to load every wounded man your ship can accommodate. They'll be packed like sardines but clear the embarkation wharf, if you can—you'll have all available boats and parties from this ship and the *Simoom* to assist you. I shall give you as many surgeons as can be spared, although I fear they will be too few for the number of sick and wounded you will have on board. But adequate medical care is awaiting them at Scutari where, I understand, a party of English nurses is expected, brought out to care for the wounded by a Miss Florence Nightingale. Women in a military hospital are a new departure but—"

"Forgive me, sir," Phillip put in. "But if I might make a suggestion?"

"Certainly. What is it?"

"The Highlanders' women, sir . . . could I not ask for volunteers from amongst their number to accompany us? They were doing a great deal for the wounded on the embarkation wharf last night, sir, and there are some skilled nurses in their camp, as I have good reason to know. I myself spent last night on the wharf, sir, and . . ." Warming to his subject, Phillip saw that the Admiral was smiling.

"I believe you, Phillip—you do not, I assure you, have to convince me. Take them, if you can persuade any to volunteer for the task . . . three or four, let us say. But you must not delay your departure for the women—or even for members of your ship's company whom there's not time to recall. Clear this harbour in darkness, you understand? *Niger* will come into your berth and, if there are Russian spies watching, they will be unable to report a change in our harbour defenses."

"Aye, aye, sir. I understand."

"I have recalled your brother," the Admiral said, almost as an afterthought. "To be your acting Master, pending a review of his case, on Captain Crawford's recommendation." He cut short Phillip's attempt to thank him. "He has earned a second chance and, in any case, I need your present Master—Mr Burnaby—to take command of one of our harbour tugs. Well"—his smile was warm—"carry on, Commander, because you have very little time. May God go with you . . . and with your passengers."

He would need that blessing, Phillip thought, as he returned post-haste to *Trojan*. With a depleted crew and several of his officers in command of gun emplacements on the Marine Heights, he had been set a formidable task. But remembering what the young Hussar had said to him so bitterly that morning, he was grateful to have been given an opportunity at least to endeavour to clear the embarkation wharf of its pathetic cargo of suffering humanity.

Back on board *Trojan*, he learnt that Captain Crawford had already departed in a boat from *Agamemnon*, leaving a kindly message of congratulation for him, and that Graham had rejoined. He took over his command without ceremony and, mustering the ship's company, informed them of what was to be done and gave his orders as briefly and concisely as he could. Normally, as commander, he would have remained on board but, on this occasion, he decided to delegate the responsibility for unloading and stowing *Trojan*'s human cargo to his First Lieutenant, himself returning to the embarkation wharf . . . and Martin Fox, with rare understanding, did not question his decision.

There was no lack of volunteers or of boats and, within minutes of his arrival there, the wharf was a seething hive of well-organized activity. The bluejackets toiled and sweated and the officers worked with their men, handling the slings and stretchers as gently as they could. A number of the boats had brought hammocks with them, slung on oars, and these were used when stretchers began to be in short supply and proved a better means of transporting the more severely wounded when the transfer from wharf to boat had to be made.

At intervals of supervising the evacuation of the wharf, Phillip searched for Catriona Moray but failed to find her. He did, however, eventually run Morag MacCorkill to earth and the Sergeant's wife promised to convey a message to her.

"Mistress Catriona is at the hospital, sir, where conditions are almost as bad as they were here this morning. But I will go to her for, indeed, it would be a great blessing if she were to leave this terrible place and never return to it. Our camp is not the place for a young lady of quality and . . ." She sighed. "You are busy and I must not detain you. But do not worry, Mr Hazard, I will persuade Mistress Catriona to go with you and four or five more besides, skilled nurses all of them now, even if they were not before. At what hour will your ship be sailing, if you please?"

Phillip consulted his pocket watch and with the aid of her lantern, looking from it to the sky, still dark and overcast with a pale moon and the promise of more rain to come. "We must sail before first light. A boat will be waiting for you at the wharf two hours from now . . . will that give you time, Mistress Mac-Corkill?"

"Ample time, sir, God willing—save that we shall not be able to go back to our tents to pack up necessities for the voyage. There will not be time for that but—"

"I can spare you a few seamen, if that would help, and you could send some of your women with them—some who are not coming with us—to pack for you."

Morag MacCorkill smiled. "Thank you, sir. Then you may expect us on the wharf, with our belongings, in two hours' time."

She was as good as her word. The wharf was clear and the last boat standing by when the little procession of women arrived and, with a pleasure and relief that surprised even himself, Phillip saw that Catriona was with them. He handed her into the boat and invited her to seat herself beside him in the sternsheets. She was, he observed, very tired, a wan, slim shadow in the darkness, with the face of a sleepwalker and the slow, laboured movements of one who had driven herself to the limit of physical endurance and beyond. But, as the boat cast off and the weary seamen bent to their oars, she said with a gratitude he found oddly moving, "Thank you, Mr Hazard, for what you have done for those poor men. They would never have been able to get away, had it not been for you."

"I am only obeying my Admiral's orders," Phillip told her. "*He* is the one those poor men should thank."

"Is he? Then I'm sure they do. But I have you to thank for making it possible for me to leave this place. I . . . I do not think I could have borne another hour there." Her lower lip trembled but bravely, Catriona bit back her tears. "Morag did not come, you know—she would not leave her husband and I did not try to persuade her to change her mind, I . . . I could not. But there is someone on board whom you will be glad to know is alive—the Indian Army officer you asked me about, the one with the beautiful grey Arab horse. I . . . forget his name, I'm sorry. Was it Sheridan? I . . . seem to be so . . . tired, I cannot remember anything."

"You are exhausted, Catriona." Phillip put his arm about her. "Spare yourself—rest a little, my dear. We can talk later. And your memory isn't failing you—the name *was* Sheridan, Captain Alexander Sheridan. I am glad he is alive."

"Yes," she agreed and with the touching trust of a child, let her head fall back on to his shoulder. She was in a deep sleep when the boat came alongside the *Trojan* and, refusing the coxswain's offer to assist him, Phillip picked her up in his arms and carried her on board. Men lay everywhere on the decks, packed as they had been on the embarkation wharf and he wondered what he could do with his helpless burden. Then he remembered that the commander's cabin, lately vacated by Captain Crawford, was still empty; there had been no time to shift his own gear into it, if, indeed, he thought wryly, he still possessed any gear. And it was, in any case, unlikely that he would be able to snatch more than the odd few hours of sleep, with his ship so overloaded and under-manned.

He carried Catriona to the cabin and laid her gently on the cot. She stirred but did not waken and he stood looking down at her white, shuttered face, his heart going out to her in helpless pity. No man's courage could, he reflected, really match hers and none transcend it; she and the other women were the real heroines of Balaclava. Drawing the blankets about her, he found her small, roughened hand and bore it to his lips in silent tribute to her heroism, his own eyes suddenly filled with tears of which—strangely—he was not ashamed. Then he tucked the hand beneath the coverlet and rose, knowing he would have to leave her now. But she could sleep off her exhaustion and, as he had told her, they could talk later, discuss and decide on her immediate future and, no doubt, arrange for her to be given a passage home . . . if she wanted to return home.

But perhaps she would not want to, perhaps she . . .

"Sorr—begging your pardon, Commander Hazard, sorr—" the voice was O'Leary's and Phillip turned from his contemplation of the sleeping girl, controlling his momentary resentment of the interruption. O'Leary's right leg was heavily bandaged, his honest, ugly face a mass of purpling bruises but he was, as always, beaming cheerfully. "First Lieutenant's compliments, sorr, and he says, with your permission, he'll pipe hands to stations for leaving harbour. And I brought you this, sorr, with my compliments, thinking you'd maybe drink it before you go on deck. 'Twill put fresh heart into you, sorr."

Phillip accepted the mug his ex-orderly held out to him and gulped down the scalding mixture of coffee and a liberal lashing of rum which it contained. "You're a good man, O'Leary," he said, meaning it. "A damned good man!"

"And so are you, sorr," O'Leary answered promptly. "If you'll pardon the liberty, sorr."

It was not, perhaps, the most graciously expressed compliment he had ever received, Phillip thought but, all things considered, it was one that, for as long as he lived, he would never forget. Buoyed up by this and by the rum, he made his way to the quarterdeck, his spirits high and—as O'Leary had predicted—fresh hope in his heart, to take his ship to sea.

As the new day dawned, grey and damp, *Trojan* cleared Balaclava Harbour and set course for Constantinople. By the time a watery sun rose to lighten the eastern sky, the toiling cooks had prepared huge cauldrons of soup and men of the watch below were moving about the crowded decks with their mess-kits, offering these to any of the wounded who could manage to swallow a few mouthfuls.

From astern, the sound of heavy guns firing from .the Crimean Upland grew gradually fainter.